# ADV
# WINNER'S CURSE

*"Winner's Curse, a smart oil and gas thriller with remarkable breadth, depth, and international intrigue, proves yet again that L.A. Starks is a master storyteller! Her characters are so true you feel like you know them. You can't help wondering how Lynn Dayton is going to deal with everything that is thrown at her, and the suspense keeps you guessing to the very end!"* —William J. Carl, Author of Assassin's Manuscript

*"Taut, suspenseful, and full of Texas flare, Stark's latest mystery will have you rooting for Lynn Dayton as she risks her life to uncover deadly secrets before it's too late. Winner's Curse is a winner!"* —Karen Harrington, Winner of the Ellery Queen Mystery Magazine Reader's Choice Award

*"Compelling characters, non-stop action, a shockingly current plot, and Starks' experience as an insider make Winner's Curse the next thriller you must read."* —Jim Kipp, investment expert

# PRAISE FOR THE
# LYNN DAYTON THRILLERS

### *The Second Law*

"Unremitting suspense throughout … Spirited characters, both good and bad, populate this engaging, often surprising thriller."
—Kirkus Review

### *Strike Price*

"If you're looking for big business wheeling-and-dealing, international intrigue, murder, mayhem and high-geared action, you've come to the right place. Toss in a charming and nervy protagonist like Lynn Dayton and L. A. Starks' STRIKE PRICE is right on the money. Well-written, well-plotted and well worth a reader's time.'"
—Carlton Stowers, two-time Edgar winner

### *13 Days: The Pythagoras Conspiracy*

"Starks has made an impressive debut with the command, passion, and insight of an insider.'"
—Michael Lucker, executive producer, Lucky Dog Filmworks

# BOOKS BY
# L. A. STARKS

*13 Days: The Pythagoras Conspiracy, Lynn Dayton Thriller #1*

*Strike Price, Lynn Dayton Thriller #2*

*The Second Law, Lynn Dayton Thriller #3*

## SHORT STORIES BY L. A. STARKS

*Robert and Thérèse Guillard: Choices (Amazon)*

*A Time for Eating Wild Onions (Amazon)*

*Gumbo Filé (Dreamspell Nightmares Anthology, edited by Lisa René Smith)*

*Josh Rosen and Bubbe (Amazon)*

*Incurable (Amazon)*

*Risk Reduction (Reckless in Texas: Metroplex Mysteries Volume II, edited by Barb Goffman)*

# WINNER'S CURSE

*A Lynn Dayton Thriller*

---

L. A. STARKS

Nemaha Ridge Publishing Group, LLC

Dallas, Texas

Copyright © 2024 by L. A. Starks

Nemaha Ridge Publishing Group, LLC supports copyrights. Thank you for buying an authorized edition of this book and for complying with copyright laws by not reproducing, scanning, or distributing any part of it in any form without permission.

Starks, L.A.

Winner's Curse/L. A. Starks

(A Lynn Dayton Thriller)

ISBN 978-09911107-5-9

Dayton, Lynn (Fictitious character)-Fiction 2. LOCATIONS Midland, Texas; London, UK; Chicago, IL; Herzliya, Israel; Budapest, Hungary; Moscow, Russia

First Print and E-book editions: August 2024, by Nemaha Ridge Publishing Group, LLC

This is a work of fiction. Names, characters, places, and incidents either are the product of the author's imagination or are used fictitiously, and any resemblance to actual persons, living or dead, businesses, companies, events, or locales is entirely coincidental.

Dedicated to my family and Diane J.

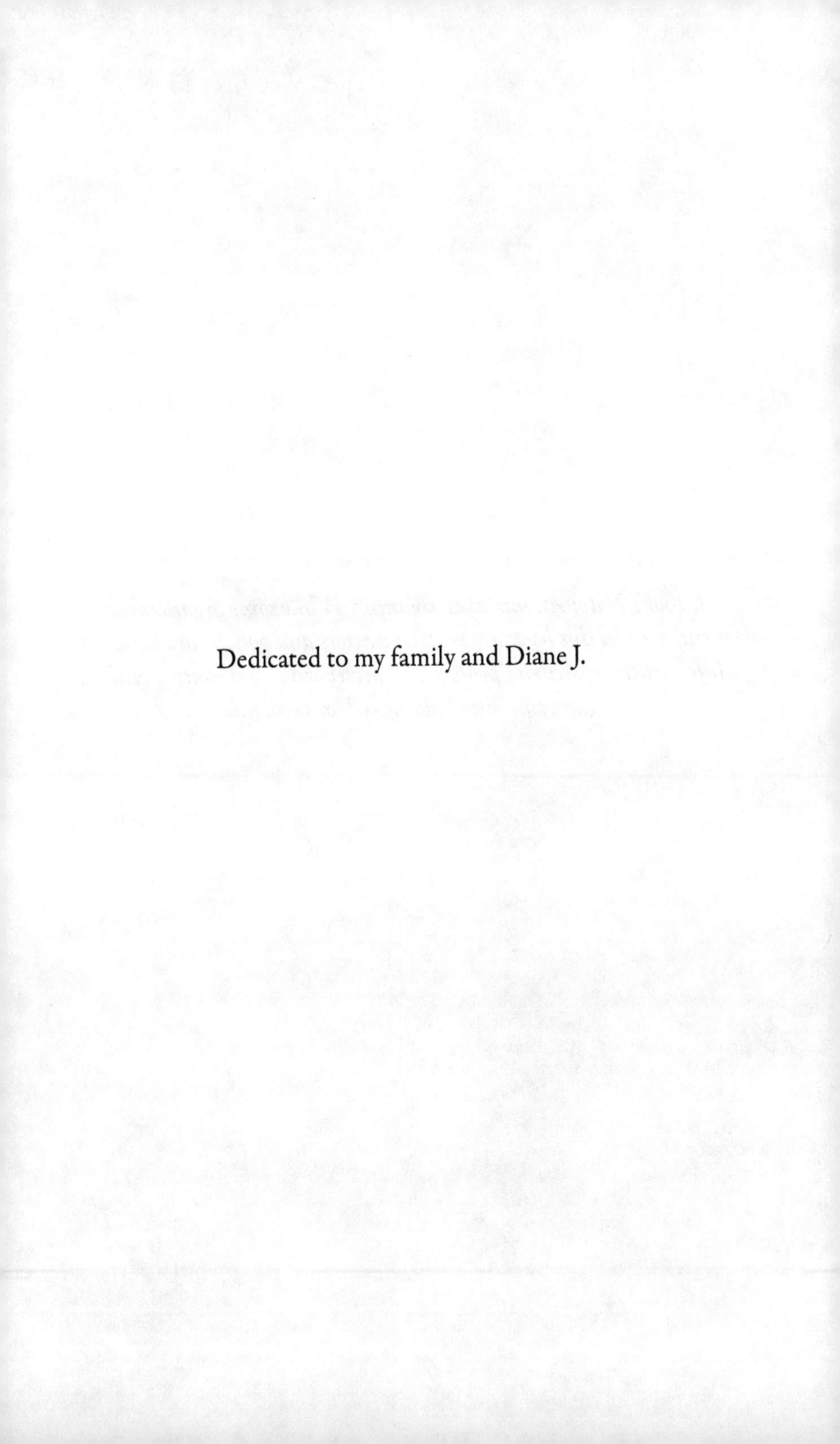

*Author's Note: All mistakes are mine. While some organizations mentioned in this book are real, characters and policies are fictional. Infrastructure, security protocols, cybersecurity, and control systems are simplified, disguised, or changed.*

"Winner's curse is a tendency for the winning bid in an auction to exceed the intrinsic value of the true worth of an item. Because of incomplete information, emotions, or other factors regarding the item being auctioned, bidders experience significant difficulty in determining the item's true intrinsic value. As a result, the large overestimation of an item's value ends up winning the auction."

—Michael Walls, **Oil and Gas Journal**

"I cannot stress often enough that what science is all about is not proving things to be true but proving them to be false."

—Lawrence Krauss, theoretical physicist

# TABLE OF CONTENTS

Chapter 1: Midland, Texas .................................................................. 1
Chapter 2: London .............................................................................. 11
Chapter 3: Israel ................................................................................. 19
Chapter 4: Midland ............................................................................ 25
Chapter 5: London, UK, Moscow and Murmansk, Russia ........ 35
Chapter 6: Midland ............................................................................ 45
Chapter 7: Herzliya, Israel ................................................................ 53
Chapter 8: London .............................................................................. 59
Chapter 9: Dallas and Midland ....................................................... 67
Chapter 10: Austin, Texas ................................................................. 79
Chapter 11: Budapest, Hungary ...................................................... 87
Chapter 12: Midland .......................................................................... 93
Chapter 13: South of Midland ......................................................... 97
Chapter 14: West Texas and Midland .......................................... 107
Chapter 15: Moscow, London, and Barcelona ........................... 117
Chapter 16: Dallas ............................................................................ 125
Chapter 17: Dallas ............................................................................ 135
Chapter 18: Dallas and Chicago ................................................... 143
Chapter 19 : Chicago ....................................................................... 147
Chapter 20: Chicago ........................................................................ 155
Chapter 21: Herzliya, Israel ........................................................... 165
Chapter 22: Midland ........................................................................ 169
Chapter 23: Louisiana Coast, TriCoast LNG Terminal ........... 175
Chapter 24: Herzliya, Israel ........................................................... 183
Chapter 25: West of Midland-Odessa .......................................... 189
Chapter 26: Midland ........................................................................ 201

Chapter 27: Budapest, Hungary ..................................................... 211
Chapter 28: Budapest, Hungary ..................................................... 217
Chapter 29: Midland, Texas .......................................................... 223
Chapter 30: Chicago ..................................................................... 227
Chapter 31: London, Midland ...................................................... 233
Chapter 32: Washington DC ......................................................... 241
Chapter 33: Israel and Spain ......................................................... 245
Chapter 34 : Midland .................................................................... 251
Chapter 35: Midland .................................................................... 259
Chapter 36: Louisiana .................................................................. 267
Chapter 37: Louisiana .................................................................. 273
Epilogue: Louisiana and Moscow, Russia ..................................... 279

# CHAPTER 1
# MIDLAND, TEXAS

*November Morning*

SHE WAS GLAD to be the only passenger boarding a company plane for Midland, Texas in chilly pre-dawn darkness. Lynn Dayton was tall and Texas-blond with gravitas matching her position in charge of hundreds of engineers. She had just accepted a new, senior position at TriCoast after her predecessor had been murdered by a jealous ex-lover.

Last week, her boss's instructions had been both sympathetic and blunt. "I understand your transition to David's job is difficult. You've been on another side of the business. It's hard to feel close to a new group of people," Mike Emerson said.

"Just remember, when you talk to the boy wonder at Bradshaw Energy—no matter what he says the terms were before, with David—don't get deal fever. We can always walk away."

"No winner's curse. Got it," Lynn replied. The phrase *winner's curse* traced to a study of Gulf of Mexico lease sales. The winning bid often was too high—a geologist or engineer was too optimistic about invisible reserves under thousands of feet of water and rock. The company was stuck with paying for a lease that would never make money.

But that was last week, before Mike was stricken with a heart attack. The board tapped the CEO of a small private oilfield service company. In a surprise, Rowan Daine was recommended as the temporary fill-in for Mike both by the board's most ardent environmentalist as well as its most conservative member, another

1

oilfield service CEO, Burl Travis. Despite the board's approval of a six-month contract for Daine, Lynn was uncertain about the man. Other women she asked described him as hard to read or else as a typical man-about-town.

At Lynn's first meeting with Rowan Daine, she found it startling to see his angular figure in place of fireplug-sized Mike Emerson. Daine noticed and was soothing. "Yes, a shock for all of us. But Mike has told me about you. He thinks highly of you. Clearly champions you with the board. You can count on the same from me."

"That's good to hear." Lynn relaxed.

"Mike and Burl told me you've led the refining division to billions in profits."

"And I expect to do the same as EVP of the drilling division. Which reminds me, will you have the regular weekly executive meeting?" Lynn asked. She almost said, *Like Mike did.*

"No. I prefer informal conversations. Less confining than a schedule." Then Daine's tone cooled slightly. "Now what about this acquisition of Bradshaw Energy? That was one of David's pet projects. You still pursuing it?"

"Yes, if Joost Bradshaw and I can agree on a price."

"I'm the new guy here, so you'll have to convince me that's a good idea."

As he ushered her to the door, Rowan Daine smiled broadly. Despite how little she knew him, Lynn was charmed.

Mike had reliably had her back. Lynn felt reassured Rowan Daine would, too.

Soon, the private jet jolted to a stop in a line of other private jets and spun down. Fast Gulfstreams were the preferred mode of transport for companies whose drilling sites could be hundreds of miles remote from any big airport.

Beau Decatur, a bodyguard who worked for several TriCoast executives, met her in the private plane terminal and guided her to a white truck. Lynn climbed into the F-350, one of many the company owned. Beau was as square as a tight end and still hard-muscled from his prior military service. Unlike other urban locations, Lynn was not expecting Molotov-throwing cocktails from environmental protesters in Midland. *But there's always a first time here, too,* she thought.

The dry, flat landscape was more Phoenix desert than east Texas verdure. Mesquite and four-wing saltbush ringed countless drill sites that shaped West Texas into an unending factory floor of oil and gas production. Midland and neighboring Odessa exuded neither southern charm nor western cool, but instead the endless anxiety of fierce competition from companies next door and countries across the ocean. Outsiders who traveled to Midland in Southwest airplanes—packed with men in the seats and hardhats in the overhead—missed the hardboiled natives' shrewdness until their egos were smeared into the dirt.

Soon, Beau parked at the TriCoast headquarters. They went inside and were directed to the office of short, chipper Roy Bastrop, the Midland district head.

Lynn steeled herself. Her predecessor, David Jenkins, had been a classically warm, friendly, and uber-competent engineer and executive. *But that didn't stop him from making bad choices,* Lynn reminded herself. One of those bad choices had been a secret affair with Dena Tarleton, a TriCoast cyber whiz. When David ended the affair, Dena killed him. As part of her revenge against David, Dena had also become involved with a shadowy international conspiracy group led from China trying to take down TriCoast and other companies from the inside.

Sure enough, it didn't take long for Bastrop to ask the inevitable question. After a few pleasantries, he leaned in. "What was it like to find Jenkins?"

She shuddered. Lynn and Beau had been the ones to discover David's bloody, cooling body in the kitchen of a closed restaurant. Dena Tarleton, the woman who had murdered David, had tried to kill them, too.

"Somehow everyone in Midland has heard both the official and real versions of the story." She shook her head. "Beau and I were the only ones in that room who survived. We've kept our mouths shut. It's one of the few things we can do for David's family."

"I hear you adopted David's pet project—talking to Vandervoost's kid about buying his little company. Stupid idea."

*Makes sense he would feel threatened, although it's more obvious why, compared to Daine's objections.* "Sound him out when you and I talk to him this afternoon. Beau will drive us since the truck he rented doesn't have the TriCoast name splashed all over it."

"Fair enough," Roy said. His next words were chilling. "And since you and Beau aren't from around here, be careful driving. Traffic's always terrible in Midland, especially in the dark. Those dirt haulers can get awfully up close and personal."

"We'll keep it in mind tonight. But right now, let's go see 'Vandervoost's kid,' as you call Joost."

"We're meeting him at lunch?" Roy asked.

Every steak house, barbeque joint, and taco stand in Midland was a familiar hunting ground. Executives ate the same scrambled eggs and told the same secrets as truck drivers, field operators, and technicians. In other cases, no one talked because everyone was listening and observing. *Who are you with? What are they selling?*

She shook her head. "After lunch. People will identify us at any diner or restaurant."

"Still very few companies here with female execs." He nodded. "They're usually doing human relations or putting a pretty face on the environmental stuff. That's if they're not the ones on the other side of the table nailing our balls to the wall for not doing *enough* environmental stuff."

*Yet another vote of confidence.* "I have just the place for us to meet with Joost."

After lunch, Lynn and Roy reviewed information on Joost Bradshaw and his company. Joost was the son of obnoxious Henry Vandervoost, once a European TriCoast VP who had been gunning to take over Lynn's prior job while she was still in it. Until last year. After he'd turned in five years of losses, at the TriCoast board's request, Lynn had bumped Henry upstairs to a non-job and installed the omni-competent Bart Colby in his place running European refining.

When Henry didn't get the signal after six months, Lynn had to tell him to find another job. Her ears still rang with his angry shouts. But soon afterward he had moved on to become a partner at a London private equity firm.

On the personal-but-still-business side, Henry's wife and Joost's mother had divorced Henry years ago. Patsy Bradshaw raised Joost in Midland in her family's Bradshaw oil business when Henry returned to Europe.

Even from across the Atlantic Ocean, Henry had made sure Joost gravitated to the right college and business school. He helped Joost find jobs with an investment bank and the same private equity firm in which Henry was now a partner. The lure of family, friends, and running the powerful Bradshaw oil business had brought Joost back to Midland.

But today Joost wanted to sell Bradshaw Energy for reasons he had told no one, except maybe the now-deceased David, Lynn's predecessor.

When David died, he had been leading a three-billion-dollar bid for Bradshaw Energy. And despite the reputation of the West Texas oil zones around Midland as being safer, can't-lose propositions than the Gulf of Mexico, Lynn knew the Permian, too, held many traps.

As they settled into Beau's anonymous white truck, Lynn asked Roy, "What do you think of Joost and his company?"

"You can't negotiate with rock, and his company does have great rock. A fair price for good rock beats a cheap price for crappy rock. Great rock only gets better. Maybe his company *is* worth buying," Roy said.

"Seems like everyone here knows everyone else. You know Joost?" Beau asked.

"We all live together, serve together, work together in Midland," Roy said as if he had recited it many times to new hires, as he no doubt had. "Joost and I go to the same church, but there's not as much camaraderie as you might expect since we're all competitors. I know more about when he's on the schedule to usher the late service than I do how much oil Bradshaw Energy is producing."

"What about Terry Gomez, the CFO he's bringing along?" Lynn asked.

"Seen him around, but I don't know much about him."

Beau stopped in a flat, sandy parking lot east of town. The three of them walked around to the front of a long, low building labeled Sibley Nature Center, and Lynn again hoped they were the only ones with this idea for keeping their meeting secret. They paid for entry and a tall, beefy man motioned them into a small room stuffed with informational posters.

"Joost?"

"The same. You didn't see Terry out there? Terry's not just my CFO, he's my hunting partner on these deals. I shoot 'em; he skins 'em."

Lynn and Roy shook hands with a man who looked more like a slightly overweight, well-bred golfer than a scion of Henry Vandervoost with his Euro-floppy haircut.

"Good to meet you, Lynn. So sorry to hear about David's death."

"We miss David," she said, wanting to head off further questions.

"I always gave him credit for meeting us halfway." In Joost's Midland-raised dialect, *credit* became *craydeet*.

"David was a good man."

"How about you? You blest with any kee-uds?"

*Everyone always gets around to that question.* "Two step-kids. They're amazing," Lynn responded.

Joost could not have been more different from his European father. Still, the son had his own set of affectations, having completely adopted West Texas mannerisms and patois.

"Let's get to the point," Joost said. "Is TriCoast still interested in acquiring my family's company?"

"Yes, but not at the price David agreed to." Lynn looked around the small room. It felt claustrophobic.

Joost stared at her. "You one of them pathologically honest folks who thinks honesty always wins the deal?"

"I'm honest, yes." Lynn shrugged.

Joost wiped sweat from his forehead, seeming to echo Lynn's thoughts about the small size of the room. "Let's find Terry first before we get to numbers. He's *onree* sometimes."

*Ornery,* Lynn mentally translated as Joost rolled up his shirt-sleeves, displaying a tattoo on his elbow in the shape of Texas. *He's taking this Texan thing pretty far.*

"He may have gone outside already. He really likes this place." Joost's brow furrowed.

Lynn, Joost, and Roy put on their coats and walked through two sets of doors, then veered right along a path.

"Feels like a maze, but if we head counterclockwise toward the outside, we won't get lost," Joost said.

Finally, above a six-foot shrub, they saw a cowboy hat suspended in the air. As they cleared the shrub, Lynn could see the large, full-featured man appeared to also be looking for them.

Joost made introductions.

Lynn jumped in, eyeing Terry. "Joost. I can't support the three-billion-dollar price now that oil is half what it was a few months ago."

"We have other offers, from companies as big or bigger than yours. So, what kind of price and timing did you have in mind?" Joost chewed his lips.

*If he's already asking for a new number, he must be anxious,* Lynn thought. *I wonder if he really has other offers.*

"We have to get a better handle on your assets, especially this technical breakthrough you're describing," Roy said.

"Many of my people have equity in the company. Would you be able to offer them a kicker?" Joost's tone was querulous.

"My team needs to look everything over and make their projections." Referring to a team gave her a way to delay.

"David told us something different," Terry said.

*Oh, here we go,* Lynn thought. "But I'm not David, and I'm the one you're dealing with. We wanted to see if you are interested in continuing to talk to us about TriCoast acquiring Bradshaw Energy."

"You're as chicken as my father." Joost's boot scraped in the path. He swung around and stared at Lynn and Roy. "You're wasting my time if you're not ready to make an offer. David was less afraid than you."

"I'm not David," Lynn repeated.

Lynn and Beau's next and final destination was a long-stay hotel on the northwest side of town at which Lynn's company kept a small block of rooms at a fixed price. It was cheaper and easier than trying to book rooms whose price could escalate three hundred percent from one night to the next, depending on how many tool pushers and vendors were in town.

The cluster of hotels and the giant HEB grocery store with its multi-pump gas station catered to tractor-trailer drivers and workers heading to Andrews, Pecos, or scrubby outposts further west. In a nod to the fieldworker clientele staying at the hotel to which they were headed, a hard-bristled brush was mounted about a foot off the ground near each entrance—a reminder to scrape off anything caked onto shoes or boots.

Midland was a microcosm of Texas—big, aggressive, fast, riding the boom, banking for the bust sure to follow. Natives were alert to events in South America, Saudi Arabia, and Russia. It was like, Lynn reflected, dry parts of Oklahoma where she'd grown up, but without cement curbs and neatly trimmed lawns.

Beau drove them past streets named for companies past and present: *Sinclair, Shell, Gulf, Stanolink*. They went by the boneyards of dropped rigs, now spares. Once onto Highway 250, he steered their truck carefully among the other ubiquitous white four-door heavy-duty trucks hurtling along the bypass. Despite the dimming light, everyone drove fast, with a loose aggressiveness.

Exits onto two-way access roads were especially precarious. Lynn hoped the oncoming trucks—many at least twice their size—would stop, as they were supposed to do.

Truckers worked 100-hour weeks with the support of cocaine and meth but then sought to break their expensive habits. Many drove for thirty-six or forty-eight hours at a stretch, caravanning their 35-ton vehicles in single file, blowing their horns to keep one another awake.

To be successful here, she thought, you had to know how to assess risks and which ones to take. *And to drive here you have to know where the hell you're going because road signs and highway exits don't exist.* Mergers of two lanes into one were sudden and unmarked. Every vehicle was a big, or bigger, truck. The Scylla and Charybdis of giant trucks could cut off the rare exit or worse, an escape from the accident occurring in front of you.

Even with the windows up in their F-350, Lynn could smell sulfur from the wells. She'd looked forward to this visit to what was really her open-air factory, a factory manufacturing barrels of oil from underground—ancient carbon capture—instead of widgets above ground.

The landscape around them faded into dusty camouflage: brown and green, yellow-brown sand. Sandy shoulders, scrub, and cacti-lined asphalt roads. The sun was setting, but streetlights were not yet illuminated. Beau kept to the middle lane of the road, but trucks whizzed by on both sides.

She looked at her phone to disguise her tension. "You didn't ask but it's called Midland because it's the midpoint between Fort Worth and El Paso—"

Suddenly, from Lynn's right, a massive sand hauler swerved toward them. She had just a moment to see the driver pull a gun and aim it toward her. "He's got a gun! Watch out!"

But a dump truck on their left boxed them in.

"Jesus!" Beau slammed the brakes. "No place to go!"

Lynn braced herself against the dashboard as she pitched forward. Pain shot through both arms. She held her breath, waited for a crash from behind that didn't occur. Other drivers had seen what was happening and slowed, too.

Angry and shocked, Lynn shouted through her window at the sand hauler's driver as he shot ahead into the space Beau had been forced to leave open.

She could see the driver of the sand hauler waving his gun in his rearview mirror. Lynn pulled out a phone to get a picture of the license plate, but the truck had no plates. It disappeared ahead of them within seconds.

"Damn. Too close," Beau said. His knuckles were white.

"Thank God for your reflexes." Lynn tightened her seat belt. "He could have killed us with his truck. Or his gun."

## CHAPTER 2
# LONDON

Henry Vandervoost stared at the encrypted email he'd just decoded. The sender appeared to be a bogus account, but the message was real. News articles about poisonings of Russian ex-pats in London. The message was unmistakable. He was next unless he paid what he owed.

He was in a foul mood, as always. Too much ... something. Stress. Too many people wanting too much money from him. He didn't have enough on hand nor the power to get more. Using the venom of his pen and voice when he'd worked at TriCoast in Rotterdam had been a satisfying outlet but now, in this new job and with the more precise language of the English, merely earned him the weak sobriquet of *snarky*.

He fumed. He felt as if his head would explode with unfairness. Well, *something* might explode. He had contacts who could make that happen.

Life had been simpler in Rotterdam before Lynn Dayton, once his rival, then his bitch boss, had sidelined him—kicked him upstairs temporarily, they called it at TriCoast. The quietly smug Bart Colby had taken over every iota of Henry's European refining authority. Colby was just another *arriviste* if a Houston engineer could even be called an arriviste.

He rubbed knuckles against his forehead. One drink had followed another and more beautiful women than he could count added up during several weekends in Las Vegas and Macau. He had been treated like the whale he was. But then he'd lost over two million pounds gambling. *Now I'm a beached whale. They'll cut me open for blubber.*

When a private equity firm had been quick to hire him after he'd been kicked up to the nice-sounding job with no authority at TriCoast, his situation became worse, not better. Now he was expected to travel to see Asian investors, eat their weird food, endure their endless stalling, gamble with them, and keep up *la flatterie*, all to raise money for the current fund. He knew plenty of people who would be happy to take the title and the money and work half-days, but he was dogged by the need, even still, to prove to his son he had *la majie*, the mojo.

When he hadn't brought in his share of the fund, his partners' expressions had become less pleasant. They told him he either needed to raise the money from investors—private investors and the big multinationals like those headquartered here in London—or kick in the pounds himself. He could afford to invest in the fund, couldn't he?

He had taken his own money and tried to double it at a couldn't-lose resort about which one of his investors told him. Apparently, he was the first to lose.

A knock sounded just before the solid oak door was thrown open so hard Henry feared its hinges would be stripped. A redheaded giant with round shoulders leaned onto the antique desk. Any more pressure and the giant would snap the equally antique desk's legs.

"Yer Henry are ya?"

Henry suspected the oaf's identity but pretended otherwise. "And you are?"

"Ya know who I am. Or what my name is today, anyway." The man laughed, as if shaking down rich guys for money rocked his world. *It does*, Henry realized.

"I hear ya got a bit o' difficulty."

"I need time."

"No. That's why the casinos and the bankers where ya

exhausted your lines told me where to find ya. Now remind me, Henry, how much ya owe?"

"150,000. Pounds."

Instantly the big man grabbed Henry by the shirt and pulled him close, nose to nose. "Don't act the maggot. Ever. I'm not one of the honeys they were usin' to get the credit out of ya."

Henry felt the man tighten his grip. "Don't tear my shirt."

"I'll tear ya a new asshole if ya don't stop lying. How much ya owe? Tell me the truth."

"A million two pounds."

The man's hands clamped around Henry's neck and began to squeeze. "A secret. I get paid whether or not you live. Try again."

Henry gasped for breath. "Two million one hundred thousand pounds."

The man gave him one final shove and backed away. "Better."

Henry stumbled, then pulled himself up straight.

"I need more time."

"Ya don't have time. What ya need now is an idea about how to make that money."

"It's in the bank," Henry said.

The man's hand caressed Henry's jaw, then grabbed his ear and pinched it. "What'd I tell ya about lyin'? If the cash was in the bank or bitcoin, you'd a paid and I wouldn't hae ta be here. You have two hundred thousand in the bank. Plus a house in Mayfair whose price you goosed for the casino records."

Henry felt sick. "If I could just get back in—anywhere—I'd win it back. My run of bad luck run is over."

"Yeah. And I believe in Santa Claus. Try harder." The man stepped away from him, frowned. As if he were thinking of the idea for the first time, he nodded. "Ya do have one asset ya keep forgettin'."

Henry looked at him, puzzled.

"Yer son," the man said triumphantly.

"What? You want my son? He's thirty-one. He doesn't owe me anything."

"The son could even buy ya some time."

"I don't understand."

"I'll talk so ya understand. What does yer son do?"

"He owns an oil company in Texas. I don't see how that helps you."

"Takin' it slow, here. Yer son just called you a few hours ago. Remember, don't lie to me."

"Yes, he did call."

"Ya don't think we overlooked that do ya?"

"He talked about research. Pie-in-the-sky stuff."

"But pie-in-the-sky turns out to be worth a lot—even enough to take care of yer two-point-one-million-pound debt—to the banks who hired me."

"When does a bank ever care about oilfield research?"

"Ya should have been listenin' more closely on the call. We were."

Henry shivered. Of course they were listening. "I was thinking about what I owed."

"All ya need to do, Henry, is get the special water cleanup technology and turn it over to me. We're not even askin' for the wells, or the oil, though that'd help ya get back into yer casinos for a while. Just the tech."

"My son hates me. He'll never tell me. Besides, it's not him, it's someone who works for him..."

The red-headed man held up a big paw, palm-forward, as if to stop Henry's stream of words. Which it did.

"Ya got the email, right?"

Henry thought about the vicious poisonings described in the message and nodded.

"Ya should have spent more time checkin' out the casino backers. Russians. They want a piece of ya, but they'd rather have the technology. My guess, they're plannin' to sell it to the Chinese. Who'll probably sell it back to the Americans."

"I'll talk to my son. They're still testing it. I don't think he knows if it works."

The red-headed man nodded. "Yer smart. You'll figure it. The 2.1 is collectin' interest at ten percent. A week. So, if I were ya, I'd try to have the water cleanup device or info really soon."

Henry shook his head. "He won't tell me."

Despite his size, the man appeared to glide to the door he'd almost destroyed on his way in. "I'll be lettin' myself out now. I'll tell my bosses your answer is *yes*."

*Maybe I should feel relieved,* Henry thought, when the door closed. *But Joost sure as hell isn't going to hand over a multi-million-dollar secret water-cleaning technology. Not to me.*

Henry began to think through how he could get the technology from his son's company. He'd kept in touch with Burl Travis, Tri-Coast board member, who'd told him TriCoast was negotiating to buy Bradshaw Energy. That couldn't be allowed to happen. Particularly since the woman he hated more than any other was leading the negotiation for TriCoast.

His face flamed as he thought of the many times Lynn Dayton had coolly dismissed his ideas, until finally one day, she coolly dismissed him altogether, telling him he no longer had his senior job at TriCoast. *I'm not a violent man, truly I'm not. But if there's anyone I could kill, it's Lynn Dayton.*

Then he recalled another nugget of information from Burl. Burl and another board member had recommended Rowan Daine to fill in for Mike Emerson as TriCoast CEO while Mike recovered from his heart attack. Henry knew Daine from his earliest days working for Bradshaw Energy, those sweet, old days when he'd married the founder's daughter and had been on track to own the company. Rowan Daine ran an oilfield wastewater disposal business. And since water was produced in at least the same volume as oil if not more, Daine's business had grown as West Texas oil production had grown.

Henry found Daine's number and called it. He expected to leave a message but was pleased when Rowan Daine answered.

"Henry, what brings you to my world? I'm driving on I-45 so make it simple for me."

"I'd think the CEO of TriCoast would get chauffeured everywhere. Congratulations, by the way."

"The company doesn't pay to have me driven to the Houston titty bars. I have to drive myself. You remember those, don't you?"

"I do. I miss them."

"So, what can I do you for. You never call, you never write."

"TriCoast is looking at buying my son's company. Don't."

"Now Henry. Whyever not?"

Henry had prepared his answer. "I remember the company's wells from when I was there."

"Long time ago. Those wells played out by now. Your son, if he's smart, has drilled a bunch of new wells."

"I'll tell you a secret. What nobody but me will explain is, old or new wells, they turn from valuable oil to worthless gas quickly. In months, sometimes weeks. And even if you can gather the gas and process it, it's expensive to process. Has too much nitrogen and hydrogen sulfide."

"Really? As much as I've been around West Texas, I haven't heard about those problems."

Despite the cool London temperature, Henry wiped sweat from his forehead.

"So, the Bradshaw wells aren't worth as much as your son and his people say they are. Or whatever crazy-ass Lynn Dayton decides to make up. She and the freaking CFO, Sara Levin. Are they both always such cool bitches?"

Henry smiled to himself. Somebody else understood the threat posed by Lynn Dayton and other women at TriCoast. "I'd say you have them both bloody pegged."

"Yes, you always were the *bloody* European. I might think about doing you this favor, Henry. But what's in it for me? And don't just tell me TriCoast stockholder value. Something I can put in the bank when my six-month contract at TriCoast runs out."

Vandervoost had remembered Daine's predilections. Daine was usually the one taking potential wastewater disposal clients out for whatever they wanted. He liked being treated the same way: boobs, bars, and big-game hunting. "I have prepaid reservations for two—you and your favorite companion--to hunt stags in Scotland, zebras in Namibia, or black bears in Alaska. What's your pick?"

"I'll take all three, Henry. Send me the dates. Get one of the girls in your office to make the flight arrangements for me and Liddy."

"Liddy's your Midland gal?"

"The same. She's always up for adventure."

Daine had answered exactly as Vandervoost had expected. Vandervoost had no such reservations yet—he had several Russians to pay off first. But Daine had just made it worth his while by removing the only obstacle—TriCoast—standing between him and the water recycling technology the Russians and the Chinese wanted so much they'd forgive his gambling debts.

# CHAPTER 3
# ISRAEL

Avi Levin kept a framed picture of the hundred-person Leviathan offshore platform installation above his desk. Everything the crew needed was on the platform: power generation, water desalination, and waste treatment. The platform was ninety-two meters tall and weighed over fifteen thousand metric tons. The platform's installation had been difficult; swells in the eastern Mediterranean were rough. Rip currents ran through the full water depth.

Next to the picture of the platform was a map of natural gas pipelines—to Israel, to LNG plants in Egypt, even a proposed pipeline north to Turkey. More than a decade ago scientists and engineers had discovered a large gas formation fifty miles off Israel's northern coast, the Tamar field. Geologists and their supercomputers then located an even larger field eighty miles off the coast and subsequently named it for its size, Leviathan. Another field, Aphrodite, had been discovered near Cyprus, overlapping slightly into Israeli waters.

Engineers had estimated Tamar and Leviathan together held thirty trillion feet of natural gas, more than enough to supply Israel for years. Over half of Israel's power was already generated from its own natural gas reserves, leaving more natural gas for export.

Even with one platform now closed, Avi was proud Israel's current level of energy security marked such a change from earlier years when he and his family worried about where their heat and electricity would come from and if it would be cut off. The proposal Avi was reviewing would add to the millions of cubic feet of natural gas Israel was already shipping via subsea pipeline to Egypt. When first signed, the agreement had been termed the most significant deal between Israel and Egypt since the 1979 treaty.

"Yes?" Avi had been dreading the call. Caller ID showed Teos Mostafa, head of a large Egyptian LNG plant. Egypt planned to liquefy the gas in big plants. The liquefied natural gas, or LNG, would be sent on ships around the world to hungry customers in Europe, India, and eastern Asia.

"Tell me why I'm calling you, Avi," the brusque Egyptian voice kept a French inflection. Teos Mostafa was a graduate of France's famously hard-to-get-into math and engineering school, École Polytechnique, or L'X.

"You want to know when we finish developing our part of the Eastern Med trading platform and when it will be online." Avi dragged out his reply to stall.

"*Précisément.*"

"We have had delays in our schedule due to the constant bombing." After Hamas launched multiple rockets into Israel's territory, Israel responded with its own barrage. Hamas then announced it would attack an "offshore Zionist gas platform." Besides Hamas in Gaza to the south lobbing missiles, Iran threatened both directly and with its support of Hezbollah to the north. Hezbollah and Hamas had shore-to-sea missiles. Both, along with Iran, had already fired at numerous Israeli inland targets in the past.

Israeli defense forces had kept the country safe, but especially now, after the latest terrible terrorist attack, Avi was on edge for the occasion when a missile somehow slipped past the Iron

Dome. As the Hamas attack made clear, no one at Avi's company, which operated in Israel's offshore natural gas fields, could relax.

Teos' voice hardened. "We have had our own problems with the Houthi attacks. They drastically reduced our normal shipping revenues. Yes, both our and your governments want our Eastern Med Gas Forum project to succeed. Immediately."

The gas trading hub, located in Cairo, also included Morocco, Sudan, Bahrain, and the United Arab Emirates, all of whom had normalized relations with Israel. US government energy policymakers frequently joined the Eastern Med meetings as observers.

"Teos, we agree. Our customers in Spain and the rest of Europe are anxious to buy our natural gas, liquefied in *your* plant, as soon as possible. Indeed, they are begging to meet with me at the upcoming Budapest gas conference." *Not exactly true since the begging goes both ways. We need twenty-year contract customers.*

"Normally this group would meet in Doha."

"Teos, we told them Israelis won't go to Doha, not with Hamas leadership there. So, they agreed to have the conference in Budapest. But you should be aware Russia has been telling our government—us—through back channels they don't like our energy agreements with your country."

The Russians hadn't liked the US shipping gas to Europe—Europe had long been exclusively Russia's customer—and they didn't like the upstart Egyptian-Israeli joint venture shipping gas to Europe either. But the Europeans, if not as desperate as they had been when Russia invaded Ukraine, were still motivated to diversify beyond Russia. Even apart from Teos' call, Avi knew he and his colleagues needed to get the Eastern Med trading platform operating as soon as possible.

Teos sounded impatient again. "Russians are always testy. You have not answered my question, Avi. We need products, not excuses. When will you finish with your part of the trading platform? And more importantly, when will we start seeing gas deliveries to our plant for liquefaction?"

"Soon, Teos. If the rocket attacks slow, then sooner."

Avi pushed his chair back and turned to a different problem. He reviewed the e-mail on the company's secure system from Lynn Dayton at TriCoast Energy. Avi had met Lynn when they'd had a weekend business school class together at the University of Chicago—she was in person in Chicago, and he participated remotely from Herzliya.

They'd met again in Washington, DC when both had helped start a research center between Israel and the US involving universities of both countries.

Her company had recently bought a small interest in one of Israel's fields. Avi had heard from his aunt that Lynn was now in charge of TriCoast's US oil and gas production, having been promoted from the refining division. He'd arranged the call with Lynn and his aunt, Sara Levin, TriCoast's chief financial officer. Sara was a no-nonsense woman who'd won Wall Street's respect with concise explanations of TriCoast's revenue and profits. Sara and Lynn were the two most senior women at TriCoast.

He needed a second petroleum engineering pro. He could look up TriCoast's experts but names on a page wouldn't give him what he needed. *What does Lynn think of them? Do they deal with international reserves? Would these west Texan petroleum engineers understand me and my company and our offshore reserves?*

Avi dialed into the video call with his Aunt Sara and Lynn.

"I've run numbers, but I want your recommendations about another petroleum engineer. What's your read on the reserve accounting firm, James and James?" Avi asked.

"Ha! What do most anal-retentive engineers do when you give them a question with uncertainty?" Sara Levin answered her own question. "They build a spreadsheet."

"What James and James does," Avi inferred.

"They're the best. David really liked them," Sara said. She paused, as if remembering Lynn now had the dead man's job.

"If Sara likes them, and especially if my folks in Midland like them—and they do—there's all the information you need," Lynn said smoothly, ignoring Sara's pause.

Suddenly Avi's picture disappeared from Sara's and Lynn's screens.

In Israel, Avi's screen locked up. It flickered off as an incoming missile alarm wailed.

Avi grabbed his laptop and ran to the steel-reinforced safe room bunker.

After the all-clear sounded, Avi returned to his office. Nothing hit, at least not nearby. He thought for a moment, then called a contact who worked with the Iron Dome, the system that intercepted and shot down incoming missiles.

"Just got the all-clear in Herzliya. Was it Hamas again? Hezbollah?"

"No. The missile wasn't fired from Gaza or Lebanon. Something new. It came from an offshore ship. In an area off Syria the Russian fleet is known to patrol."

## CHAPTER 4
# MIDLAND

*"Hydraulic fracturing and horizontal drilling involve high pressure stimulation using water and proppant (usually sand) to create small cracks in tight shale rock that allow oil and gas trapped in the formation to flow more easily into the well and up to the surface. The most popular proppant is raw sand."*

—RBN Energy, rbnenergy.com

Lynn met Beau in the hotel's parking lot. November morning fog softened the look of the Midland and blurred its edges, but a brutal wind whipped Lynn's hair across her eyes. She tied it back and put on a cap and gloves. Wrapped against the numbing cold, they ran west on paved side streets away from their hotel and toward Odessa. A flat vista opened all the way to the horizon since so few trees could survive the wind and aridity. Cement drives interrupted sandy soil which, in places, was carved into big plats.

Another set of apartment buildings was under construction, testament to the city's growth from its streets named for oil companies to signs pointing off one of the main drags toward a former president's house.

A man walked a skinny dog on a sidewalk nearby. The sun through the dog's hair outlined him with a halo-like aura. Lynn remembered how her stepchildren had been begging for a dog, spotting them everywhere.

"Did you notice there were no road signs or exits from I-20? As if road signs and exits are for scaredy-cats."

Beau laughed. "There are no scaredy-cats in Midland."

After a few more miles of fast jogging in the freezing air, Lynn realized her feet had become not just cold, but wet. *Nothing like cold, wet feet to make me feel poor again.*

She signaled to Beau. They turned around and ran back to the hotel.

In the post-run shower, hot water splashing onto her head was cooled by her cold skin by the time it dripped down her ankles.

Beau called her to say they would be delayed leaving to go to the field operation in Stanton that Joost had reluctantly offered for an inspection visit. "Our new boss, Rowan Daine, is in town—he has a house here—and sounds like he has questions. Let me call him back. Shouldn't be more than fifteen minutes."

Fifteen minutes was just enough time for Lynn to call her husband, although he was moments from having to wake his (*our*—she corrected herself) children.

When Cy answered her video call, his unshaven face told her he, too, had only a few minutes to talk.

"Good morning, love. First, you need to know Marika's asking for a puppy again. I say we say yes," Cy said.

"And she will—"

"Yup. Take care of it. She'll learn she's committed herself to more clean-up than she realizes, but I think she'll take it on."

"Have you studied—"

"—breeds? Yes, but we need to look further. She wants—"

"—a puppy from a rescue group. What do you think?" Lynn found being able to complete one another's sentences was something she cherished about her still-new marriage to Cy, so different from her first marriage.

"I'll have to look by myself first. If I take her and Matt with me, we'll end up with five dogs. I'm not sure I trust even myself once I start looking at those big eyes."

"Theirs or the puppies?"

"Both."

She smiled. "I understand."

"This could be the right time to get a dog for both. Some of the eight-year-old girls at school are friendly with Marika. Others want to be in control. They're not too subtle about it."

"She needs help surviving pre-teen Psy Ops."

"Exactly."

"How's Matt?"

"At night he wrestles his pillow into submission. When he wins the match, he can go to sleep. It's his turn to bring snacks to preschool. Which means it's my turn. Gotta leave."

❖

"Daine asked what we were doing. When I told him, he explained he wanted to go with us," Beau said as they got into his double-cab truck. "That's why we're picking him up, too."

"Can't turn the man down. But I wish he'd called me," Lynn said.

Beau and Lynn arrived first at Roy's house, a large, frame two-story. Lynn shivered as they waited.

When he climbed into the back seat of the truck, Lynn told him Rowan Daine would also be joining them.

"Good. Since he's one of TriCoast's wastewater contractors, as well as the big boss for right now, I've been to his house on business. Friendly guy. Rumor is, he's got a mistress here and a wife and kid in Houston. Haven't met the mistress."

She told Roy about their near accident the night before.

"Everyone's on the road, and off the road, at the same time—we all line up for breakfast tacos and barbeque lunches. A few of the companies have modeled every major intersection in the city because there's so much traffic. They're trying to save their truckers' time. Then you've got all these straight roads. A car going 110 miles an hour on a 70-mile-an-hour road is in trouble when the road turns."

"We've had a spate of problems. When the first truck driver

crashed and died, we all assumed it was the stay-awake amphetamines he was taking. The coroner confirmed it," Roy explained.

"Most of the accidents are just accidents?" Lynn asked, adjusting her seat belt.

Beau slowed to allow a bigger truck to pass them.

"Yes," Roy responded.

"Beau and I don't, not after what happened last night. I was on the passenger side. The driver of the hauler pulled close, like he was going to push us in the other lane."

"Seen it many times," Roy said.

"But how often does the driver also point a gun at passengers? That's what happened to us. Looked like he was ready to take a shot."

"You sure you saw a gun?" Roy asked.

"Yes. Thank God Beau has top-notch reflexes and the other trucks behind us were watching out for us."

"That *is* shocking. Everyone around here has a gun for protection. And many people have road rage. So, I shouldn't be surprised someone would pull a gun on you, but I am." Roy shook his head in disbelief.

"What I remember in those few seconds, the man didn't even seem angry. The opposite, very deliberate," Lynn explained.

"I'm sorry that happened to you here," Roy said.

Beau drove slower than the speed limit. They had plenty of time to get to the operations centers for the drill sites. The plan was to visit Bradshaw sites, fortunately all close together. The core Midland basin comprised only six counties, but decades in, they still held millions of barrels of oil.

"Remember, you always want to have a meal before you go into one of these prospect meetings. Otherwise, you'll agree to anything," Roy reminded them.

"Because you're hungry?" Beau asked.

"If you weren't you would be fast. The prospects have names like Chimichangas, Salsa, and Powdered Donuts."

Lynn laughed. "Fighting Okra, Dos Equis, and Spud Muffin."

Roy smiled. "Goldirocks."

They pulled up to the driveway and gate of what had to be one of the biggest houses in Midland, near the Midland Country Club. Beau pushed a button on the security box. After he was verified, the gate swung open. Then it was several hundred yards to an enormous Tuscan-style mansion with a six-truck garage off to one side.

Beau pulled the truck around on the circle drive. Lynn recognized Rowan Daine from their brief meeting in Dallas as he bounded out of the house.

He greeted everyone and slipped into the second row of seats in the cab. Nodding toward the house he said, "Yes, it IS over-the-top, which is why my customers love the parties here. So, Roy, good to see you again. I'm looking forward to seeing these Bradshaw wells." He reached over the seat and shook hands with Beau.

Rowan didn't say anything to Lynn until she turned in her seat and offered her hand. "Good to see you again."

"And you." But nobody in the truck could miss it when Daine didn't take Lynn's offer of a handshake.

"So Roy, tell me what you think of Joost's company so far," Daine said.

Lynn turned again and looked at Roy, allowing a slight edge in her voice. "Yes, Roy, do tell us what you think."

Roy nodded and blushed, acknowledging Daine's slighting of Lynn but didn't hold back. "As I've told Lynn, who'll be the decisionmaker by the way, I'm concerned we're offering too much for the company, despite the supposed bonus of this great new water clean-up technology he has. Plus, since Joost Bradshaw is Henry Vandervoost's son and Vandervoost used to work for TriCoast, Joost probably has all the intel on TriCoast from his old man."

Beau drove away from the Tuscan mansion, through the gate, and east on busy Highway 250 toward the even busier I-20.

"Henry doesn't work for TriCoast now, though," Lynn said. *And I'm the one who let him go.* Thinking this brought up the memory of every person she'd known hired in a boom and let go in a bust—the subdued expressions, the meetings that went on forever because no one had anywhere else to go. Million-milers put on a brave face but were stunned to find themselves stuck at home saying, "Now I'm a consultant."

"—word here in Midland is Henry and Joost aren't close," Daine said, lightly.

"You're a wastewater CEO, Rowan. What do you think of Bradshaw's water technology?" Lynn asked.

"Have to see it in action. Maybe we will today. Honestly, I'm more interested in what he's been doing with AI."

"You're experimenting with it?" Lynn asked him.

"I am, for all the well detection. TriCoast should, too. You could get rid of folks in investor relations and HR."

*Maybe he's right but that will be touchy*, Lynn thought. She looked at Roy. "Roy and I are also interested in how Bradshaw and his contractors operate his wells, which is where the money is. And Henry doesn't have to like his son to tell him everything about TriCoast. What about his CFO, Gomez? What's the 'word in Midland' on him?"

Roy spoke up. "Standard issue top-of-line Texas A&M engineer with an accounting master's for extra gloss. He's done his best to assure Bradshaw Energy doesn't become a zombie company or another dead carcass by the side of the road."

"Why're they selling?" Lynn asked.

"They have private equity funding," Daine said. "Private equity has the money but then you're beholden to them. Surely you already knew that, Lynn, or have you not spent enough time in Midland yet to understand how things work here?"

"Mmm, in fact, I did already know about the quick private equity timetable." *Daine is a freaking jerk. This will be a long day.*

"It can't make Joost feel great that the money could come from a fund his estranged father is running. Talk about being under your daddy's thumb," Roy said.

"Maybe it's the other way around—maybe Henry is under pressure to do business with Joost," Lynn suggested. She looked out the window. Even with the windows rolled up, the smell was a faint mixture of sulfur and hydrocarbons from the many wells off toward the horizon. Nearer the road, low bushes and mesquite trees in the sandy soil were interrupted at intervals only by telephone poles.

"Frankly, I like that both Joost and Gomez are young," Daine said.

"What do you mean?"

Daine leaned forward from the back seat of the truck, looking directly at Lynn for the first time. "I'm like a baseball scout looking for talent. Have a friend in the scouting business. He wants big, tall teenagers without much hair on their legs. Not much hair means they'll grow even more."

"You're saying we should get Joost and Gomez to parade in front of us in shorts so we can examine their legs?" Lynn smiled.

"Not a bad idea." Roy laughed but Daine didn't react. "They'll feel exposed anyway once they cough up their financials."

The truck slowed as they encountered another jam of trucks on I-20.

"*Beeping and creeping* is what we call this," Roy said.

"*Onlooker slowdown. Lots of friends out here. Heavy brake tap. Slow roll through the Mid-Cities.* KRLD-Dallas," Beau said.

"*Gapers' block.* Chicago for the win," Lynn replied. "No euphemisms for that town."

Cold rain greeted them after Beau made the final turn to the drill site. Dusty trucks like theirs clustered around a couple of trailers, one with the license plate, OVERRIDE, which meant a valuable share of production. The lines of pressure pumpers looking like the industrial machines they were, the several-story rig resembling a narrow-based Eiffel Tower, and the cylindrical silos of sand to one side dominated the view. A US flag was draped down the side of the rig.

Several feet off the ground near the base of the rig was a big box-shaped office. They climbed up a staircase to it.

Inside, Roy introduced Lynn and Beau to the drilling contractor chief. "Great guy. This is a Bradshaw site, but he's done good work for us at TriCoast, too."

Rowan Daine joined the group and nodded. "Chief, good to see you again. You've probably heard I'm temping at TriCoast for Mike until he recovers from his heart attack."

"Matter of fact, I did." The drill chief nodded back at Daine, then pointed to his own engraved silver belt buckle. "Deeper Cheaper. That's us. You came to see Bradshaw manufrackturing in person, hey?" he asked.

"Thanks for taking the time," Lynn said.

"Word is she's a refinery gal, not a petroleum engineer," Daine said in a stage whisper.

*No question. Daine's an asshole.* "Engineers are engineers so we can learn anything. Still, I might have a few easy questions for the chief. Why don't you give us an overview of what you're doing and tell me what I need to know?"

"Sure. We're turning dirt, we're drilling; someone else picked the site and zones. The landing zone is super important. So's the rock. You can't fix bad rock, but no problem. All the rock around here is good." The chief spun through several computer screens to show them the well's progress. The lateral had already been drilled four thousand feet.

She nodded, relaxing in the presence of technical terms. *Mechanical problems are so much easier than people problems.*

Outside, the drilling chief guided Roy, Lynn, and Daine to a corner of the rig where they could watch the pipe feed down through the deck. Lynn asked questions about cementing and casing.

"You got your rig, your drill bit, your casing, your frac crews, electricity, pumping horsepower, and sand. Last few years, oil production graph looked like a damn hockey stock until it went off the rails and we didn't have enough pipelines for the oil and gas. But all that's fixed now, at least for the next few months—we got more than enough takeaway pipes. We hit our targets 97% of the time—not like the old days."

"I gotta interrupt here," Rowan Daine said. "You left out the most important part. For me anyway. Water! The chief here gets flowback and produced water—millions of gallons of it, about the same volume as oil—from every well. And it's all non-potable—you can't drink it. What comes up when he fracs the line is oil, gas, AND water. They all have to be separated and sent on their way. My company takes care of all the dirty, salty water for him."

"You're also testing Bradshaw's new water recycling technology on this well, right?" Lynn asked.

The chief glanced at Rowan Daine and said, "Yes, we are."

"But it's not public yet, so you can't tell us if it works? And it's super-expensive, I hear," Daine said. "I can't see it replacing our existing system of deep disposal wells."

"Hate to argue with a water company guy like you, but I have to disagree," the chief said. "So do the regulators and just about everyone. Too many earthquakes we didn't used to have."

"You know this ESG bullshit isn't proving out. Too expensive and does a worse job." Daine glowered but then stepped back as if telling himself to calm down.

Lynn watched his sequence of reactions. *Touchy guy.* She turned back to the chief. "How do you plan for enough pipes or trucks?"

"It's hard. Sometimes you've got so much coming out and not enough pipes in the field, especially to the west of us where they haven't drilled as many wells. Then you have to use fleets of trucks each day to take away the oil and another fleet of trucks, like Daine's, to take away the water."

"Again, Lynn, if you had more experience out here you wouldn't ask such a dumb question. You never know exactly what's underground until it starts coming up in the pipe," Daine said.

*He's getting way too angry about a technical discussion.* Lynn thought. *Where's the Rowan Daine salesman geniality? What is he hiding?*

## CHAPTER 5
# LONDON, UK, MOSCOW AND MURMANSK, RUSSIA

Hannah Bosko was celebrating with her mates at the pub.

A forensic geologist—"Who knew that was a job?"

She laughed, remembering her interview with Scotland Yard a few months ago.

Then her group chuckled about her Chicago accent. "They won't understand you."

"No problem. Most of what I'm 'interviewing' are literally plants and dirt."

The pay for occasional Scotland Yard projects beat the salary she'd been earning as a water quality inspector, so she signed on when they made her the offer.

Forensic geology is an American idea we've adopted, she was told.

*And since then I've learned so much about shoes,* she thought.

About the same time, her neighborhood pub had ordered a case of very fine, very expensive single-malt Scotch whiskey—bought for the holidays and paid in advance because it was so valuable, the owner told her—from a new, reputable vendor who supplied many London neighborhood pubs.

George, the pub owner, celebrated the day of its arrival with a special, invitation-only party for his favorite customers. Hannah had skipped two environmental protests she'd planned to attend, honored to be included in the owner's party.

But when George opened the four boxes, to gasps and jeers of the men and women crowded around, instead of cases of fine Scotch whiskey he found cement blocks packed in newspaper.

George was pink-cheeked with embarrassment. "Go on then. Get some other bevvys. Happy hour prices," he muttered. Hannah felt for the hard-working man of sixty who'd recently reopened the place.

Everyone drifted to the bar to take him up on the offer except Hannah, who stood by while the man called the delivery company.

When George clicked off his phone, he shook his head. "They say they picked up from the company, same place as always. No one else has complained."

"Save the boxes for me," she offered. "Whole thing's dodgy."

"Bloody right." He sighed. "I'll call my insurance company tomorrow."

"Let me look into it for you," Hannah said.

"You're daft. Invisible elves and goblins will tell you what happened?"

"Simpler. The dirt, grit, and dust will."

George shook his head. "I need whatever help I can get. This could clean me out."

❖

Energy minister Zaitsev kept his face impassive. It wouldn't matter what he thought but it would matter if his face communicated dissent. Russian President Maksim Egonov considered himself first all-powerful and, close second, an oilman. He was proud of his doctoral dissertation on minerals development. Any whispers of plagiarism had been snuffed out, along with their authors. The steppingstone served its purpose: Egonov had gotten others in OPEC oil negotiations to accept Russia's importance. Indeed, Zaitsev had to credit the man as he was credited in the West—during periods of low oil and gas prices Egonov had played a weak hand well, reaching out to China, building pipelines, funding anti-hydrocarbon groups in the EU, UK, and US.

Beyond its borders, its oil and gas revenues allowed Russia to project power into the Middle East, Africa, and Venezuela. Russia was no longer a bystander to Saudi Arabia on oil nor to Qatar on gas: Russia was now a world leader in both and a key trading partner to China. And had to be, because Russia was first and foremost a petrostate. Which pleased Zaitsev. No matter how many sanctions packages Europe and the US passed against Russian energy, Russian energy remained a force.

After the big meeting, Zaitsev trailed Egonov back to his enormous office. Kir Zaitsev didn't like disagreeing with President Egonov's ideas. To protest could mean being replaced and then quickly executed, or perhaps in reverse order. Egonov would find another to take Zaitsev's place. Worse, it was possible Zaitsev would not be killed quickly. It could occur slowly, after months of isolation and torture. It had with others.

*But surely Egonov will realize this is for the good of Russia. And I prefer to risk my life for Russia. I could be in just as much danger by not speaking up if events turn out poorly.*

"Mr. President, most of your ideas and policies are excellent. So I was surprised to learn we had ordered a missile strike on Israel." Kir Zaitsev took a deep breath.

"You sound disloyal by assuming it was our missile strike," Egonov said coolly. "I'm told it was brave Hezbollah fighters who fired the missiles."

"Hezbollah listens to us. If we suggested even one missile, they would fire twenty. We are already hurt by the expenses of the Ukraine war in rubles and men."

"Are you suggesting, Kir Zaitsev, that Russia could not fight our enemies on many fronts?"

"Of course we can, but should we? Mr. President, what should we do to avoid being associated with the bombing of Israel, as many are already saying we are."

"The Western press will say anything they are fed. What do you think we should do, Kir?"

"Denial. Distraction. If we are going to destroy competitors, we should make it count."

"What do you have in mind?" Egonov leaned forward.

"There are far too many LNG terminals, both terminals to send out LNG and terminals to receive it. In addition to rebuilding pipelines, we have an excellent LNG facility ourselves here in Murmansk. Perhaps it is necessary to send a message to those who have been slow to commit to buy Russian LNG."

"A message. Yes, Kir. Send a message. One they will remember. Now, leave."

"Mr. President." Kir Zaitsev nodded and left.

❖

The bigger risk was after decades in the job, Egonov would get bored and start looking for new entertainment, a new challenge. No more of his usual *hut-hut-hut* laughs. He preferred a situation where people had to guess what surprise he might spring, especially the final card—whether he would use nuclear weapons. With the most menacing atrocities, he sent signals that he couldn't be ignored: *the West's red lines mean nothing.* Instead, battle plans were drawn to reclaim land and population that had once been theirs. *And the oligarchs lost their yachts and billions,* Zaitsev thought.

The relationship with China and the CCP was uneasy. Russia had paid for the construction and infrastructure for The Power of Siberia —a big new pipeline with a grandiose name delivering gas to China—yet China had a huge advantage in the contract terms. And another pipeline was planned, through Mongolia. It wasn't about rubles or dollars, only Egonov's political power. Even the remaining gas contracts to Europe were underpriced—Russia could have made more on the spot market but Egonov instead chose to punish the Europeans by withholding gas. Everything was hostage to Egonov's political calculations.

Egonov had many ideas—often brilliant, Zaitsev admitted—and he wanted all of them done now. Zaitsev's task was to figure out which of them could be done as quickly as the Russian President demanded and to be certain Egonov got the credit publicly.

He craved a cigarette. Later.

He turned his attention to recruiting another asset. He knew exactly the woman he wanted to recruit. Unfortunately, it couldn't be the beautiful Lynn Dayton at TriCoast, although his operatives kept tabs on her and every senior energy executive. No, this other woman was perfect. She'd grown up in Chicago and so was known by the Russian and Eastern European diaspora there. She'd also lived in Alaska. She was a firm environmentalist, another of the categories of useful idiots he recruited. Environmentalists, particularly ones from Europe, wanted all hydrocarbon production and consumption shut down. Many foolish Western governments had moved hard to just do that, then discovered their citizens wanted the heat, electricity, and jobs that could only be fueled with hydrocarbons. As they got desperate, they turned to Russia, to him, to meet their needs for natural gas, oil, and distillate so they could have heat, electricity, and jobs.

His phone rang. He might wish for a private line or a burner phone but those would be tracked by the FSB no differently than this one was.

"I've delivered the first message to Henry Vandervoost," the man growled.

"What happened?"

"Not much resistance, but he will have trouble raising the money."

This was bad news. Zaitsev had agreed to collect Vandervoost's debt to the Chinese and the CCP in exchange for a small cut of the euros and a big contract for Russian gas. It was supposed to be easy because Vandervoost had access to capital, contacts, and several pressure points with both. Zaitsev had cleared everything with Egonov, who liked the idea.

"Why a problem?" Zaitsev kept his voice firm.

"Up to eyebrows in debt and no cash. Says the banks have lent him and his company everything possible."

"Actually, he can help with something else," Zaitsev said. *Would the Chinese take payment in kind if not in euros?* "Can he get to his son's company? Get what we need from it?" Zaitsev asked.

"He doesn't believe so but he doesn't know his own talents. Although perhaps he needs to be further convinced of those talents."

Zaitsev sighed. Thugs' limited skill set did not include deep thinking. Muscle often didn't realize a softer, steadier touch could be more effective.

"We need him. Nothing rough," Zaitsev said.

"Me?"

"Henry can be useful another way."

"Now you're making me work," the man said.

"It's work you'll like. Henry will like it, too. There's a woman who can help us. An acquaintance of Henry's," Zaitsev said.

"*Umnyy* or *shlyukha?*" the man questioned.

*A Scottish thug pretends delicacy by speaking Russian?* Zaitsev thought. *What a joke.* "Brains or whore? She's both. You will give Henry the message?"

"Yes."

Zaitsev told him what to do next.

❖

## *Murmansk, Russia*

Zaitsev went by private jet to northern, much colder Murmansk. He had promised President Egonov he would report on one of their new prized projects—a liquefied natural gas plant to solidify Russia's position as a premier global natural gas supplier. Kir Zaitsev felt it was a particular show of loyalty to visit Murmansk at the beginning of winter, a time during which the sun never rose for days, and the cold was even more bitter. Fuel from this project would meet vast Chinese needs and would further persuade the Europeans to continue relying on Russian gas while they built out their renewables. Whether pipelined through southern Europe or coming in on tankers, it was all about keeping the EU at least somewhat dependent on Russia, even if they weren't buying as much as they had before the war with Ukraine.

Zaitsev had often explained to his counterparts in other countries that one couldn't understand Russia without understanding oil and gas—the two were as inextricably tied as in Saudi Arabia. Egonov's trademark had been the nationalization of Russia's oil and gas companies. Technically private, they answered to the state, as was true in many countries throughout the world. Egonov's friends had made palaces and dachas and jet fleets of money from oil and gas. They had been a pillar of the foundation destined to keep Russia stable and Egonov in power for another ten or fifteen years. But now that was uncertain.

Zaitsev had been with the president when he'd been asked by an impertinent Western analyst whether Russia was an energy superpower. Egonov had, uncharacteristically, demurred, unwilling to admit Russia was as much a petro state as Venezuela, but said, "We have more oil and gas than anyone else in the world. No one should underestimate us." He could cite energy statistics without looking at notes or asking Zaitsev for answers.

Indeed, Russia's gross domestic product was almost half due to oil and gas extraction, as was more than half of its exports. After a few price wars, Russia had come around to working with OPEC on oil.

But Egonov, and Zaitsev, were also determined to remain the world leaders in natural gas. It was an important reason one of Zaitsev's deputies focused on encouraging solar and wind and funding disinformation campaigns to oppose fracking.

His jet flew past the giant statue of Alyosha Arctic Defenders. A brilliant yellow and green aurora arching over this part of western Siberia was visible outside his jet window.

In the wintry darkness that didn't lift until spring, Zaitsev idly reread the notes on his phone. The notes would disappear within a few hours. People who knew the notes existed would require days to reconstruct them.

An Egonov-favored bill had passed by an overwhelming margin. Of course it did, Zaitsev thought. Because no one ever voted against Egonov.

The people—men mostly—building this plant were doing heroic work. They were like Valergy Legasov and the brave men and women at Chernobyl who had sacrificed themselves for their countrymen either directly, or in Legasov's case later, when he committed suicide.

Russians were tougher in the cold. Tougher than the soft Europeans, Chinese, or Americans who had never experienced Arctic cold. All of them agonized so much about freezing they became willing to pay any price for Russian gas.

Zaitsev had had survival training, as did most of his countrymen. In one brutal exercise, he had been locked out of a building—a few meters away, he could see the lights and nearly feel the warmth—and—so that he would recognize them—been forced to identify and endure the first few steps of freezing to death. Despite gloves and thick boots, his fingers and toes quickly got cold as blood fled inward to vital organs. Then he began shivering so hard his muscles ached.

As he pounded on the door separating him from light and warmth, his exposed skin began turning white. He found the urge to urinate unbearable, until he didn't, preferring frozen pee-stiff pants to uncovering any skin. It became more and more difficult to move his muscles.

His comrades were watching—at least the few who hadn't passed out—and decided Zaitsev passed the hazing when he fell unconscious. At least that's what they told him later, when they dragged him inside and warmed him back alive.

Zaitsev shook the memory from his head as he exited the private jet. In the dim light, he was pleased to see only a small delegation there to meet him. He wanted people to work, not entertain him.

"How is everyone?"

The project manager who gripped Zaitsev's gloved hand in both of his understood the question. So dark and cold, for so long.

"Eh, like the Norwegians in Svalbard. We do not fight the dark. We keep to routines, socializing, lots of lights, and we're all looking forward to time off across the border in Finland in a few weeks."

He wheeled the big, black SUV up to the huge construction site just north of the town of Murmansk. It was bright and busy, the busiest site this far north. The manager pointed out the dock and the names of several of the over one hundred vendor companies.

"The first train—" Zaitsev began, referring to the first big module that would liquefy Siberian gas for shipping.

"—nearly ready. And the second and third will be too, shortly," the project manager responded. "Our workers are from here, but also China and Central Asia."

*Appropriate,* Zaitsev thought. Although Russia was the largest sponsor, others included companies in China, France, and Japan. China especially would want employment for its people, and it was a major customer for the LNG. Egonov had fostered cooperation with China across several spheres, not just energy: trade, joint military exercise, and high-tech.

"You have talked to the chiefs of the Geofizicheskoye and Salmanovskoye fields."

The manager nodded. "They're ready to ship us gas as soon as we say."

Zaitsev was satisfied, especially as he looked across Koa Bay. Russia's important Northern Fleet had its main base in Severomorsk, with a waterfront length of one and a half kilometers. This site had almost twice as much waterfront length.

Later, Zaitsev, the construction manager, and others joined in vodka toasts.

*"Za druzhbu,"* Zaitsev said. To friendship.

*"Za nas,"* the project manager added. To us.

"Ah. *Za lyubov*," countered Zaitsev. To love.

## CHAPTER 6
# MIDLAND

THE EMBED, JOHN Cooper, pretended to be like so many other oilfield contractors in West Texas—a sunburned recent hire from out-of-state with a trimmed beard who was red-eyed from lack of sleep and blowing dust.

After the three-hour drive from his small ranch in south Texas, near Alpine, he checked into the enormous man camp near Odessa. They didn't call it a man camp, but that's what it was: hundreds of rooms, a roof, air-conditioning, blackout shades for each tiny window, superb cable connections, and protein-rich meals.

"Welcome back, John. You here for a while?" The front desk clerk handed him a card.

Cooper relaxed as he realized the clerk hadn't really recognized him, just read his name off the sign-up form. John Cooper often felt at his best when he wasn't known, wasn't recognized, wasn't remembered.

"A few weeks, thanks."

"I see Daine Environmental Water Services is paying your freight. We'll charge back to them. Look around, Daine's got a few other fellows staying here. Y'all could be friends."

"Sure," Cooper lied. Being friends with his fellow employees was the last relationship he wanted, even behind being a "temporary boyfriend" to a Houston waitress.

He left a suitcase in the room, returned to his truck, and headed to the Odessa HEB. Not for food, not at first. He parked his black Silverado among all the others, went to the corner of the store featuring the state's best barbecue, and ate. There would be plenty of time for camp breakfasts, dinners, and brown-bag lunches. After dinner, he shopped for the soda, chips, and cereal he liked and knew the camp wouldn't have. He filled a thermos with coffee.

After dinner but before it got dark, he drove east of Midland to Daine's field office. He exchanged his truck for one of Daine's big water tanker trucks, one that held sixty thousand gallons.

His job—part of it—was taking some of the millions of gallons of wastewater produced with the more valuable oil and gas and then separated from it—to deep saltwater disposal wells. The Daine field office manager gave him a list for the night of pickup and drop-off addresses, not much more than coordinates on a map.

He drove to the first well site and was admitted when he flashed his badge. He was directed to one of the settling ponds used to separate oil from the water that came up to the surface with it. The pond was near capacity, and the hydrocarbon smell was as strong as at the drilling platform itself.

His was the fifth water truck in line at the pond. At his turn, he showed his badge and his phone with the pickup instructions. Other Daine employees working onsite piped water into his tanker. Even though Cooper knew Daine prided himself on operating cheaply, the interior of the tanker had alternating dividers to keep the water from sloshing all the way from the front to the back. Cheap was one thing. Big interior tanker water waves rising from back to front and throwing the truck off the road was something else.

By the time Cooper left, it was dark, and another four water trucks were waiting at the pond. He put the delivery coordinates into his phone, which ginned up directions for him.

*A new place. Must have filled up the old one, or somebody turned it in.*

At the gate to the wastewater disposal site, Cooper waved his employee ID card. Somewhere, the code was validated, and the heavy-duty gate swung open. He didn't know if this was an approved or unapproved site and didn't care. Site selection was up to Daine. He just knew he needed to pump the water into the ultradeep wastewater or saltwater disposal well. The wells were drilled far below the oil and gas zones so as not to contaminate them. Deep, dirty, salty groundwater out at one well back to deep groundwater back at another site. What could be environmentally wrong about that? He hooked up the high-volume hose to his tanker and it began to empty water from his truck.

The pick-up and delivery sequence was one he would repeat all night. The nighttime schedule was due to the wells and disposal sites operating 24/7. At night there was far less traffic on the road. Less waiting meant more loads meant more money.

The next several days John Cooper would appear equally at ease at a breakfast of eggs, ham, and doughnuts or a dinner of steak, potatoes, and cake. But he knew the firethorn shrubs and chitalpa trees of West Texas also hid a killing floor. Sometimes it was also part of his job to make it so.

❖

In the next nights of water pick-ups and drop-offs, he noticed far less traffic at the saltwater disposal wells designated in his coordinates. And, even at night, the field office manager told him to call ahead before making deliveries. One evening, he arrived ahead of schedule, early enough to see the disposal site's operator take down a sign from the gate reading "Closed by order of Texas Railroad Commission." He didn't ask for an explanation, and the man didn't volunteer.

At the next wellsite where he went to make a pickup of thousands more gallons of water that evening, he asked another water tanker driver about the sign. "I saw a closed sign. What's that mean? Temporary, right? Or closed for good?"

The burly man gave him a hard look and then stared at his

badge. "Daine Environmental Water Services, hunh?" He spat off to one side, close enough to Cooper to signal an insult.

"Hey. Stop spitting. I'm just the driver."

"Don't get your panties in a wad. They shouldn't be asking you to make those deliveries."

"What do you mean?" Cooper asked, although he then knew exactly what the man, and the sign, meant.

"That disposal well's closed because they think all the water already in it is causing slabs of rock to slide around. Otherwise known as earthquakes."

"Well, son of a biscuit. Who knew? To me it's just water out of the ground, water back in."

"You must be new to the patch or you'd know every place with the super-deep water wells has had problems and had to shut down some of them. Pennsylvania. Texas around Fort Worth. Oklahoma—especially Oklahoma. Now here in West Texas. I don't agree with much they do in California, but California already has so many natural earthquakes I understand why they don't want to chance more from the super-deep wastewater wells."

"You sure? What's your name?"

"You think I'm going to tell you? Have you turn me in? In fact, I should turn you in." The burly man gave him another hard stare.

Cooper rocked back on his heels. "I'd rather you didn't."

"You, Cooper," the man's voice rose. "You AND your company, Daine. Environmental my ass. Fools like you get us all in trouble, get the feds to shut down anyone doing anything, even when we're doing it all the right way."

"I think you're up now," Cooper said, keeping his voice even calmer than usual. "They're signaling you."

When the burly man climbed back into his truck, Cooper took note of the license plate, the company name on the truck, and several other details so he could identify the burly man in the future. Soon in the future.

❖

Cooper didn't know how quickly the man would get in touch with the regulators, or if he would, but he doubted the righteous-sounding man would delay long.

After calls and conversations the next day, pieced together with what he knew, John Cooper learned the burly man was a contract trucker from Kermit—wife and three kids, little ranchette house, deacon in his church, one son a football player—who transported various loads, depending on what was needed when and where, and how much the load paid. Pipe, sand, and chemicals were trucked all the time. Oil and water were trucked when the pipelines were full or hadn't been extended to a new wellsite.

Cooper explained to Rowan Daine what had happened.

"Can you take care of it?" Daine asked.

"I need you to put a word in for me at PipePod."

"Sure. We buy pipe from them. I'll explain I've got a contract driver needs extra hours."

The following day, Cooper was assigned to carry a load from PipePod on an early shift. The industrial pipes each weighed more than a ton.

When he arrived, he found his truck and that of his target. He slipped around the target truck and quickly loosened the restraints.

When the burly man arrived and saw Cooper, he said, "You again! Making trouble here, too? I haven't forgotten. I'm turning you and your company in tomorrow."

"Please don't."

The burly man looked at him. "What a pussy."

Cooper said no more but followed the burly man's truck out of the pipe yard in his own loaded truck.

Truckers and drivers in West Texas were in a constant hurry. On Highway 349, the burly man's load shifted.

He pulled over and radioed for a truck with a forklift to help him re-secure the pyramid of pipes.

Cooper pulled up behind him at the side of the road.

"Heard you're having a problem. Maybe I can help." He reached casually into his jacket pocket.

"Sure, I'd appreciate that. Hey, aren't you--?"

His question was cut short. In one quick motion, Cooper pulled the Glock from his jacket and shot the burly truck driver in the chest.

"No! Take—" he gurgled, spat up blood and fell to his knees. Blood spread across the front of his shirt.

Cooper grabbed the man from behind in a fireman's carry and pulled him into his own truck. He'd already covered the floor mats and seats with plastic sheeting.

He dumped the man onto the floor, climbed into the driver's seat, and headed for the special remote place he'd spotted recently. A place perfect for leaving a dead man. And if he wasn't quite dead yet, he wouldn't be able to escape before dying.

Cooper drove carefully for a while on the narrow highway. Once he reached the intersection with I-20, he accelerated to the speed of the other 18-wheelers around him. In a touch even he found fitting, his destination, or rather the final destination of the dead man in his truck, would be a hidden-in-plain-sight location not far from the man's hometown of Kermit.

After about an hour, he pulled up to the long-abandoned site. Once it had been hot, important, useful. No longer. Cooper opened the rusted door to the place.

He unloaded a construction wheelbarrow from inside his truck. The burly driver no longer had a pulse, but his body was not yet rigid. Cooper stabilized the wheelbarrow with rocks and pushed the man's body out of his truck cab onto the ground near the wheelbarrow. He then lifted the man's body, first his top half, then his bottom half, into the wheelbarrow. He removed the rocks and wheeled the body inside the abandoned structure. He worked quickly—the stiffer the body got, the harder it would be to move. He'd already made all the necessary preparations.

Within fifteen minutes, John Cooper was back in his truck, driving away.

❖

A PipePod truck with a forklift arrived at the site of the pipeline-hauling truck an hour later, but the burly truck driver was gone. At first, it was presumed he'd been crushed under the one-ton pipes that had somehow slipped further and tumbled off the side of his truck. But no body was found. After restacking the pipes onto the truck and radioing for a new driver, the forklift driver saw a few spots of blood on the ground. He radioed in the driver's absence and the blood, saying, "Maybe someone else already picked him up and took him to the hospital."

But hospitals in the area reported no new wounded drivers.

When the story made the rounds later in the day, John Cooper shook his head. "Tragic. So many accidents out here."

# CHAPTER 7
# HERZLIYA, ISRAEL

AVI DROVE TO the unmarked garage for a three-building complex in downtown Herzliya, near Tel Aviv, the high-tech park and its restaurants, and the coast.

He waved his badge at the reader and the rolling metal gate lifted. After parking on the third floor and taking the elevator to the lobby, he waved a different ID card at another reader, which flashed green and opened a gate. He walked past two security guards. On the sixth floor, another guard checked his identification and nodded him through. He finally reached his office, unsure of whether he was happy or unhappy that at work he was never alone, never unobserved. *Safety or panopticon?*

It was just past several religious holidays and nearly the weekend, so he hoped payment processing—specifically the auto-deposit of his paycheck—had remained on schedule.

Avi reviewed his company's bids for the next set of natural gas drilling leases in Israel's exclusive economic zone, or EEZ, in the eastern Mediterranean. About two dozen exploration blocks had been mapped and grouped into five clusters. None were too close in: the energy ministry preferred to keep operations at least seven kilometers offshore. Unlike an oil leak, a natural gas leak wouldn't harm beaches or birds; still, every centimeter of the coast was vital.

Israel and Cyprus had finally reached an agreement over Aphrodite, the pleasantly named natural gas field located in the offshore waters of both countries. Israel's claim was small relative to its large Tamar and appropriately named Leviathan offshore natural gas fields, but Avi knew it had been diplomatically important to negotiate for every cubic meter of reserves. The negotiations had taken years. Cyprus was strategic, particularly to countries like Russia and Turkey. The UAE was better aligned with Israel than Cyprus, but in another complication, the Chinese could move into UAE ports as they had successfully done in other countries.

And there were two other important elements to the relationship: Cyprus, Israel, and Greece had agreed to build a subsea power cable to connect their electricity grids. The government of Israel had become comfortable about having enough gas to meet its own country's needs and was willing to allow Avi's company to export gas to Egypt and there convert it to LNG. But there were always nay-sayers, those who wanted to leave the gas in place under the sea and begin a decades-long build-out of solar instead.

The marketing side of the transaction was easier since all knew the reserves actually existed there in the eastern Med. Avi was pleased to see solicitations of interest to buy the gas—should Avi's company win the bid—from European power companies. They sought natural gas supplies to back up their intermittent solar and wind electric generation and to replace the Russian gas they now officially shunned.

Avi saw the shadow of the old man's forward lean before he stepped into Avi's office. *The last man I want to see now.* The bald spot on his head looked like a groom's white kipa.

"Avi, what do you think about the Cyprus deal to sell our gas from Aphrodite to Europe?"

"The deal is accretive on all key metrics."

The old man scratched his cheek. "You mean it makes money."

Avi nodded. "Very accretive."

"*A lot* of money."

Avi nodded. "We've got a steady upwards trajectory—volumes increase over the life of the deal and," in a point Avi hoped would win the man over, "we can do green bonds—sustainability-linked bonds to finance our part of it."

The old man shook his head. "The bond interest rates will be too high or there will be too many restrictions. I've been on many roller coasters with natural gas prices. It's easy to find yourself making far less or even losing money with plans like yours."

Avi waited for the old man to finish. "I've run scenarios at the strip. They look good."

"Sure, the futures prices look good today. They could suck tomorrow. I'd bet anything your Aunt Sara at TriCoast prepped you with all these fancy phrases. So, I've got one for you. How about if you *provide me context around the deal*? Which means, explain what the hell you're really doing!"

The old man turned as slowly as a turtle and left without another word.

Avi drummed the table with his fingers. *Tsuris.* Problems.

❖

While Avi's video call with the Spanish energy minister also meant problems, they were good problems, *the kinds of problems I signed up to solve,* he thought. Avi was anxious—Spain was the first customer for Israeli natural gas. It would arrive in Barcelona from Egypt after being transformed into liquefied natural gas. Good or bad, Israel's performance—Avi's performance—on this contract would send a signal to Spain and other European countries about Israel's reliability as a supplier.

Moreover, the Spanish energy minister was rumored to be friendly toward Russia. Indeed, he had protested the diplomatic cut-off of cheap Russian gas supplies to Spain.

Avi opened the door and greeted attractive Miriam, a translator he had requested. All official business in Spain was required to be conducted in Spanish. Avi understood basic Spanish, but this conversation was too important to trust his limited vocabulary.

Although Miriam hadn't said so explicitly, Avi surmised her job of working for a tourism agency was a cover for Mossad assignments. No doubt the entire conversation would be reported to them. *Even more pressure.*

Avi motioned to Miriam to sit next to him, at an angle. "Thank you. Give me plenty of time to respond if you would, please."

"Of course." Her smile was lovely.

When Avi initiated the call, an English-speaking assistant in Madrid appeared on-screen and adjusted the settings. He remained, apparently also acting as the minister's translator.

After a few minutes Alejandro Garcia, Spain's energy minister, appeared on screen and sat down. Señor Garcia represented the reason Avi had worked late every night to finish the trading hub software. With a flourish, Garcia's assistant announced, "The Honorable Alejandro Garcia Fernández, Minister for the Ecological Transition and the Demographic Challenge."

Avi felt as if he should salute. "Minister Garcia, welcome. My company looks forward to supplying your country with the first liquefied natural gas production from our newest offshore fields. As you know, our joint venture with Egypt means our gas will be liquefied at one of Egypt's LNG plants and then sent to your Barcelona terminal for your country's use."

From Garcia's knitted brows, Avi surmised Garcia had understood most of what Avi had said. Still, Garcia waited until Miriam had translated. His reply was brief.

"He wants to know if your delivery will be within a week, as promised," Miriam said.

Avi was conscious not to indicate his dismay. *Much less time than I expected.* And all future business, with Spain and with other European countries, hung on his answer. He ran through timetables in his head. "*Si.*"

Rapid Spanish followed. Miriam said, "He asks if you are certain Israel can deliver. Minister Garcia says he could return to Russia, his preferred supplier for natural gas, if Israel cannot meet this timetable."

Avi nodded vigorously. "*Si. Si.* We will get the gas to you on time, as promised." He waited while Miriam translated.

Garcia listened but did not respond. Instead, he and his English translators rose from their chairs and disappeared from the screen.

After they left, he and Miriam could see an empty bookshelf in the energy minister's office. Empty except for a flag stand holding a red, black, white, and green Palestinian flag.

## CHAPTER 8
# LONDON

As suggested by *le voyou*, as Henry Vandervoost thought of the man who'd threatened him over his gambling debt, Henry began visiting a pub near Canary Wharf, the one where he'd been told he would be likeliest to find the woman the thug had *suggested* he recruit. She was apparently working on a problem for her friend, the pub owner, who'd received cement blocks packed in newspaper in a recent shipment, instead of the fine Scotch he'd ordered.

He mused further about how to get money from his son. Ironically, he had been doing something similar—he had been raising money for a fund investing in, among others, his son's company. But that money was walled off in accounts he couldn't access.

He fumed again as he thought of his last days at TriCoast. *La putain,* the bitch, Lynn Dayton had dismissed him like trash. First, it was the non-promotion, to executive chair of special European refining projects, of which there were exactly none. She'd moved in a Texan to take his place as head of European refining. As if a Texan could understand Europe. And then she'd been the one to tell him he had six months to find another job. He had done so—his contacts through the industry were happy enough to bring him on, although more than a few alluded to expectations of Henry bringing in business from both TriCoast and his son's company.

Despite the chilly, rainy weather, his cheeks burned at the memories. He shoved his bulk into the pub's dark corner he'd claimed as a favorite and reviewed what he knew about the woman he was supposed to recruit. Raised in Alaska and Chicago, she wouldn't shrink from cold-weather assignments the thug said she was needed for. She was a geochemist. Her father had died in a pipeline explosion, which had transformed Hannah into an environmental activist as well as a science expert.

"George, mates, gather round. Your man's been got!" The low, excited voice came from a woman Henry hadn't seen before.

"What'd you learn, Hannah?"

"Found the man. He's been charged. Not fired but fined and reassigned. Insurance company got involved, too. Believe the distillery now owes you several cases of fine Scotch." The woman's dark hair swung into her face. She shoved it back.

George said, "Round for everyone on me, now." The pub rocked with a cheer, followed by loud chatter as orders were shouted. "One at a time. Tell us the story, Hannah."

"Locard's principle."

"Explain, lass."

Her grin was particularly American, Henry noted.

"Whenever two objects come into contact, material is always transferred. Helps link people to scenes."

"Seems a bit. Detailed."

"Insurance company needed it. Different insurance companies cover different legs of the trip, so they want to know which of them has to pay."

"On my Scotch!" Henry could see the satisfaction as George stood up straighter.

"That valuable, yes. So, I compared dust in the box and from the bricks to ports, found the port of origin. Turns out there's a quarry near the distillery whose dust matched the dust in the box. And one of the distributor's employees had been seen at the quarry."

"You're a clever one, Hannah. Double shots for you!" George couldn't keep the smile off his face.

*Brilliant woman*, Vandervoost thought, momentarily forgetting his hatred of other brilliant women like Lynn Dayton. He crowded in to shake Hannah's hand and introduce himself.

Hannah's brilliance would make recruiting her both harder and far more interesting.

❖

As he stood in line to shake Hannah Bosko's hand and congratulate her on solving the whiskey mystery, Vandervoost checked his phone for notes he'd been sent about recruiting her. *Hannah Bosko—consulting forensic geologist for Scotland Yard. US citizen. Grew up in Alaska and Chicago. Father died in pipeline explosion when she was twelve. Now an expert chemist and an anti-pipeline protestor. Had a London steady, a married man. They recently split.*

"Ms. Bosko, excellent work," Vandervoost said, beaming at her. "You must have lined up another dozen consulting projects tonight at this pub."

"I wish. You are?"

"Henry Vandervoost." He observed she was appropriately impressed when he named the private equity firm at which he was a partner, a place where he'd perfected the casual one-upmanship necessary for positioning in any group.

Something the text hadn't mentioned. Hannah needed more money than she was making on occasional projects from Scotland Yard.

He leaned closer. "If you're done here, let me take you to a quieter place. I have easily six months of full-time projects in the US. We can work out terms." He added a phrase he thought she would like. "For real."

"Not tonight."

He had no time. He had so little time. But she'd refuse if he pushed.

"I'm on a short leash, as Americans say. This all starts soon. Work in Chicago and Texas. Meet me at 7 PM tomorrow night at the Bull and Last. I won't even ask you for a phone number. Here's a card so you can verify everything I've said."

She nodded as he slipped away. He didn't look back.

❖

He'd find a way. Despite growing up in Europe, Vandervoost had been attracted to Texas freedoms he found when he earned a chemical engineering degree there. He'd stayed on for a while, climbing the ranks at big Texas oil firms where people were charmed by his Dutch-accented English and soon sending him back to Europe to do deals there.

One day, more than thirty-five years earlier, he'd looked across the porte-cochere at the Houston Country Club to get the attention of Patsy Bradshaw, only child of a Midland oil billionaire. One conversation led to another, then dates, and finally an engagement. Within a year, he'd both married Patsy and become second-in-command at her father's company.

He managed to sire one son before Patsy found out about the affairs.

The only time he'd heard her shout was when he explained, "Affairs are common in France among the wealthy. I don't understand why you are offended."

Her pride had kept her in the marriage and him in the job at Bradshaw Energy for a few more years until Patsy explained the situation to her father. Immediately, Henry was no longer second in command at Bradshaw Energy. Patsy took his place.

Henry's affairs continued until her family's patience ended. Their billions were enough for a couple of local toughs to explain to Henry he needed to divorce and decamp to a location far away. Rotterdam was suggested. And so, he went.

Patsy remained cool but oddly devoted. She never remarried and assumed full control of Bradshaw Energy when her father died. She was eager to integrate Joost into Henry's life, often sending him to Europe for weeks in the summer. Later, Henry helped Joost get investment banking jobs in London and introduced him to the many pleasures of brothels not just in Paris and Amsterdam, but also Singapore and Bangkok, Antwerp and Hamburg. By his late twenties, Joost was known about Europe, Asia, and the States as a restless, generous playboy.

Yet when Patsy entered treatment for cancer, both she and Henry persuaded Joost to return to Midland to help her. No one was willing to say it, but Patsy knew statistics and management well enough to realize her survival odds were small and that she needed a fully trained replacement. Not just a replacement, but a family member.

Once Joost learned the truth of his parents' marriage breakup, he became more distant, rarely answering or returning Henry's calls or texts, though still finding plenty of female companionship not only in Midland, but also in Dallas, Houston, and San Antonio. His friends jealously remarked he always had two or three women on a string within a week after arriving in any city.

Henry observed all this from abroad, waiting for Patsy's call. In the month before she had calculated she would die, she urged Henry to return to Midland and stay with her and then Joost through her funeral. He did, sharing tears and hugs with her, and then with his son Joost.

Henry was in Midland just long enough to understand what he was missing: Macau was no substitute for his ex-wife's—and now his son's—game at Bradshaw Energy: high-dollar wells coming in every time and generating five times what had been invested. In their last conversation a few months ago, Joost let slip that Bradshaw Energy's market value was in the billions, and a few of the secrets its scientists were developing as a side business could be worth hundreds of millions more.

But Joost had refused his father's calls since then.

More emails and texts, brazen in their threats, had lately arrived in Henry Vandervoost's inbox:

"Dutch pull out of Dutch-Russian gas company over threats."

"Top engineer in Russian-English joint oil venture found shot dead in Siberia."

"Former chief of Russian-English joint venture slowly poisoned over weeks by Kremlin to force him to leave Moscow and over a hundred employees also targeted."

"State-controlled Russian company takes over Russian-English oil company."

"Russians believed behind poisoning of Chechen in Germany."

Henry slapped his desk so hard it shuddered. He couldn't forget the conversations with his son. He needed, he deserved, control of Bradshaw Energy. Patsy was dead. He owed money to Russians. Gaining control of Bradshaw Energy and its secrets was his only option for saving himself.

❖

To his relief, the next night Hannah Bosko showed up. The Bull and Last pub, on a corner of Hampstead Heath with a stunning view of London, had started off as an inn in 1721 and had become one again, with rooms named for locals like John Keats. While the fish and chips at the inn were good, Henry counted on a leisurely meal of several courses in which to make his case. He needed Hannah's expertise. He needed her to go to Midland, meet his son, and pave the way for Henry to take over Bradshaw Energy and get the secret water recycling technology to pay off his gambling debts.

After drinks and entrees, Vandervoost said, "I need your expertise for work, mainly in Midland, Texas. Perhaps a project in Chicago, although that's less certain."

"Why me?"

"I've looked into your work. Unusual and impressive. What I'm concerned about falls into your area of expertise."

"What do you know about my work?"

*I can look at your face and body and see my son will be totally taken by you. But I won't tell you it's one of your qualifications,* Vandervoost thought.

"You understand water, sand, soils. I'm thinking of your case in Rotterdam, where I lived before moving to London. Man drowned, no identification. You did a multi-isotope analysis on his teeth and bones."

She nodded. "Water sources were part of the analysis. The water isotope signature of tooth enamel is set early in life, but the water isotope signatures of bones is set later."

Henry continued, "You concluded the man didn't grow up in Rotterdam and didn't move there as a child. Instead, from the isotopes left in the bones by the water he had likely grown up in Poland, Russia, Bulgaria, or Scandinavia."

"I finally narrowed it to Poland, Ukraine, or Slovakia." She smiled.

"And you were right. The man was ultimately identified as being from Slovakia."

"You're almost as good a researcher as me." Hannah smiled more broadly.

"So, I'm interested in water and chemical analysis for this project in Texas for which I'd like to hire you."

"Be more specific."

Folding lies into the truth, he said, "My son owns a company in Texas, wants me to invest, and has a new wastewater membrane filter process for recycling dirty water out of wells so it can be used again. But from what I gather and want to know before investing, the process requires dangerous chemicals. And there are other environmentally hazardous chemicals being filtered out from the water—like arsenic and heavy metals—they don't seem to be addressing. He and his scientists don't understand those potential problems, though."

To Vandervoost's alarm, Hannah pushed back from the table. "I don't believe you. The scientists I know are meticulous. You're describing them as sloppy."

"Don't leave. They aren't sloppy. They found something that works well, and they started using it to make money without fully understanding the chemistry or the environmental hazards."

Hannah pulled back closer to the table.

"Chicago?"

"Maybe a legal protest. You grew up there; I think you may be acquainted with the utility manager. Gas pipeline analysis. I know you'd want to save anyone else from being killed by a gas pipeline explosion."

"The way my father was."

# CHAPTER 9
# DALLAS AND MIDLAND

*"The idea of injecting random noise into a system to improve its functioning has been applied across fields. By a mechanism called stochastic resonance, adding random noise to the background makes you hear the sounds (say, music) with more accuracy."*

—*Nicholas Naseem Taleb*

LYNN HAD TAKEN a TriCoast company jet to Dallas, grateful to spend a night with her family.

Early the following morning, she and her bodyguard met a hard-muscled self-defense trainer at the gym near her house. Although the trainer had been vetted, Beau's presence was an extra precaution. Lynn was one of TriCoast's most senior executives.

They practiced barefoot on the gym's wooden floor.

"Knives can be deadlier than guns," the trainer explained. "Remember if you're faced with someone with a knife, first try to run away. If you can't, you can't control the knife. Instead, try to control the *hand* with the knife." They practiced several moves.

"Do you remember Krav Maga?" the trainer asked.

"Only a little," Lynn confessed.

"You only need a little. But let's refresh. Particularly since you don't usually carry. You could end up looking down the barrel of someone's gun. Not the last thing you want to see."

Lynn nodded and hated remembering the times she'd faced someone who had wanted to kill her.

"Stand beside me and do what I do," the trainer said. "Beau, you hold this plastic water gun. Start with it in one hand."

Although plastic, the gun was painted gray and shaped like a real one. Lynn restrained a gasp at the close resemblance.

"Aim it at my head," the trainer instructed. Beau did so. "Lynn, do as I do. Notice I have my hands partway up, in a surrender position."

Lynn raised both hands.

"No, not all the way up. More like, in the ready position. And you're watching Beau's tiniest movement. You may want to speak slowly to him—you must read him, though."

"Beau, you don't want to do this," Lynn said.

Beau looked slightly sheepish. Lynn felt the same way.

"No. Serious." In one smooth motion, the trainer grabbed the barrel of the gun with his left hand, pointed it down and away, and punched toward Beau's nose with his right hand, but not making contact. "I was lucky. Good as Beau is, he was slightly distracted. Now you do it."

Lynn tried several times. Beau, alert, would not allow her to force down the gun.

The trainer whispered to Beau, who readied the gun with both hands. Then he whispered to Lynn. She nodded.

"Again."

This time she grabbed Beau's left wrist with her right hand, simultaneously taking the plastic gun with her left.

"Good. Point it at him. You have control of the situation now."

The trainer showed her several similar moves, all aimed at gaining possession of the plastic gun. After several repetitions, they began feeling more automatic.

"This next is a judo move, the arterial choke," the trainer said to Lynn. "I'll explain it, demonstrate it on Beau while you watch, and then you'll practice on me.

"You are the aggressor. You both are right-handed?"

They nodded.

"Me too. You approach your victim from behind and pull him

back with your right hip to him. Wrap your right forearm around his neck from behind. Put the inside of your wrist against the left side of his neck with your thumb up, other fingers curled. With your left arm, reach under the armpit and lock your left hand's curled fingers with those of your right hand."

Lynn could see Beau tense as the trainer got behind him and walked through the moves. Lynn noticed the trainer was careful to avoid actually touching Beau, likely knowing her bodyguard's response would be instinctive, and possibly deadly.

"Do you see what I'm doing?" the trainer asked her.

"Yes."

"Then pull your right arm tightly against him and push your right hip into his back while doing it, so you're angled to him rather than directly behind him."

Again, the man carefully mimed the move without touching Beau. "You've presented a narrower profile for his elbows. By being tight against him—which I'm not, here—he can't get as much leverage for punching or elbowing you.

"Hold those hands together and let the pressure of your right wrist cut off the blood supply to his brain until he passes out. Now you try it on me. I want you to grab me tight and try to choke me."

"Really?" Lynn swallowed.

"You need practice for muscle memory. Don't worry. I've defended against this before. And Beau will be watching in case one of us gets overzealous."

Lynn got behind the trainer, angled, pulled him against her right hip, and wrapped her arm around his neck. He positioned her hand against his neck.

"Thumb up! Curl your fingers!"

She did. Then she reached under his armpit, ready to lock her left hand's finger with her right.

He pushed her left hand away. "Since I know the move, I'm protecting myself. But now go ahead. Lock your hands together and push your right hip into my back."

She did.

"Harder! I won't break."

She tightened her grip, then pressed her wrist against his neck.

He jerked sideways out of her hold. "Not bad, but you need to work out with weights for more upper-body strength."

"In all my spare time."

"It could keep you alive. And so you know," the trainer said, staring hard into her eyes. "People have died from this hold."

"Got it."

"You didn't plan on this, but Beau and I did. You also need gun range practice."

"I don't have time."

"You do. If Mike Emerson were here, he'd tell you it's a job requirement."

Beau took her to a nearby range, handed her his Glock, and said, "Half an hour. Go!"

She donned ear protection and safety glasses. Beau corrected her stance and aim. She shot at the targets mounted on a far wall.

After several minutes, he pulled her out of the booth. "Move around. Try to hit the target from different positions. I'm already seeing improvement."

Lynn focused, aimed, and shot round after round. Sitting. Squatting. From the ground. Her arms and shoulders burned from holding the same firing position.

"Looking better. That's enough," Beau finally said.

"That was more than a half hour." She snorted to clear the smoke and haze from her nostrils.

"Range practice is like wearing a seat belt. You hope to never need it."

Lynn was glad to leave the serious self-defense lessons for a shower and a ride to one of the TriCoast's private jets at Dallas Love Field for the return trip to Midland. When she checked her emails while waiting, she saw one from a sender she didn't recognize, Hannah Bosko. Hannah must have known about Lynn, however, and quite a bit more: Lynn was surprised to read Hannah wanted to talk to her about the Bradshaw company. The email closed with, "Meet me at Scott Tinker's environmental talk in Austin." *Who is Hannah Bosko? How does she know about Bradshaw? Or is this just something bogus and I'm being set up by a crank?*

The plane flew over white square pads west of Fort Worth, signs of the earliest horizontal drilling successes. Further on, farms hinted at their perfect business combinations of cattle, water, oil and gas, as well as wind and solar leasing. Aqua-green stock and plastic-lined blue treatment ponds trailed one after another, checkerboard-flat to the horizon.

The copilot told her there was so much fog ahead near Midland that they might have to turn around and go back to Dallas. "But at least you paid attention to the safety briefing!"

After many tense minutes, they cleared the ground-level fog and the pilot announced they would be able to land.

Now that they were closer to Midland, Lynn could see hundreds of smaller square pads closer together—sometimes just a few hundred feet—with working or abandoned horseheads showing the region's oil roots. Then came straight yellow section line roads and gray-green brush with hundreds more trails to well sites. Oil storage tanks and natural gas liquid spheres filled in.

Finally, there was the perpetual housing construction from booms past, current, and expected. Blocks of lookalike houses stood in rows, with empty rows in the grid showing where more houses would be built. The lack of trees testified to soil too poor for growing much other than mesquite.

Jackup rigs were visible on the landing approach and a line of black tank cars south of the airport suggested the overflow option if pipelines filled up.

❖

Roy picked Lynn up at the airport for the drive northeast of Midland, near Stanton. They had arranged to see another of Joost

Bradshaw's drilling sites, part of the diligence for TriCoast's proposed acquisition of Bradshaw's company. *At least we're still negotiating*, Lynn thought.

After initial pleasantries, she couldn't restrain herself from the question that had bothered her while she was on the plane. Hydraulic fracturing pumped millions of gallons of water and chemicals at high pressure to break shale and prop open the cracks with sand, letting oil and gas flow up a well. So TriCoast bought literally tons of sand.

"Roy, we have to talk about this new sand contract TriCoast has. I don't know what David was thinking when he made it. It's a terrible price. Too high."

"He wanted to secure a supply of sand for all the drilling that we—which now includes you, too—are doing," Roy explained.

At the intersection of the asphalt highway with a less welcoming gravel road, Roy turned carefully, keeping the tires in the icy, mudded ruts other trucks had made.

"We require thousands of pounds per horizontal foot of drilling, so tons a day. But there are dozens of other companies we can get sand from. Actually, the phrase 'infinite supply' comes to mind," Lynn said.

"Not anymore. Many of them shut down in the last bust. We can make the contract work. I don't want it to crater or have to lay people off, just because *you think* David made a bad deal." His emphasis suggested he didn't agree with her.

"Right in one. And I'm sure we can sell the excess sand to other companies, but it's a complication we don't need," Lynn said. "And honestly, it makes me question how good a deal he was making with Joost Bradshaw to buy Bradshaw Energy."

"Well, David's not around to defend himself."

"I wish he was." She sighed. "Different topic. How about saltwater disposal wells?"

"They got a few problem ones here that the Railroad Commission's told 'em to shut in."

"Is Rowan Daine Bradshaw's water contractor?"

Roy nodded.

"Daine's not trying to use the closed wells, is he?" Lynn asked

"You'll have to ask him for sure, but rumor is, he does."

"Will be a hell of a problem for Bradshaw. And for him. And for us since he's the temp TriCoast CEO for now and we're looking at buying Joost's company."

"Yes, but everyone around here is tangled up in one another's business, so there are always these kinds of conflicts. Another reason I don't like the idea of buying Bradshaw Energy," Roy said.

The truck bumped down the gravel road and they arrived at the massive, precisely arranged drill site.

They met the site foreman, who gave them operating stats. "Sand's running eighteen hundred pounds per horizontal foot. The fracking stages along the laterals are spaced about two hundred and fifty feet apart. Each stage requires four hundred thousand pounds of sand, so twenty-five stages is ten million pounds."

"Wow. I'm always amazed at how much sand is used," Lynn said. She looked at Roy, thinking of their conversation about David's sand contract.

The foreman continued, "We're recycling over half the water, soon to be three-quarters, and expanding the gas gathering system to reduce flaring to zero. Drilling time's just ten days for 15,000-foot laterals."

Unexpectedly, Lynn felt movement under her feet. She put out a hand to brace herself against a desk. *Am I dizzy? Sick?*

But when she glanced around, everyone else looked surprised, too. Except the foreman.

"Little earthquake. We've had a few. Someone must still be loading up the saltwater disposal wells when they're not supposed to."

"But not from this drill site, right?" Lynn asked.

"Not that I know of. Of course, I don't follow the contractor's trucks to see where they go. But I have to assume they follow the rules. Should be someone here now. I'll ask."

Then the blare of the shutdown alarm drowned out every other sound.

"Stop the pumps!" The foreman shouted, then jabbed buttons on the control panel. Next, he spoke and the outside loudspeaker echoed. "Manual override. Shut down everything now!"

"Stay here!" He ordered Lynn and Roy. But as he exited, Lynn could see a dwindling arc of a steaming oil-water mix from a broken steel pipe. Two men on the platform had pulled a third away from the pipe.

"Not my site, but I assume he's called an ambulance. It'll take a while to get out here," Roy said.

"Let's grab water and a blanket," Lynn said. She filled a bucket with tap water and found rags, a blanket, and the burn kit. She and Roy raced out to the site foreman and the injured man.

"Heard a creak when the ground rattled and next I knew the damn pipe was spraying right at me! Glad I wasn't any closer." The injured man sat several feet away from the busted pipe, whose spray had finally slowed to a trickle. He poured the water Lynn had brought onto his hands, but they had already reddened. He winced from pain at the slight pressure of the flowing water.

"You see anything else?" The foreman looked at the other two men.

When they shook their heads, the foreman squatted down and talked to the injured man. "Ambulance should be here shortly."

"It's not bad. I can keep working."

"No. You need to get your hands checked and treated more than we can do here."

When he stood back up, the foreman did a double take and motioned one of the other two men closer. "You're from the water disposal company?"

A brown-bearded man in nondescript jeans and work shirt nodded. When he saw Lynn, he said, "Ma'am."

"No need but thank you. I'm Lynn Dayton and this is Roy Bastrop. We're from TriCoast. You're?"

His nametag was clipped onto his shirt rather than a lanyard.

A lanyard could too easily be caught in rotating equipment, causing an accident even worse than what they'd just witnessed.

Lynn was surprised to recognize the logo and the name of the company on the nametag. Daine Environmental Water Services. *Rowan Daine's company. Daine's overlap here keeps getting more and more curious. And it's a problem for TriCoast.*

"My name is John Cooper."

"Mr. Cooper, we're checking on operations here, though we didn't expect to be in time for this shaker. You're one of the ones driving the water disposal trucks with all the hot water separated out in these wells." She smiled in as encouraging a way as she could muster.

"Yes, ma'am."

"Just Lynn, please," Lynn said. "I have to ask, where are you taking the water?"

"I don't know the name of the place," he lied, "but I can give you the coordinates." He checked his phone and scribbled them on a piece of paper. Using coordinates was shorthand for identifying locations that otherwise had no identifying traits, not even a tree or fence post. And Cooper knew anyone who needed could get his routes. He didn't expect this woman to be so fast, though.

She frowned at the numbers, then at him. "I wish I didn't recognize this location, but I do. It's one of the shut-in disposal wells. Nobody should be putting more water into it."

She turned to the site foreman.

He shook his head. News to him, too.

"Thank you for your honesty, Mr. Cooper, although this place has a name which you should know. It's Deadman's Draw. We'll pass the word through the chain but you're hearing it from us, too. Please find another disposal well for your saltwater drop-offs. Not just me talking. The Railroad Commission would say the same."

Lynn pulled Roy Bastrop aside. "Cooper confirms it. We do have a conflict problem with Daine."

"Forget Bradshaw. If he's dumping wastewater into closed disposal wells, that's illegal," Roy said.

Lynn completed his thought. "And Rowan Daine is the wrong man to be filling in as TriCoast CEO. He could get us in trouble fast."

❖

The embed hated confirming his name to the woman but doubted anyone would suspect anything. He ground his teeth to keep from snarling. Finding another saltwater disposal well would cut into his time. But worse, now this woman knew who he was. He needed anonymity above all. He'd have to think about how to address this new person who'd become an additional problem.

As he left, Cooper saw a dust fantail from the approaching ambulance. More important, he heard Lynn's side of a phone conversation. "Joost, you've got an issue with your water disposal. It has to be fixed before we can negotiate further.

Once he was on the road, Cooper called Daine. "Hey, sorry to bring bad news, but we've got another problem. The TriCoast people—particularly the Lynn Dayton bitch—know I've been making wastewater deliveries to closed wells."

"Damn. Why couldn't you keep a lower profile?"

"Didn't know she'd be here. I had to have my badge on to stay onsite, and she cornered me."

"Cornered you? You wuss. She's not so tough. I don't believe you."

"Doesn't matter if you believe me or not. She does. And she looks like she could take you to the TriCoast board."

"Well, this may just play right into my plans. Ol' Lynn may have the hots for buying Bradshaw Energy, but plenty of people around her, including me and I think Roy, think it's a terrible idea. Maybe now she'll back off. And if she does, she's got no reason to run to Austin and be a tattletale."

"I like the way you think, Rowan, but we need to keep an eye on her."

"Coincidentally, I'm well-placed at TriCoast to do so. You watch her, too. Maybe it's time to get more tracking data on her." After he hung up, Daine laughed to himself. *Two birds with one stone, by God. I have my own reasons for bankrupting Bradshaw Energy.*

# CHAPTER 10
# AUSTIN, TEXAS

IN THE EVENING, Lynn went to a talk by Dr. Scott Tinker that TriCoast and a few environmental groups had sponsored about energy economics in less developed countries. She wondered if the mysterious Hannah Bosko would turn up. Lynn had found little online about the woman.

She slid into a chair at the back of the room, glad to be out of the winter wind.

"Quality of life is based on the fundamental "food" of energy. Energy poverty is tied to economic poverty. You see it in clothing, education, food, shelter, health.

"There's not good and bad energy or clean and dirty energy. They all have their challenges, and they all have their positive impacts. Oil and gas are the fuels for every other industry. The wealthier the economy, the more it can afford to invest in the environment, clean-up, regulations, and laws. Where air, water, and soil are the cleanest is where it's rich. That's why the barrels of oil produced here are the lowest carbon-emission barrels in the world. The dirtiest environments in the world are usually also the poorest ones.

"Most of the world looks to fossil fuels to grow themselves out of poverty. They'd rather burn propane or coal or natural gas instead of their people killing themselves from respiratory diseases because they're burning dung for heat. All these countries are building their nations on fossil fuels just as we and the UK did. Half the world's population lives in southeast Asia. They get their energy from coal because coal makes electricity cheap.

Cheap electricity means manufacturing, wealth, and, eventually, a cleaner environment.

"It took us a hundred and fifty years to go from all renewables—that is, wood for heat and horses for transport—to what we have now, which is about ten to fifteen percent renewables."

He nodded to a young man who had raised his hand. "What about batteries storing solar and wind?"

"They work well but right now, the US electric grid has only twenty seconds of battery storage for the whole country. Batteries are expensive and they discharge unevenly, but I agree we need to build more."

"What about EVs?"

"The good thing about EVs is they use whatever fuel you use for electricity—solar, wind, nuclear, coal, hydro, natural gas. The challenges, as some of you may have experienced, are range anxiety and time to recharge. And electricity takes about three times as much generating fuel as what you get in output. Same thing for car batteries as for utility batteries—takes thousands of pounds of mining since you're mining, and separating, solid minerals rather than oil.

"Natural gas will continue to play a huge role. You can use it directly for cooking and heating, or to make plastics, or to make electricity. Oil is important because it's liquid, dense power for our vehicles. You fill up your SUV or truck in three minutes and drive again for three hundred miles.

"You can't get out of poverty without energy. There's an energy-economy-environment waltz. All three must work together.

"Those billions of people in the world won't keep eighty-five percent of the world's energy in the ground. And it would be a disaster for the environment if we did because then you keep people in poverty for much longer, so they can't invest in the environment."

*Many would agree with you,* Lynn thought.

Some in the audience booed.

"We're not transitioning away from one form of energy to something else. In the next fifty to a hundred years, the transition includes oil, it includes more natural gas, and it includes more renewables, more nuclear, and more geothermal. That allows lifting the world out of energy poverty. I'll take questions," engineering professor Tinker concluded.

A young woman with an accent from who-knew-where? Chicago? England? asked the question Lynn found most relevant: "What about emissions from these fields in West Texas? What about solar?"

*Is she Hannah Bosko?*

"In the companies with whom I've worked, they find if everything is in underground pipelines instead of being trucked, it helps enormously. Fewer trucks, fewer accidents, fewer emissions," Tinker replied.

Afterward, the woman made her way to Lynn.

"I'm Hannah Bosko. Thank you for being here."

"How did you know who I am?"

"Your picture is all over the TriCoast website. And you're one of the older women here."

"Oh."

"Older. I didn't say oldest."

"Stop. You're digging the hole deeper. Where are you from, Hannah?" Lynn didn't ask the question she most wanted the answer to. *How do you know about Bradshaw Energy?* Since Hannah had requested the meeting, she would wait for Hannah to bring up Bradshaw.

"I'm from everywhere. Those questions people were asking were rather odd. After all, we're all just carbon ourselves, aren't we?"

Lynn concentrated on Hannah's accent. Midwestern but burnished with the tone of someone who had spent time in England. She almost missed what Hannah said next.

"I do generally agree with him."

"What do you mean?" Lynn asked.

"Energy poverty is real. It's incredibly hypocritical and colonialist to deny poor countries access to energy."

"We're on the same page. The regs are important and we follow them. On the alternate energy question, we often find adjacent projects, like a solar array in a New Mexico field far from the electricity grid."

"Awesome," Hannah said.

"And you? It sounds like you have interesting experience."

"Consulting. Environmental, sometimes chemistry. Most recently I worked in forensic chemistry and geology for Scotland Yard."

The lights blinked in the auditorium, a signal to leave. "Can I buy you a drink? Or a drink and tacos?"

"I had the last, best Scotch I'll ever have in a pub in London, so no, no sticky margaritas. But tacos yeah," Hannah said.

They walked through a bitter wind to Cain & Abel's, a campus sports bar. Lynn found a booth near a pool table.

Hannah watched the action as three impossibly tall, gawky students clustered around the table with their pool cues, calculating too-elaborate bank shots. "Physics students."

Lynn turned and smiled as one of them pumped his fist after shooting into the pocket. "Did you skip dinner like I did?"

"Yes. I'm trying to decide between fajita tacos and crawfish tacos."

They got orders of both, along with draft beer. Hannah sat forward, brushing hair out of her eyes.

"How do you like Austin?" Lynn asked.

"I used to come to gamers' conferences here. One of them grew from five hundred to thirty thousand people in just a few years. Speaking of, those people would be good to have around at TriCoast for risk assessment. They're always thinking about what bad stuff could happen and how to get out of it."

"Thirty thousand! I have a mental image of a gamer. You don't match it."

"You mean your stereotype. You're thinking big, square people, meaty endomorphs with cankles and black t-shirts. Plastic black-frame glasses. People watching other people play video games or waiting three hours in line to hear a one-hour panel."

"Yes."

"Sure, many of those people. But other types, too. Including me."

"Do you mind telling me about yourself?" Lynn asked.

"You first."

Lynn hesitated, thinking about the last time she confided in a younger woman over drinks. *Dena, the woman who killed David and who tried to kill me and my bodyguard. But I have to move on from it.* "Grew up in Oklahoma. I have one sister. She works for the International Energy Agency in Paris.

Hannah nodded approval.

"My mother was an accountant. She's passed away. So has my father, more recently. He was a pipeline inspect—"

"I can't even! Mine worked in the oilfield too, until he was killed by a gas pipeline explosion. That's what they told us."

"I'm so sorry." Lynn paused for several seconds. "I'm a chemical engineer. Do you mind my asking what happened?"

"The company told my mother it hadn't been pigged correctly."

*Pigged. Cleared and cleaned.* "Again, I'm so sorry. How did you and your mother handle it?"

"It was horrible," Her voice caught. "He was so badly burned the coroner had to take impressions of his teeth to verify his identity. They wouldn't let us see his body. What's odd is my mom said my dad was so careful. Gas is very combustible and she said he was safety conscious on and off the job. He even had safety checklists for repairs he did around the house, she said. I wanted to see the accident report, but the company wouldn't release it since my mother had settled with them."

Lynn shook her head. "Again, I'm so sorry."

"The settlement kept my mom in the medicine she needed and

paid for my school. I added environmental studies to my chem undergrad." Hannah shrugged.

The noise in the bar escalated. Lynn leaned across the table so she could be heard. "Geology and chemistry forensics. Give me an example."

"Shoes at crime scenes. Often my investigations now center on shoes. And soils. Dirt. I try to avoid bodies but it's not always possible." Hannah explained how she had solved the mystery of the stolen Scotch at her favorite London pub.

"Cool." With the noise now ear-splitting and the bill paid, Lynn leaned over and said, "It's cold outside but it's quieter."

Hannah explained she was staying with friends not far from Lynn's hotel, so they began walking.

"And you? Doing your best to –what?" Hannah asked.

"Keep people moving around the country and keep them warm—especially now. I have a new job so I'm meeting the people in the division. Funny, we talk often about dirt, too," Lynn replied.

"I didn't want to shout in there and have everyone hear me, but I get called in often on crime scenes."

"More than missing bottles of whiskey." Lynn turned to look at her.

"Whiskey's important!" Hannah tightened her scarf. "But a bomb scene, for example. Many soil samples would be taken. Or a US federal agent who was killed and buried in a country south of here I won't name. Officials in the country said it was a suicide. He was found in a desert. But the material stuck to his body—and there's always material stuck to a body—was from a different area a hundred kilometers away, in the city. Basalt. Green glass, among other things. Turned out the country's police had teamed up with a drug cartel to get rid of him and dump his body in the desert."

"Oh my God."

"I worked on the case and helped solve it, though I don't know if his killers ever went to jail. So that's a country I can't go back to."

"What about in London?" Lynn hoped she would never need to ask for Hannah's, or anyone's, expertise at crime scenes.

"I attended with the bobbies at Scotland Yard and watched them. They observe everything. Decomposition starts fast, so you can usually smell it. The metallic copper sensation—blood. And bloodstains aren't always pools—sometimes they show the body's been dragged."

"So, what are you doing here?" Lynn asked. "Your email said you wanted to talk about Bradshaw Energy. How do you know about them? What do you need to tell me?"

Hannah paused before she answered. "I'm investigating the company. Working for a man out of London named Henry Vandervoost."

Lynn stifled a yelp. "Vandervoost. I worked with him when he was at TriCoast in Europe. He has so many ego scars. He wasn't a fan of me or any American, especially not women. He wanted to take over my job. It didn't happen."

"I had a sense of those scars, yeah. But what you're saying otherwise is odd because he was married to an American at one time. He's paying me to look into his son's company in Midland. Bradshaw Energy. He said his son wants him to invest but the company has a new water recycling technology using dangerous and environmentally destructive chemicals. He says he particularly wants me to check into that."

*Oh Christ. We're talking about the same person and I'm on a different side. Since when does Henry Vandervoost worry about technology or chemistry? Does he really have money to invest or is that just a cover? But I should confirm with Hannah.* "Yes, Henry's son is Joost Bradshaw. I know."

"In London, Henry told me TriCoast was considering buying Joost's company. You're leading that, right?"

"How did you figure it out?" Lynn asked.

"Process of elimination. I'm a good researcher."

"I shouldn't tell you this, but there's plenty of opposition within my company to acquiring Bradshaw Energy. Despite the due diligence we've done, it's hard to know what problems we might be acquiring."

"Maybe we're not on opposite sides. Maybe Henry and his fund can invest alongside TriCoast if you decide to go ahead with the acquisition. And if turns out the special Bradshaw recycling process he's telling me about is not really so harmful." The wind turned chillier as Hannah pointed toward a small cottage. "My friends."

"Thank you for arranging for us to meet. Hannah, perhaps you could come with me on my next trip to Midland?"

"Brilliant. Yes. Text me your phone number," Hannah said.

# CHAPTER 11
# BUDAPEST, HUNGARY

MEN IN RED and white ghutras and thobes—headdresses and long gowns—thronged the streets of commercial Budapest.

Kir Zaitsev was blunt and not one to make small talk—no Russian was—he was merely glad, though wary, to be allowed at this first of two natural gas buyers' and sellers' conferences. Without humiliating himself or his country, he'd dialed down from the show of wealth his Middle Eastern partners typically preferred. That included picking only penthouse rooms for himself and a single floor for his security entourage at the conference hotel, Four Seasons Gresham Palace. It was close to the convention center, the financial center, and shopping.

At a different time, Zaitsev would have chosen an even more luxurious and even more private location overlooking the Danube, although he had to admire the view from the Gresham.

Egonov had charged Zaitsev with recovering the sales Russia had lost after its deadly international incursions. Easy to request, hard to accomplish. Re-establishing ties with the twenty European and Baltic companies Russia had supplied before the conflict wouldn't happen quickly, and not at all with some. But if he, Zaitsev, didn't accomplish it, others would. Zaitsev could only guess at the form his banishment would then take.

Yet Russia's partnerships with other natural gas producers had survived the conflicts, just as had Russia's membership in OPEC+. Fewer gas buyers did not mean no gas buyers, particularly not with China and India in the orbit. For Europe, he would focus during this conference on those already favorably inclined toward him, like Alejandro Garcia of Spain. Success with Garcia would provide the wedge for negotiations with others, especially Germany.

Zaitsev also would have to arrange to cross paths with Israeli Avi Levin. He wanted to evaluate how strong a competitor for Spain's natural gas business Levin would be. He'd heard the outlines of Israel's initial contract with Spain. Garcia had made certain everyone had.

A second benefit of meeting Avi was that he could assume anything he told Avi would get back to his nutty aunt, Sara Levin, CFO of TriCoast. This would kill two hares. Or what the English called "killing two birds with one stone."

Budapest was not as cold as he expected, and of course warmer than Moscow or Murmansk. And then there were the city's baths. He'd been to one and looked forward to trying others.

Zaitsev glanced through his memorized list. Before the Ukraine difficulty, Russia had been well-positioned with Western Europe, supplying over half the gas consumed to countries like Germany, the Czech Republic, Greece, and even independent-minded Poland. Finland, Slovakia, and Austria had depended completely on gas imports from Russia. The way to win back customers would be through an extraordinary discount. The discount would be temporary, and—he grimaced—would have to be deep. But improving the relationship with Spain, and then others, would eventually allow Russia to return to normal, non-discounted pricing for its natural gas exports.

As part of the plan, he also had to signal his seriousness to his competitors—those who had displaced Russia. They included Qatar, the United States, Poland, companies drilling in the North Sea, Australia, Canada, Norway, even Mozambique.

He would start with Israel. Upstart Israel had been producing gas in the eastern Mediterranean and sending it to Egypt, which then liquefied it and sent it to other countries for regasification and further resale. He had to stall the Israeli-Egyptian partnership and their plans to sell to customers who had been, and would again be, Russia's customers. Especially Spain.

❖

"Avi Levin, come in."

Avi had been coached enough to not be offended when Russian Kir Zaitsev didn't shake hands with him at the door. It was Russian superstition that a handshake over a threshold could lead to a quarrel.

The muscular man offered him vodka and said, "Here's where the dog is buried."

"Already I don't understand you," Avi said.

"The essence of things. Skipping the small talk." Zaitsev's mouth twitched in a sneer.

"Yes?"

"Your essential utilities may be at risk should you go ahead with this Egyptian partnership to sell gas to Spain and the rest of Europe."

"Again, explain."

"Rather than compete with us and risk, say, Israel's electricity grid or banking system from cyberattacks, you should join the Gas Exporting Countries Forum. We have an excellent service. It can help you line up buyers for the natural gas you wish to sell."

"I don't have the authority to make the commitment."

"You make an elephant out of a fly. You take me too seriously."

Avi waited. So did Zaitsev.

"Israel does not need to join the forum. Even some of your buyers are talking to us."

"You mean Alejandro Garcia of Spain."

"You know him?"

"Everyone vital to Spain, as I am, has heard about your discussions. Señor Garcia called Russia immediately after his last con versation with you. He believes Israel may not be able to move its gas to Egypt, liquefy it, and get it to Spain on schedule."

Avi masked his surprise. *Everyone talks to everyone. It's negotiation. I should have expected it.* "We'll meet the delivery schedule, as we discussed with the Honorable"—he tried not to choke on the word—Alejandro Garcia."

"You are no doubt aware Egypt is experiencing a catastrophic loss of revenue because of rebel attacks on ships in the Suez Canal and Red Sea. Ship owners are picking different routes now. And my sources tell me that even Israel experienced another attack from a new direction."

"Then the attack on Israel from an offshore ship near Syria *was* Russia!"

"No. But we do have many allies who might, at a word from us, take such an action." Zaitsev leaned forward. "Avi Levin, for the sake of Israel and your Egyptian partners, perhaps you should rethink this contract with Spain." He leaned back. "Accidents happen. There's no harm in backing out, or just missing a deadline due to an accident. I'm sure you could explain your change of heart to Señor Garcia."

*He wants me to react.* "I will not have a change of heart, as you call it. The only thing I will be explaining to Señor Garcia, and our Egyptian partners is how quickly we will meet our contractual obligations. Further discussion with you is not fruitful." Avi stood to leave.

Zaitsev's expression remained deceptively warm. "There, Avi Levin, you are wrong. Discussion with us is always fruitful."

❖

Despite the cool air outside, Kir Zaitsev again remembered the far colder air in Murmansk as he settled into the octagonal Turkish Bath at Rudas. It was a weekday morning, which meant Rudas Thermal Bath was relaxingly men-only. Fed for centuries by hot, deep, mineral-rich spring water from beneath Gellert Hill, Rudas, and the other nearby thermal baths were the choicest destinations for everyone attending the Budapest conference.

Yet it was also the perfect place for a private meeting.

*Mineral-rich.* The salts and minerals were part of the much-desired healing properties of the Turkish baths. *Why would technology to remove salts and minerals from water in West Texas be desirable? Is it worth anything at all? What do the Chinese want with the Bradshaw Energy water clean-up technology?* He would ask Vandervoost, Zaitsev thought.

A man splashed in beside him. Despite the dim overhead light, every extra kilogram of weight from dozens of diplomatic dinners was evident on the Spanish energy minister's body.

"Alejandro. Welcome."

"Excellent idea, Kir. I have been to other baths here and wanted to try Rudas. Thank you for arranging it."

Kir Zaitsev's expression was as genial as he could make it. "Only the best for our best customers."

"Two fat men in hot water. Seems like many situations."

"Speaking only for yourself, I hope."

"But Kir, you are enjoying Budapest?"

"Yes, in every way. Do you want—?"

"No, no girls, but thank you."

"So how can I persuade you to resume business with us? Russia is a good, affordable supplier of natural gas."

"We work with the EU. They look over my shoulder."

"But why do you care?"

"You are from a huge country. I am not."

"But at what cost? Everyone is marking up prices to you, including the Israelis with their LNG from Egypt, as you told me."

"Kir, I am required to follow my president, even when I do not agree with him."

"But how will it look in a year when you've paid double for the Israeli gas compared to what I would charge you?"

The Spanish energy minister nodded, splashed water on his arms. "Long-term. I understand what you are doing in Ukraine, but my government does not want to aid you by buying natural gas from Russia."

Kir paused as if Garcia's Spanish accent was difficult to understand. "They are not the same issues."

"Kir, I agree with you. But I am bound by my government... Let me think. We can perhaps make a brief agreement."

"We will consider whatever you might request. Call me once you and your government have a proposal for us. Now, let's enjoy this warm water."

## CHAPTER 12
# MIDLAND

She started with a voicemail. Hannah figured if Joost heard her, rather than just seeing a text, he might be more willing to respond. She doubted she could get all the data she needed about the water recycling process Henry kept mentioning, but she would try. "Hi Joost, Hannah Bosko here. I'm a project evaluator working for your father, Henry Vandervoost, at his private equity firm. He's interested in putting several hundred million more into your company, but he said the two of you haven't been speaking recently. He figured you wouldn't take his call. I'd like to sit down with you and talk about your company and its prospects. Due diligence, too."

Joost called her back later the same day. "If you are really Hannah Bosko and you are really representing my father, he guessed right. I don't want to talk to him at present. But who are you? Text me your credentials. If they check out, you can come to our offices in Midland. Where are you now?"

"Austin."

"Bane of my existence."

He had been satisfied with her credentials. A few days later, she was in Bradshaw Energy's offices on Big Spring Street in Midland.

More than one source had described Joost as a particularly eligible man, recently divorced from his first wife. When he came to retrieve her from the outer lobby of the building, he looked her up and down.

*Hmm. This one may be much too entitled,* Hannah thought.

But she worried more that her true mission—to learn about

the secret water recycling technology Joost claimed—would be revealed.

In a small conference room with high-back leather chairs, Joost introduced her to his chief financial officer, Terry Gomez.

*Great, CFO as well as chaperone.*

"You probably know we're also negotiating with TriCoast," Gomez said.

She nodded. She could be truthful about that, at least.

"So, we're happy to take money my father's raised, but we can't offer him much in return. A small stake, not too liquid. We'd need a two-year lockup," Joost said.

"You know your father, so it's best if we let him be the judge of what's right for him and the firm. He's backed by several banks and funds. They're interested in making energy investments here in the Permian basin."

"Where was he six months ago, when we really needed him?" Joost's tight-lipped smile suggested he wasn't interested in nuance.

"I only just met him myself." She shrugged. She then named other large funds reversing course, well-known financiers who had become interested in making hydrocarbon investments again.

"And where were these guys, too?" Joost insisted. His tone softened. "You probably don't have the history here to know how tough it's been."

"So will you consider the $750 million enough to answer due diligence questions?" She tried her most serious look. *God, he's awesome-looking. He must have all the single and divorced—and married—women in Texas after him.*

Joost glanced at Gomez, who nodded.

"What do you want to know?"

She had memorized her checklist. "Water handling?"

"Water coming in is on pipe. No trucks so we limit truck traffic. Produced and flowback water coming out of the well are mostly recycled with a new process we've developed. So we use saltwater disposal wells as little as possible. From just one zone, like the Wolfcamp, we can get several thousand barrels of water per stage. With 25-75 stages, we can wind up with half a million to a million barrels of water. You bet we think about water."

"But the oil-water ratio only goes up, so your water flows will be increasing, particularly since produced water from the formation is at least twice as much as what's used for fracking. Any seismic issues?"

"Okay, I'm impressed you know about oil-water ratios. Seismic. You mean earthquakes?" Joost leaned toward her. She stared back and nodded.

In past years, earthquakes up to a 5.3 magnitude had struck nearby. The earthquakes were similar to what had happened earlier in Oklahoma and for the same reason. As they were filled, the ultra-deep wastewater disposal wells could lubricate underground faults, which then started slipping. An earthquake. In response, regulators in Oklahoma and then Texas limited the volume of wastewater that could be put into the ground in certain deep wastewater disposal wells.

"None that track back to water disposal from our leases. Since we recycle so much of our water, we have very little exposure."

"Fresh water for drilling?" She felt a little breathless. *Why do I feel breathless?*

He shook his head. "Like I said, we recycle. Ours and others. We had to adapt our process to it, though. We do have to blend fresh water in to make it work."

"How much?"

"About half," he admitted.

"As a geochemist, I'm interested in the water specs—what goes into and what comes out of your recycle process: chloride, hardness, sulfides, iron, oil, total solids, pH, bacteria."

"I don't have it at hand. We can make that available to you later." He smiled at the level of detail she was requesting.

*Or is he smiling about something else?* Hannah wondered. She made a note. "Contracts for gas, oil, liquids, gathering, processing and transportation?"

"Yes, everything. We sell oil to refineries here and on the Gulf Coast, natural gas liquids to chemicals plants, and natural gas to electric utilities and plants in Texas and in the Midwest. We have big contracts with the Chicago gas utility."

"How big?"

He paused, and Gomez elaborated. "About a third of B a day."

A third of a B meant over three hundred million cubic feet per day. Even out here in the field that contract was worth at least a million dollars a day. Worth much more in Chicago.

"Hedges?" Hannah looked to Gomez for this answer, too.

"Only when the banks require it, but they do for the Chicago volumes since they're so big," Gomez said.

The wind picked up and a few snowflakes appeared outside the conference room window. The glass made a cracking sound as it flexed and contracted in the cold air.

"Look, Hannah, maybe you and my father are for real on this financing and maybe you're not. Say you are. How about we take you out of town, further west. You can see how we run things. Where the money my father says he's raised would be going."

"Sure. When?" *Gives me more opportunities to find out about the water treatment process so interesting to Henry. Spending more time with Joost is not hard duty, either.*

"Tomorrow, same time? I'm headed out with Lynn Dayton and Roy Bastrop from TriCoast. Maybe all of you will see fit to buy out my company."

Later, after Hannah told Henry all she had learned, a small part of her wished she hadn't. She had expected her conversation with Joost would be a straightforward interview, in which she got as much information as she could about Bradshaw Energy. She'd been successful at that. But in equal parts horror and anticipation, she realized she really wanted to see Joost again. Just to look at him.

*Damn.* His attraction was as magnetic as advertised. *I don't want to fall for Joost. He's not paying my bills. His* father *is my client.*

# CHAPTER 13
# SOUTH OF MIDLAND

They stopped first at one of TriCoast's pipeline control rooms near Midland. "So, you can see what you'd be selling into," Lynn explained to Joost.

They saw twenty controllers, twenty consoles, two shift supervisors. "We're staffed here 24/7/365," Roy explained. "We have eighteen thousand miles of pipeline to move crude and natural gas liquids from the field to refining, other pipelines, and export ships. We can monitor flows from all over the US."

"So, you're saying my small system would fit right in with what you already have here?" Joost asked.

"Exactly," Lynn replied.

Then Joost, Lynn, Roy, and Hannah drove west toward one of Joost's well sites. Near the highway they saw cows with calves as frisky as big dogs. Further down the interstate off to the side, a scatter of big feathers spoke to a fight between Canadian geese or, more likely, a goose and a coyote. Lynn looked for a goose carcass but didn't see one.

"You might not have an earthquake monitor next to your water well or a dust and gas monitor next to the line into your house, but we have all that and more on our wellsites. We've cut flaring and emissions leaks," Joost said.

"How much did you cut?" Hannah asked. "And what?"

"On flaring, greenhouse gases—primarily $CO_2$ and methane—we're down half from our baseline and we'll achieve a 75% cut by next year."

Hannah nodded.

"On emissions leaks, we aim to get all of them. Like with flaring, no point in letting money escape into the air. We have a quarterly drone program in place now to check methane emissions from our whole system."

"Only methane?" Hannah asked.

"Good catch." Joost grinned at her.

Hannah's face lit up in response. *Why am I grinning at him like a bloody idiot?*

"We don't want leaks of any hydrocarbon gas, but it's usually methane because methane's the lightest, and that's what's mainly in the gas. And we're field-testing our new water recycling technology.

"We hope to hear more about that," Lynn interjected.

"You may eventually if you and I agree on how much Bradshaw Energy is really worth. What is TriCoast's environmental profile?" Joost asked.

"We talk to the Dark Skies people at McDonald Observatory south of here to make sure we're cutting our light pollution," Roy said, agreeably. "They say we're good. We use LED lights, shields to keep down the glare, or switch to softer yellow lights."

"Gotta love the people in Alpine and Marfa. They're so cooler-than-thou they're like Austin," Joost said. "But I do like the pitch-black night skies. Perspective. Helps me think."

"We answer to seven counties nearby on light pollution, in addition to the observatory," Lynn added. "The astronomers at the observatory want to be able to see the Milky Way clearly. Used to be the brightest things were El Paso and Juarez, which are over 150 miles away. Fortunately, the mountains do a good job of blocking light from the fields, in addition to all the ways we've been able to cut the light."

She wished Dwayne Thomas was here with her instead of working in Pennsylvania. Part of Dwayne's job was to oversee the construction of equipment to clean and pressure up natural gas so it could be shipped out from the field in massive, commercial trunklines to customers. Although the processes were not as complicated as the oil refining to which he and Lynn were accustomed, they were keys to selling the gas. Raw natural gas right out of the ground couldn't be used the next day by a Chicago or Houston or Mexican grandmother to heat her house or make tortillas. Fresh-from-the-fractured-rock natural gas, or methane, also contained undesirable hydrogen sulfide, carbon dioxide, water vapor, mercury, and nitrogen, as well as slightly heavier organic gases like ethane, propane, and butane. Each had to be removed to make the natural gas—the methane—transportable, saleable, and safe.

"Same. Though like David says—used to say—" Roy blushed and glanced at Lynn, "We look for opportunities in the white space." *White space* referred to the space shown on a map in between well markers.

"The banks are comfortable with their risk on your company?" Lynn asked Joost.

"Yes. You know what they say about risk: 'No shots, no ducks.' How about TriCoast? A few big customers or several little ones for your production?"

"California and Mexico, Houston, and LNG export for the gas and NGLs. We recycle some of the gas back to the wells for pressurization. For the oil, a few refineries out here, more refineries in Houston and the Midwest, some export."

"We'd like to drill in Mexico. A lot of the same geologic trends that are here continue there. But it's too violent. Can't risk our people or theirs," Roy said. "Still, I'm glad they buy a bunch of our production. A lot of Bs."

As he spoke, Lynn wondered how safe her workers were from the cartels, even here on the other side of the border. People traveled back and forth for legitimate work constantly, especially further southeast for the Eagle Ford shale field.

Roy turned to Hannah. "Sorry, Bs are billions of cubic feet. But I suppose you're one of those folks who think we shouldn't use energy at all. Make the rest of us apologize for having grandkids."

"Nope. Not me. You have me confused with someone else. I've seen the African mommas coughing from smoke when they cook over a dung fire. I know their daughters get attacked and raped when they go out to gather wood. Those are their "biofuels." They need natural gas and especially the propane and butane you just talked about separating from your oil here. I hope you're thinking about ways to get it to them."

She looked at Joost. To her surprise and secret delight, he was nodding at her comments.

"But lighter topic," Hannah continued. "I'm amused by how you name your wells and fields. For giants, for history, for ghosts, for whatever the topic of conversation was when the field was identified. There's Blood Rock even, name of a sandstone in Pennsylvania."

"I like the name Phantom Field," Lynn said. "Many projects are named for food or football. Sometimes it depends on what lunch was that day. The Permian basin is huge. Thirty thousand square miles. Eighteen million acres. That's a lot of names to come up with."

They stopped for lunch. Joost probed Hannah's background further.

She explained she'd grown up in Alaska and Chicago, was a consulting chemist and forensic geologist, had previously worked on crime scenes in London for Scotland Yard, and had met Lynn in Austin.

"How can we be sure you're not really one of those ESG folks in disguise, looking for ways to screw us?" Roy flashed a grin, but Lynn knew his question was serious.

"Now wait a minute, Roy. Let the woman talk," Joost said. He nodded at Hannah. "I want to hear what she has to say."

"Look," Hannah said, simultaneously exasperated, pleased at the attention from Joost, and suspicious of Roy. "I agree with all of you. Oil and gas are all biofuels. We're just talking about compressed plants here. Just like you can get oil out of algae." As she spoke, she drew chemical formulas on a napkin. Mostly they were lines connecting the letters 'C,' 'H,' and 'O.'

"Hannah, you're way ahead of us. What are those?" Joost asked.

*I'm glad he's interested but this seems like a con he pulls on women,* Hannah thought. Before agreeing to take on the project from Henry Vandervoost, she had researched his son's background. As a particularly eligible billionaire, Joost's name had been linked with several women, but after his divorce, he claimed no interest in long-term relationships. *And why would he?*

"Fruit formulas," Hannah answered. "Like these winter grapes we're getting. Methyl anthranilate. The oranges and pears I wish we could have but they're out of season. Octyl acetate and pentyl acetate."

"How do you know such stuff? You grow up in the chem lab?" Joost asked, a note of admiration warming his voice.

"My father worked in the oilfield, yes. But it's my own experience. I'm a geochemist, duh. Organic chemistry. Honestly, it's kind of basic, gentlemen. See this?" She pointed to a segment in each drawing. "C-O-O. Group of one carbon, two oxygens. Its presence is vital to the kind of smell."

"Organic. Whoa. I always stayed as far away from it as I could. It's how I wound up in petroleum geology," Roy chimed in. "No o-chem requirement."

"Your loss. Organic chemistry explains everything. But Joost, you're diverting me." She gave him a small smile suggesting she didn't mind the diversion. "It's important to tell you this fruit smell, or a bleach smell, also suggests someone making triacetone triperoxide. It gets into clothes and hair."

"Now that *is* outside anything I ever studied. What's triacetone triperoxide?" Lynn asked.

"TATP. An explosive."

Joost's eyes widened. He took a deep breath, then turned to Lynn. "Less grim subject. Your company has a fleet of Gulfstreams. Are your payments for those coming out of the purchase price you're offering me?"

"Whoa. Back up. First principles. We do not have a fleet of Gulfstreams. Two or three. Mainly we just have Learjet shares, which cost about a fiftieth of a Gulfstream. If you think I'm negotiating from a Middle Eastern level of wealth, then we're far apart."

"I'm still not sure little ol' us would fit with big ol' TriCoast in terms of company culture," Joost said.

"False modesty, and you know it. Your company is as sophisticated as they come. I've seen it in other acquisitions I've done. People don't want to work on new accounting systems. They want answers to big questions like, Do I have a job? What IS my job? Who do I report to?"

"Okay. Fair enough," Joost said, settling back in his chair. He stared again at Hannah. "I'd rather be hearing about oranges and TATP and organic chemistry from her."

Roy noticed. He rolled his eyes at Lynn, indicating Joost with a tip of his head, then prompted, "Joost, we all know your reputation. If you can take a break from trying to seduce Hannah, I've paid the bill. Let's go."

❖

Hannah stared at glistening stars already crowding the winter sky above Pecos, Texas. The McDonald Observatory was ninety miles distant—*nearby* in Texas terms—so, as they'd discussed, everyone within a large radius kept lights low for the benefit of the observatory and the Big Bend Dark Sky Reserve. Despite the cold, she'd hoped to see the big, spring-fed swimming hole at Balmorhea. *Balmorhea, Balmoral. Were the Scots here first?* Hannah wondered. She looked it up. *No.* The town, pronounced bal-mah-RHEE, had been named by combining letters from the last names of its three founders: Balcum, Morrow, and Rhea.

She'd also wanted to stay at a new Alpine Air BnB she'd heard about, famous for its finely detailed new construction, but even for long-driving west Texans, Balmorhea, and especially Alpine, were too far away from today's work sites in the Permian Basin.

*Honestly, what Joost told me yesterday is correct.* His operation was all just sand, water, oil, and gas. After he finished extracting oil and gas, a wellsite contained more sand and water and less oil and gas. But she reminded herself, there was the produced and flowback water. Dirty, salty, mineral-laden undrinkable water Joost said he and his company were trying to recycle. But were they?

*Joost.* She needed to think of the oil company scion as the enemy he was supposed to be, but it was difficult. He was her age, attractive, and single. *Too much interference with my job.* She decided to compartmentalize him as a likely-wayward exec out in the middle of treeless West Texas.

For a moment, Hannah felt the stab of loneliness, of missing her London friends and not knowing anyone in West Texas. The vibe here was brusque, borne of male competitiveness and deal-doing. *Of course.*

But as she turned to go to her room, Joost himself appeared next to her.

"Even though it's dark, it's still early. Food delivery out here isn't very fast. Could I take you to try out barbecue ribs?"

"Yes." *Whatever I think of Joost, I'm here to learn about Bradshaw Energy.*

His reply was a blinding smile. "I have the truck right here. Hop in."

She climbed into the front seat.

"Everything here is a bit of a drive. Hang on," he said, pulling out of the motel's parking lot.

"Tell me about yourself. How did you end up in Midland?" Hannah asked.

"Easy. Bradshaw Energy was my mom's company. Well, started by my grandfather. My father, who's not really a bad guy, just kind of well-educated Eurotrash, thought if he married into the family, he'd wind up controlling the company. I mean, I do think he loved my mother too."

He gave a two-finger wave as another truck roared past them going in the opposite direction.

"But he couldn't stay away from other women. My grandfather—and my mother—got fed up with him and told him to leave town, not too long after I was born. They divorced, but neither one ever remarried.

"As my grandfather got older, he gave my mother different positions in Bradshaw Energy, and after a few years, he asked her to run it. He stayed on the board, and I think they battled, but then horizontal drilling and fracking came along and suddenly Bradshaw Energy was able to grow much bigger."

He wheeled the truck into a jammed parking lot, finally finding a place at the back. The one-story diner was crowded with picnic tables inside and out. They stood in line, then ordered. Hannah ordered brisket, macaroni and cheese, and cole slaw. Joost got ribs and potato salad and Shiner Bock beer for both of them.

He pointed toward a half-occupied picnic table. As they walked over with their plates, several people stopped him and spoke to him. Some looked expectantly at her.

She overheard one of Joost's acquaintances say, "The latest?"

"A work acquaintance," Joost said.

"Yeah, right."

After they sat, Hannah said, "You must come here often." *With many other women.*

"Bradshaw Energy does an enormous amount of business in these counties." He shrugged.

"They like your money."

"Everyone does." He had soon finished the ribs. "Tell me more about yourself. You've had such an interesting life."

*The oldest line in the book.* But Hannah explained her father's death in West Texas still seemed mysterious to her.

Joost nodded. "Of course. I would wonder, too, in your place. There are *so* many industrial accidents here, though."

Hannah didn't want to dwell further on it and asked a few test questions, to which she knew the answers. "You went to college at Texas A&M? Then came back to help your mother run the company?"

He shook his head. "My father made certain I had all the right credentials. Princeton. Harvard Business School. Then time at an investment bank. We traveled throughout Europe and Asia. It was a good experience, in every way." He snorted.

"Do you ever feel stuck or isolated now in West Texas?"

"Not when I'm in the company of beautiful, smart women like you."

*Jesus. I'm disappointed his lines are so dated. It's what comes of being such a rich bloke in West Texas. He doesn't have to try hard to get what he wants.* "Joost, look, we've eaten. I'm full. It's dark. I'm not interested in being your latest, no matter what you tell your acquaintances here. I'd call an Uber or a taxi, but they don't usually make sixty-mile round trips. Please take me back."

"You misunderstand me." But he got up from the table.

"I understand you all too well." She frowned. "You're another git. You and dozens like you."

Both were silent on the return trip to the motel. Once they arrived, she got out, nodded at him, and closed the door. He spun off toward the parking apron behind the motel.

*It will be a long day tomorrow.* Hannah sighed.

Still, staring at a brilliant night sky was definitely a benefit. *But I'm not here to measure stars. Only gas flows.* Specifically, flows in the Wahalajara Pipeline between Waha in West Texas and Guadalajara, Mexico. The jubilantly labeled line connected to the equally exotic Tarahumara Pipeline, named for a dusty area of Mexico whose long-distance runners were legendary among Hannah's running friends.

She crossed to the lobby of her new-from-the-last-oil-boom three-story motel, regretting she had to go inside to sleep. The rooms were nice, and—since their cost followed the oil price—cheaper this month than last. But she would have preferred to stay outside and watch the million-star sky until it faded to dawn.

# CHAPTER 14
# WEST TEXAS AND MIDLAND

Lynn thought back to the call she'd made last week to Rowan Daine, after seeing the Bradshaw well. She'd done more research on John Cooper and discovered he'd been cited for illegal dumping several times.

When she called last week, she'd said, "Hey Rowan, sorry to call you outside of work hours, but you need to know we ran into one of your water company employees at a Bradshaw well site. John Cooper."

"Cooper, Cooper, yeah John, great guy!"

"Then you may not be aware he has a problem. I wanted to warn you, so he doesn't get your whole company in trouble."

"What do you mean, Lynn?" Glasses clinked in the background. Cocktail hour.

"He's been doing illegal dumping—putting wastewater into deep wells that are supposed to be closed. Not just the day we saw him. He's been cited a half-dozen times. He'll get banned from pickups by some companies and Daine Environmental Water Services could be looking at massive fines."

"Oh Lord. Lynn, thank you for telling me. I will talk to Mr. Cooper about following the rules and regulations. I don't want a problem. How's everything else? How's Bradshaw Energy looking to you?"

"Interesting. We'll be ready to make a new bid soon."

"Keep me apprised. I want to know all about it before we bring it to the board."

"Will do."

"And Lynn, thanks again for notifying me about Cooper."

❖

Moments after Lynn disconnected the call, Daine called Cooper. "We have a problem."

"I'll bet money I can identify who. Lynn Dayton."

"Yes. She thought she was doing me and my company a favor by fingering you as a driver with an illegal dumping history."

"What a bitch. Lucky you, she hasn't made the connection."

"And she shouldn't."

"I might have a solution. It'll cost you, same as always."

"I'll pay, same as always. I can't lose my company to an overzealous girl who doesn't understand the business."

"Besides the money, I need one of your best tech gurus to work on something for me ASAP. Someone fast. You need to pay him whatever price he quotes me."

"You got him. Besides your fee, throw in an extra 50% for yourself on the tech guy since this needs to happen yesterday." Daine listed a name and number.

"No promises, just based on what I overheard them saying about stuff they're checking out."

When Cooper hung up, he called the number Daine had given him. "Rowan Daine recommended you. Here's what I need you to do."

❖

In the morning at the motel in West Texas, Lynn shook her head. She wondered what Daine had said last week to Cooper. She hoped Cooper hadn't lost his job. *But wastewater dumping into closed wells? More earthquakes. More trouble for all of us.*

Lynn met Hannah and Joost after breakfast. Roy had been

with them the day before but had departed back to Midland. Unlike yesterday, Hannah and Joost were quiet, giving her one-word answers to her questions and not speaking at all to one another. Lynn wondered if something had happened between them.

Still, Joost had promised to show them around another well-site, a sand mine, and a sand loading silo to verify his operations met or were better than the safety and emissions targets she was now using for TriCoast operations. Missing the targets could lead to too much dust at the mine and silo. Using deep well disposal for wastewater—especially in the wrong places—instead of recycling could lead to earthquakes.

Given her training as an engineer, these were simple metrics. But even one site whose operators couldn't get simple metrics right could result in hazards that could maim or kill people.

The drill sites were functional—gravel and brown scrub, pipe, the rig itself. Solar panels for electricity, although they were backed up by electricity from the grid, which was especially important in the winter. All had tragically learned electricity for producing gas was essential when, during the worst, longest ice storm in memory, so many generating units went down ERCOT had to implement rolling blackouts and cut electricity to non-essential uses. Turned out natural gas production—to make the very electricity they needed—was far more essential than the grid operators had understood.

Lynn wondered at Hannah's grim look but shook it off. "Joost, your sand. Is it local or northern?" Northern sand was considered higher quality but had to be shipped in from Wisconsin, so was more expensive.

"Local. In-basin."

"Physical security?"

"No incidents."

"Vendors?"

"All vouched for."

Here was a key question. Lynn hoped he would give her the

answer she needed. "New technologies? All technologies patented?"

As she asked it, Lynn saw Hannah had turned to Joost, also waiting for his answer.

He looked at Lynn suspiciously. "Why would you be asking that?"

"On my checklist."

"No comment."

*Crap. Okay.* She moved on. "Drill crews and frac crews?" Because of the ups and downs of prices, it had become more difficult to reserve the labor and parts to drill a well. Everything and everyone were in short supply. Having drill and frac crews under contract was thus a big deal.

"Two of each contracted through next year. Our largest project is over twenty wells drilling in six zones."

Lynn sat back in surprise. His project was as big as projects by much larger companies.

Joost signaled and pulled right toward an exit.

"Cybersecurity?"

"It's good," he said. He'd stopped at a four-way stop. Though no other vehicles were in evidence, his eyes flicked left and then right. "Sometimes the drivers floor it on these roads, and they blast through these signs."

"What do you do for all-around security?" Lynn pressed.

"Like a lot of folks here including your new TriCoast boss, Rowan Daine at his water company, we're hooked up with a service that uses permit applications, landowner records, satellite imagery, cell phone pings, and just plain old jawboning about who's doing what. Satellites can apparently "see" metal, so the service knows when a frac crew is onsite. They know when roads go in, when the drill pad goes in, how big it is, when sand goes in. Since you can also see water squares from space, satellite imagery lets this service see well pads, lease pads, reserve pits, frac ponds, frac roads, and rig movements. Well pad plus permit equals drilling. Cell phone pings show where the crews came from and what they do and who they work for—by where the crews go back to."

Hannah spoke up, finally, from the back seat of the cab, sounding impressed. "All that."

❖

By mid-afternoon, Joost and his operators had shown Hannah and Lynn everything but the sand mines and sand-loading silos. He'd fed them a beef brisket-and-potato salad lunch with iced tea, even though the temperatures outside were just above freezing. He'd also explained the company's motto was to *move quickly and fix things*.

"It's okay if we get it 80-90% right. Doesn't have to be perfect. Same as with relationships." He turned a warm, fierce stare on Hannah.

Hannah returned his stare and spoke. "For anything safety-related, it *does* have to be perfect. Same as with relationships."

Lynn wondered again if something had happened between Hannah and Joost the night before. Apparently so. Judging from their reactions to one another, it hadn't gone well.

The entrance to the sand mine—really, just hills of sand dunes—was busy. *Too busy*, Lynn thought, noting nonstop truck traffic.

"While we need to avoid the science experiments, or long-drawn-out processes—we've found the more sand we put in a well, the more oil and gas we get out."

"Sure," Lynn said. "More proppant—more rocks propped open."

"So how much?" Hannah asked.

While the typical horizontal oil well once took four million pounds of sand, Joost explained, he was now using three times as much. "And we've heard of folks using even more. But these trucks are hell on the roads and there's not many roads around here, so they're crowded, too. I've owned sand mines before, and lost money on them every time. It's embarrassing. I'm supposed to be smarter." He shook his head.

To Lynn, Hannah appeared to take pleasure in imagining an embarrassed Joost.

"So now we buy sand from others," he continued. "Depending on how fast a well is fracked, we need up to three thousand tons of sand a day. The trucks load up at the silos and unload just as fast at our well sites, sometimes with a hundred-mile drive in between. Serious time pressure. But they also have to obey the speed limit. Driving over the speed limit will get you banned from a well site for good. Applies to me and everyone."

He drove them to the sand loading silos, located on a big pad cleared of brush and mesquite.

Heavy-duty belly dump trucks passed them in a steady parade—empty going in, full coming out.

Each of the four giant silos had a truck-sized tunnel at the bottom. Trucks were pulled into and aligned in three of the four. Each silo contained five thousand tons of frack sand, Joost said. At ready signals from the drivers, chutes above the trucks dropped down. Rattling rivers of yellow-gold sand thundered into the open truck beds.

Joost took them to a nearby office trailer. They watched as a dispatcher monitored the increasing weight of each filling truck on video screens.

Lynn marveled at the size of the chutes, the rush of the sand at high velocity, and how quickly each truck was filled. Every driver followed the same drill.

The dispatcher turned to them and said, "Just five minutes start to finish. Good, hunh?"

"It's hard to believe how fast this all is. And how precise," Lynn said.

Hannah grinned at her, her first happy expression of the day. "Spoken like the engineer you are."

More numbers flashed on the screens. As the totals

approached 45,000 pounds, the dispatcher hit three buttons, one after another. Sand waterfalls stopped.

"Alright trucks, you're loaded. Okay truck one, okay truck two, okay truck three. See you later." The dispatcher leaned forward and rolled his shoulders as if to relax them.

When the trucks pulled away, three more took their places. They too were filled in only a few minutes in this exquisitely timed dance of elephants. Yet even the big trucks and their drivers appeared small and vulnerable compared to the gargantuan waterfalls of sand coming from above.

"The chutes have automatic shutoffs, right?" Lynn asked.

The dispatcher nodded.

Joost answered her question with his own. "You mean, has anyone ever been buried in sand? The answer is no. I've heard about it happening elsewhere, but our safety record and protocols are better than that."

Fifth in the line of waiting trucks, the brown-haired embed, John Cooper, looked like every other truck driver, and in fact worked as one on the days and nights Daine didn't need him. But as requested, Daine's tech guy had broken the code for the automatic safety shutoffs and reset them to manual operations and higher, faster sand volumes. Cooper could change their settings with commands from his cell phone.

The man hoisted binoculars up to his eyes. He watched Joost and the two women come out of the office trailer.

All he needed was for Lynn to walk through a silo. He didn't care about the other two, although if Joost was collateral damage, Daine wouldn't like it.

The three of them walked into an empty truck bay at one of the silos and stood directly beneath a chute. Yellow guard rails on either side of the roadbed through the silo kept the driver steering a straight line, like a car wash.

The embed pressed the command on his phone to disable the safety shutoff and open up a sand surge to bury the three of them.

The button stuck. He shook his phone and pressed the command again.

Silence.

Cooper stared in disbelief as the three targets walked away from the silo. Fifteen seconds later—the control program had a built-in time lag the tech guy hadn't bothered to explain to him—the chute opened.

As Lynn left the truck bay beneath the silo with Joost and Hannah, a sound behind them started as a waterfall of silken glass. A cloud of sand dust billowed toward them, and they began coughing.

The noise accelerated, sounding like heavy rain with chunks of hail, then turned into a deafening roar. Lynn grabbed Hannah's and Joost's hands. The dust was making it hard to see. "Run!"

She yanked them forward another hundred yards. Then she turned to see what had happened.

Where they had been standing seconds earlier, a Niagara of frack sand flooded the silo floor for five minutes. Twenty-two tons of sand formed a new, colossal mountain in the middle of the silo.

"Jesus. That was close!" Hannah said.

"I don't think Jesus had much to do with it," Lynn replied. She turned to Joost. "You and Hannah need to come back to the control room. Let's find out how the hell that happened."

Joost nodded and the three of them spun around, giving the new mountain of sand in the truck bay a wide berth. Workers from the loading site joined them staring quizzically at the now-quiet funnel above them. Trucks waiting for sand had all been halted in their lanes.

They found the grizzled dispatcher. His face relaxed although he didn't smile. "Not hurt, were you?"

"No, but only due to incredible luck," Lynn said. "What happened?"

"My system stopped functioning. I couldn't make the controls respond. It was like it was taking instructions from the outside. I couldn't even get the safety override to work. Whatever bug it was vanished, though. Now it's as if nothing was wrong."

"You ever been hacked before?" Joost asked. "You have normal safety checks, I thought you said?"

The man shook his head. "No, no prior hacking. We have layers of security to head off normal human operator mistakes, but also to prevent something like what just happened."

"Seems to have been aimed at us. Do we have any enemies here? Anybody complained to you about our visit?" Joost asked.

"No. Look, I'm shutting down for a while. We're behind on loading, but I've called my IT guys to come and examine the system. Can't take a chance on it happening again to anyone. Unfortunately, the IT guys work everywhere in the county so it will take them an hour to get here, even though I've told them it's an emergency."

"Give me a call once they've diagnosed it," Joost said.

Lynn still felt shaky. *That was so close.*

# CHAPTER 15
# MOSCOW, LONDON, AND BARCELONA

ZAITSEV THOUGHT ABOUT what he had learned from Spanish energy minister Garcia. Despite what the man had confided to him at the Rudas bath in Budapest, it was clear Spain was going through with its long-term purchase and delivery of Israel's natural gas. The pipeline from the offshore Israeli platforms to Egypt's liquefaction plant was operating, the liquefaction plant was operating, and the LNG had begun shipping to Barcelona.

It was time to force the issue with everyone involved.

"Hello Zaitsev," Vandervoost said when he answered the video call.

"Have you progressed in acquiring directions for the Bradshaw water recycle technology?"

"The woman you recommended I recruit is in Texas with my son learning his operation."

"The technology?"

Henry's forehead creased. "Not yet."

"The Americans and the Israelis are helping the EU too much and too often. I need you to do a project in Spain, make it a less hospitable customer."

"What do you mean?"

"A few clicks, you should be able to take down the Barcelona terminal, yes?"

"If you loan me one of your hacking geniuses."

Zaitsev was silent for a moment. Everyone working for him was busy. But this would be worthwhile. "I can give you Armen.

He had experience 'liberating' the Ukrainian power in Kyiv a few years ago, followed by an attack on a Saudi chemical plant—before the Saudis were our friends in OPEC."

"How?"

"He studies the plant's operations. He also studies how engineers respond to emergencies. He usually starts with a loss-of-view attack so the engineers can't see what's happening and what he does next. In Ukraine, after switching relays to stop the flow of electricity, he also used code that caused damage when the staff restored power."

"He destroys equipment, but not people, yes? I don't want a killer."

*Vandervoost is too soft,* Zaitsev realized, disappointed. "People can be collateral damage. In particular, he used malware to disable the plant's safety shut-off system."

"The ones that are an automated safety defense for an industrial facility?"

*Vandervoost is soft and stupid. I should not be explaining this to him.* "Yes, the systems otherwise prevent equipment failure and incidents such as explosions or fire. Armen will call you. Prepare the site details for him. He will do the coding."

Yet after a few days, Armen reported back to Zaitsev he could not reach Vandervoost. Vandervoost was not returning his calls or texts. Zaitsev texted Vandervoost. "Armen has not been able to reach you. I will send Armen to meet you for tea tomorrow. He will text you the time and place. Be prepared to speak with him about the terminal. Your life will be worth nothing if you continue to refuse to speak to Armen."

Vandervoost bristled at being ordered around by a man he viewed as a Russian throwback. Yet Vandervoost was afraid. But he also felt loyalty to the Spanish, who had always treated him fairly. He compiled all he knew about contacts, IT systems, capacities, interconnects, and gas unloading dates for Spanish terminals, using an untraceable browser and committing all the information to paper. He toyed with the idea of changing a few numbers throughout to throw Armen's calculations awry.

The next day, he went to one of London's finest teahouses. A short, anonymous-looking man motioned him over to a small table in the corner. "Henry. At last. You have what I need?"

Henry Vandervoost nodded and handed him the papers. "The terminals are physically well-guarded. Electronic communications are the only way in."

The man had already poured tea for both. "Please. Drink."

Henry sipped, looked over his teacup to see Armen doing the same. Within moments, he felt nauseous.

Armen observed him, unconcerned. "You have received a dose of poison. I have the antidote. If the information you have provided me is accurate, I will give you the antidote. If not..."

Henry gasped. "It's all correct. Call the first number." He started to choke.

Armen slowly, deliberately, put his cell phone on speaker and called the first number Henry had listed at the top of the papers. It was the main number for the terminal. When a woman's voice answered, Armen hung up.

"I can assume the rest of your information is also accurate?"

"Ye..." Henry choked.

Armen got up from his chair, shielded Henry from the view of the rest of the tearoom, and jabbed a needle into Henry's neck.

"I think that is the correct antidote. Next time I contact you, do not wait to respond." The anonymous-looking man pushed in his chair and left.

Henry rushed for the men's room, making it just in time to throw up. He took several deep breaths. The nausea began to fade but he still felt weak. And more afraid than at any time in his life.

❖

Ernesto was happy with his job monitoring systems at the Barcelona re-gas plant. He worked nights, leaving the days free for the beach, and parties, but usually sleep. Big LNG tankers arrived and unloaded their liquid—liquefied natural gas, under high pressure. His plant turned the liquid into gas and sent it out in pipes to Barcelona, Madrid, and on to other EU countries. Families kept warm with gas heat and showered with hot water. Utilities burned the gas to make electricity.

This was a vital operation, Ernesto knew. His country depended more than ever on LNG from Israeli gas via Egypt produced at the other end of the Mediterranean, LNG from Algeria, and LNG from the States.

He had trained often on the threat of foreign actors: thousands of hackers, especially Russian ones like Xenotime and Kamacite, developed by the Russian Ministry of Defense's Central Scientific Research Institute of Chemistry and Mechanics. Cyber units from Russia's FSB and GRU led the attacks. They repeatedly tested not just bank systems, but digital systems of LNG terminals like the big one in Rotterdam, key to all of Europe, and, it was rumored, one of the LNG facilities in the States.

Sometimes GRU and FSB merely took the cash route: funding anti-hydrocarbon environmental groups and protestors.

Ernesto had been told hackers had even gained access to the FBI's InfraGard, a database of critical infrastructure in the US.

Especially now, LNG exports from the US and imports to the EU remained a particular threat to Russia's remaining hold on the gas market.

The flicker of lights was the first sign something was wrong. Then Ernesto noted automatic safety overrides were attempting to engage but unable to do so.

He gasped. Pipes were rupturing and gas clouds were forming as liquid in the LNG transfer line suddenly gasified and exploded to six hundred times its liquid volume. The far larger volume of gas couldn't be contained in the heavy-duty pipe. Pieces of pipe launched and whizzed, like shrapnel.

Pressure spikes were occurring all along the main gathering line from the ship dock into storage tanks.

Other pressure spikes were occurring on the main gas discharge line. It was a Xenotime-like attack he'd feared: malware designed to take over industrial controls that also defeated associated safety systems and safeguards.

Lines were over-pressuring everywhere, especially along the discharge line. But safety valves to release the gas harmlessly into the air weren't triggering as they were supposed to.

More pressures built to five times what the lines and equipment were designed for.

Gas explosions ricocheted through the plant.

Fireballs rocketed into the air.

Ernesto worked desperately for thirty minutes, sweating through his clothes despite the chilly winter. He finally got a few of the manual overrides to engage.

After he'd done as much as he could to stop the gas flow so it would no longer fuel the explosions and fires, he stepped out of the control room to assess the damage. Parts of the plant were flattened. Its big, beautiful steel structure was torn and melted in places. The place would be shut down for months if it could even be repaired.

They'd be calling for backup gas from everyone. Even if they couldn't buy from Russia, gas prices would go up, helping the Russians. And when you were desperate for heat, you cared a little less that the gas you were receiving from China might have started out as LNG from Russia's northern steppes.

Ernesto gathered with others on the overnight shift near the plant's main gate, ready to direct firefighters who'd arrived to quench the flames.

No one knew Zaitsev's local operatives had been collecting ordinary chemicals through small shell businesses like nail salons and pool cleaners.

No one knew they'd used the chemicals the EU outlawed for ordinary citizens to make triacetone triperoxide or TATP. TATP powder was unstable and prone to exploding. Explosions could be triggered by mild shaking, heat, knocking, grinding, or even just friction.

Indeed, TATP had been found in the accidental explosions preceding the years-earlier Barcelona terrorist attacks. TATP had been used to make the improvised explosive devices that killed over fifty people and injured hundreds more in the 2005 London bus attack.

No one saw the pads on the cement by the gate or the powder underneath it. The pads had been placed there only minutes earlier.

As Ernesto stepped on the pad, forty other men and women were crowded around him, ready to direct the firefighters toward the smoldering steel inside.

No one, including the firefighters, was left alive in the tangle of bloody bodies and limbs when the TATP blew up.

❖

While details on the international news sources were murky, it was conjectured that a hacker had invaded the terminal's electronic communication system, shut it down, and then—from the outside—rewired its industrial control system so valves that were supposed to fail shut instead failed open. And fail they had, because the last step before the explosion was another change in the safety system allowing the pipes in the terminal to become vastly overpressured. Dozens had been killed. The resulting fireballs could be seen from many kilometers away. And no one yet realized a secondary TATP explosion had killed many more.

❖

In Madrid, energy minister Garcia was stunned and heartbroken. He called the head of Spain's security services to investigate.

As he prepared to go in front of the press to describe his horror and to explain the steps in investigating the heinous crime, he received a conference call from a consortium of five banks. They expressed their distress at the attack and told him given the risks, they were pulling their agreement to fund new billions of euros in long-term LNG import contracts. Like the one he had just negotiated with Avi Levin.

❖

Updates to the nightly news on every continent featured the terrible accident at the Barcelona liquefied natural gas terminal that would prevent it from receiving any more desperately needed natural gas, likely for months. A day later, the largest Russian gas company offered Spanish energy minister Alejandro Garcia, a two-year contract for pipeline gas at twice the normal price to replace the natural gas the terminal explosion had burned up and the much larger volumes of liquefied natural gas it could no longer receive.

❖

In Israel, Avi Levin put his head down and groaned at the news of the Barcelona terminal explosion, then wiped away tears. In working with Spanish energy minister Alejandro Garcia, Avi as well as his Israeli and Egyptian colleagues, had spoken with several of the men at the Barcelona terminal. They'd exchanged bantering phone calls in mixed Spanish and English, along with promises to trade visits.

Most of those men had died.

He mourned them.

He thought about his conversation with Zaitsev and slumped

at the signal the Russian had sent. Zaitsev had pushed back against Israel's LNG contract with Spain, saying Spain was Russia's customer. Now the Russians had killed innocent Spaniards over it.

After the warning attacks on Israel from offshore Syria that had come from Russian warships, and Zaitsev's warning to Avi in Budapest, Avi was certain Russia would attack Israel and its offshore gas platforms soon.

## CHAPTER 16
# DALLAS

*"Anything you can do to get your opponent or enemy to weaken themselves benefits you."*

—*Sun Tzu*

AFTER THE LONG trip to West Texas and the narrow escape from being buried alive at the sand silo, Lynn was relieved to be back in Dallas with her family. But her mind was still in West Texas. A nightmare of drowning in sand caused her to startle awake, breathing hard. *Christ, I almost died!*

Her husband stirred beside her. "You okay? You were crying out. Like you had a bad dream."

"It *was* a bad dream." She wouldn't tell Cy what had happened. There was nothing he could have done or could do now. *And his reaction would be to tell me to get a different job.*

Cy had cut back on his legal work to spend more time with Marika and her younger brother. They all depended on Lynn's salary.

"Move closer to me."

She did and they began kissing. Lynn tried to lose herself in the moment, but flashbacks—the thunder of the flood of sand—kept replaying, a deadly earworm.

"You seem distracted." He pulled back.

She forced a smile. "You're distracting me. And I want to be distracted by you." *I do. I don't want to keep reliving the accident right now.*

She closed her eyes, consciously relaxed, compartmentalizing the overwhelming memories to examine later.

They made love urgently, before their children awoke.

Afterward, she sighed, moved slightly away, and listened to the expansion joints from a nearby bridge sing in the steady frequency of the cars and trucks rolling over them. Her mind returned to the scenes in West Texas and she wondered what signals she had missed. *What was out of place? Or who?*

Cy gave her a long kiss. "Life is just one missing ingredient after another. I'm showering, then going to the grocery store, especially since I can go now without taking Matt and Marika. Anything you need?"

*Answers. I need answers.* But she smiled at him. "Got it already. I love you, Cy."

"That *was* fun." He laughed. "And when I come back, I'm putting the door between the kitchen and the den back on. Matt's been taking apart the door hinges again. I don't want one falling on him."

While Cy showered, Lynn's thoughts returned to the sand avalanche. Not only had Joost said such a thing had never happened, but Hannah in her anger—in what Lynn now understood triggered Hannah's investigative mode—had vowed to get to the bottom of what had happened. *And I can't forget the man in a sand truck waving a gun at me! What's going on with these sand companies? Why didn't David tell me anything about them? Or is this a redirection to keep me from looking into Daine's wastewater disposal company?*

Her stepchildren soon yanked at her attention. Marika was up first and dragged Lynn into the kitchen. "Did you see?! Did you SEE outside?"

"What?"

"Frost dusting on the grass and frost smiles on the leaves!"

Lynn pulled the shutters open further to look at where Marika was pointing. The frost outside *was* beautiful. She pulled on her new, red jacket and stepped onto the front porch, still relieved at the cool air after what had seemed to be a six-month summer.

Pecans, sumacs, and red mulberry trees had lost their leaves. English ivy that had burned the previous summer was gone. Only the live oaks were still green. They wouldn't lose their leaves until spring.

When Lynn came back inside, Marika touched the sleeve of her jacket. "So dank! Can I have it when I grow into it?"

"I'll still want it then. You're growing so fast it may fit you next week!"

When Cy returned, he said, "I told my friends I'd have lunch with them. Can you take Matt and Marika to Marika's basketball game?"

"Yes."

Cy had already had several days this month of solo parenting. Marika interrupted. "Lynn, LYNN! Guess what?"

"What?"

"I had a dream about star sharks!"

"What are star sharks?"

"They jump out of the water and eat the stars."

"I've seen how tall the girls are on the other team. You probably need some star sharks on your team. Are you sure all the girls on the other team are all nine?"

"Dad! Stop teasing! Some of them are ten."

Matt appeared, still rubbing sleep from his eyes.

"Lynn, I'm no friend of pajamas." Matt squirmed restlessly as she picked him up, hugged him, and put him at the table.

"And they're no friend of yours?" Lynn asked the three-year-old boy. "Let's get you breakfast. You're going with us to Marika's basketball game."

"Is your game going to be longer than halfses of an hour? I get tired of it."

Lynn reminded herself to pack extra toys and snacks for him.

She got both kids ready, put Matt in the car seat in the back of her Porsche and Marika in the front, and drove to a nearby gym for the game. Lynn found the immediate noise, focus, and excitement of the girls and their parents a welcome change from adult worries about drilling in West Texas.

❖

While at the game watching Marika, Lynn remembered her recent visit to Austin to meet members of University Lands and the Texas Railroad Commission, both groups significant for Tri-Coast's Texas production. University Lands, which had been surveyed between 1838 and 1923, was a one-stop shop for the state. Texas earned money on over two million acres it owned from oil and gas royalties, sand mining, solar, wind, and surface activities like ranches and grape-growing. As the name implied, its revenues helped fund Texas' public universities.

When she spoke to a Railroad Commission staffer, he asked, "Did you feel the earthquake yesterday?"

"Yes."

"We've traced it to disposal wells that are supposed to be closed. You know anything about those?"

*How to answer?* "The rumor I heard is there's still traffic to those disposal wells."

"Who? Bradshaw?" His gaze turned sharp.

"Like I said, rumor. Do you have security tape?"

The man shook his head. "The monitor stationed there says no one's been coming or going."

"Sure."

"Are you saying yes or no?"

"I leave the interpretation to you."

"You wouldn't want additional inspections of TriCoast flaring or wellsite procedures, correct?"

"On the contrary. I invite them. At TriCoast we follow all regulations," Lynn said, keeping her voice even.

❖

After the game, she relished the chance to take her stepchildren to another of her own favorite restaurants, one she'd first read about in a book by Texas author Julie Heaberlin. The owners had kept it open through many ups and downs, finding the same workarounds small restaurants often navigate so that people and money continued coming in.

As they pulled up to Flying Fish in Addison, Marika and Matt cheered. They too liked the restaurant's fried shrimp, chicken strips, and hushpuppies.

It was too cold to sit at the outside picnic tables, so they crowded around a table inside.

Matt looked at her seriously. "Dad said I can touch God."

She wondered how Cy had explained that.

"How?"

"By touch a stone."

"You mean a tombstone? Like for your mom."

"You're our mom. But so was she," Marika said. "We went to see your dad's tombstone, too."

Lynn found herself tearing up. Her father hadn't been dead for long. She missed him every day.

"Don't cry, Lynn."

"I miss my father the way you miss your mother. I miss your mother, too. I wish I'd known her. She was a wonderful woman." Lynn wiped her eyes and wished talking about relationships was subject to the same rules as basketball—no more than three seconds in the key.

Marika seemed ready to change the subject, too. "And I dreamed I time-traveled to dinosaur times to fight evil and even the T-Rex needed help."

"You really have the dreams, Marika. First star sharks and then T-Rex. So, what did you do?"

"I tossed the bad guys in the T-Rex's mouth. Snap!" she exclaimed.

Lynn smiled at her stepdaughter.

As she drove them home, she considered what Hannah had revealed about her plans. *Is Hannah only checking out Bradshaw Energy and Joost Bradshaw so Joost's father—Vandervoost of all people!— can invest in it? Or is there more going on with Hannah and her work for Vandervoost than what she's telling me?*

*And do the sand problems tie into Daine somehow? He knows everything and everyone in Midland. Didn't Joost tell me—yes, he did—sand truck drivers sometimes drive wastewater disposal trucks to fill out their work week? It makes sense, because truck drivers are so much in demand in West Texas.*

❖

As they had arranged by text a few days before, Lynn met Tri-Coast's CFO, Sara Levin, at the bustling Farmers Market food hall on the south side of downtown Dallas. Lynn arrived to find Sara already there, her froth of frizzy curls smoothed into obedience.

"I know it would be faster to order in, but I need a break from the four walls," Sara had explained.

Sara ordered sushi. Since she'd already had lunch, Lynn ordered just iced tea. Afterward, they walked the several blocks to TriCoast's offices. Next up was a teleconference with Avi Levin in Israel before the bigger TriCoast board meeting to discuss Lynn's bid for Joost Bradshaw's company.

Sara stopped and pulled at Lynn's arm. "Been meaning to ask, after visiting all those field offices to catch up on what David was doing, you won't make me do a restatement, will you? Those wells drop off so quick they could give TriCoast's financials and stock price a kick in the ass."

"No. The teams have been good about keeping everything on time and under budget." Lynn sighed.

"What?"

"Nothing."

"It's never nothing," Sara said.

"Just thinking of how to position for the board meeting." Lynn hated revealing weakness, even to Sara. Especially to Sara. "You'd think we'd be decades past it, but we aren't. Anyone I don't know who looks at me automatically thinks I'm a novice, that I don't know what I'm talking about because I'm female. He—and it's always he—thinks I look like his wife. Yet men automatically assume other men DO know what they're talking about. It's relentless. Wears me out."

Sara nodded. "Some of us have a heavier lift than others. I'll bet Burl and Mike and them have other issues they deal with. The guys are always measuring dicks. For me, it takes me as long to get ready for a video call as an in-person meeting." She mimed running an imaginary comb through her hair.

"Hell, I bet they barely had to make up your face when you were on the cover of Oil and Gas Royalty. You're the most beautiful CFO in the business."

"The competition with dudes isn't too tough. In the meantime, work on your management philosophy."

"What's your jibe about my management philosophy?" Lynn rolled her eyes.

"Let me see if I can paraphrase it. 'Shit happens. Be ready.'"

"Not only did I learn it at TriCoast but it's highly effective."

Sara laughed. "You're in better shape than you realize."

"Why?"

"Price sets the narrative, and right now—last week anyway—the prices favor producers like us. You're not playing small ball anymore."

"I wouldn't call my old job, being in charge of hundreds of millions of dollars of refining equipment, *small ball*."

"But now you're in charge of billions of dollars of assets. To keep my favorite baseball metaphor going, you need to swing for the fences."

Once at TriCoast's office, they dialed in Avi for the video conference. When he answered and appeared on their screen, Lynn said, "Avi, we heard about the terrible Barcelona attack."

He shook his head. "I still can't believe it. It's so horrible, so tragic. So many people killed. Not sure what Garcia, the energy minister, will do."

"And you'd just started your contract with them?" Lynn asked.

"Yes. We'd just unloaded our first tanker of LNG. We pipelined it to Teos Mostafa's plant in Egypt, he liquefied it, and we shipped it to Barcelona. Barcelona is—was—Spain's busiest import terminal. I don't know what they'll do now. We only had permission to unload there, not anywhere else."

Sara looked at Lynn and nodded. Lynn said, "Avi, we can backstop you. We have spot, short-term LNG from our Louisiana terminal that needs a home. We've already been talking to Garcia because he wants spot volumes, not fixed, to back up his wind and solar renewables. Plus at one of Spain's other regas terminals, the one in Bilbao, he gets better economics because he uses LNG directly to make electricity. It's more efficient. We have the ships reserved and we already have permission to ship to Bilbao and Cartagena. You revise the terms with Garcia. Like I said, he knows us because we've already talked to him. Include us in your revised contract as a co-supplier for you to him and tell us the details as soon as you have them. We'll loan you the gas for now and ship it to Bilbao until you get permission to ship to those terminals yourself. Then you can pay us back."

His lower lip trembled slightly but his voice was steady. "Lynn Dayton, you're a *mensch*. Perfect for us. I'll make the changes with Señor Garcia and tell you when they're final."

As they closed the call, Lynn noted a glance of familial affection between Sara and Avi, but Avi saved his bigger smile for her.

"A *mitzvah*! I'm sure it's not your first or last, Lynn Dayton," Sara said.

"I'm glad we have the supply and the ships. It will still take a few days to arrive, but they could load tomorrow."

"We have a bigger capital structure and well-developed banking relationships," Sara said. "I hear some of Spain's bank funding for their regas terminals have been pulled so Garcia is in a spot, too. Helping Avi gets our foot in the door as a trusted LNG supplier to Spain and the rest of the EU."

# CHAPTER 17
# DALLAS

As Lynn walked with Sara to the conference room, Sara shook her head. "You should have set this up better. Just telling people we're making an offer won't cut it. Everyone will object."

"Remember the conversation you and I had about Bradshaw Energy?"

Sara nodded, her curls bouncing.

"I've had one-on-one conversations with all the TriCoast execs at this meeting and answered everyone's questions."

"Well, I have another one. Do they have a debt tower that will tumble down?"

Lynn shook her head and tried to ignore a cramp threatening to seize up her leg, as happened when she was particularly stressed.

"Who else is at this meeting?"

Lynn ticked off on her fingers, "Burl Travis, Rowan Daine of course, Tyree Bickham, Claude Durand, you, me."

Lynn had named a key board member, the temporary CEO he'd hired to fill in for Mike when Mike had his heart attack, the company's chief legal officer, and the French-born head of Tri-Coast's communications.

"And Sara?"

Sara looked at her.

"Since David's gone and I've taken his place, everyone is moving in and trying to cut my budget to give it to themselves. I need you on my side."

Sara was disturbingly noncommittal. "If your budget makes sense."

She and Sara took seats at the board table.

Burl Travis lumbered in. "Hey Lynn, you gettin' the oil price up out there in West Texas?"

"Sure. Me, the Saudis, and the Russians."

"We'll juice our oil production? Keep the investors happy? Our properties are making more oil than gas?" Burl continued his inquisition.

"Unlike Pennsylvania, the gas in West Texas comes out of the same wellbore as the oil. You understand that, Burl. It's associated. But sure, we're emphasizing oil production."

After the meeting began, Lynn was surprised to see Rowan Daine rubbing his eyes. "I'm beat. But I'm anxious to hear what you have to say, Lynn."

Tyree drummed his fingers, his Howard University ring clanking against the table. "Just don't spend too much time saying it, though. *My* son's playing basketball in an hour, his first varsity game. We'll be done. I'm making a statement, not asking a question."

Lynn pushed away her own exhaustion and began. "You've received my division's information on a TriCoast bid for Bradshaw Energy in Midland. I've spoken with each of you. In a nutshell, I'm following up on David's proposed acquisition of Bradshaw Energy. He first approached Bradshaw several months ago, and they were open to it. Prices cratered in the meantime. Then David was killed, as you know.

"No other serious bidder has come along, although a few private equity guys are sniffing around. I'm proposing TriCoast acquire Bradshaw Energy in Midland for two billion dollars, combine it with TriCoast's existing operations in Midland, and otherwise leave everyone and everything in place. We'll get economy-of-scale savings, talented engineers, firm transportation contracts, more oil and gas revenue, and Bradshaw's new water recycle technology."

Daine leaned forward. "If we're paying extra for water recycling tech, I'm against it. The systems I use in my business work just fine. More important, they're affordable for the operators out there, especially with the Permian producing over fifteen million barrels a day. Of water. In fact, I don't understand why Bradshaw's selling. I'm suspicious we're the only offer. Joost doesn't appear to be running a business so much as he is running FROM a business."

*Daine feels more threatened than I expected.* "If you mean, is he underperforming or losing money, the answer is no." Lynn kept herself from wincing as she raised her heel to work out another sudden, fierce leg cramp. "I have David's notes. His assessment was Joost had grown the company but wanted to start over again. Serial entrepreneur. He'll have no trouble getting financial backing.

"And Rowan, I've been impressed with what I've seen of Bradshaw's water recycle technology. It's a good model for us and all oil companies, one we should think about incorporating quickly in our own operations. Overall, we obviously need to focus on what's best for TriCoast." Lynn let the silence fill in the blank. *Not what's best for your water disposal business.*

"Now, I know you two will want to hear about Mike, missing him and all," Burl said, apparently convinced the acquisition discussion was over, or at least wanting to cut it off. "He texted me he's got another few weeks of rehab. Anything else?" Lynn *did* miss Mike Emerson's steady hand on the tiller. His approach was less emotional and more analytical than Daine's. TriCoast couldn't continue to rely on Daine's seat-of-the-pants instincts.

Daine winked. "Now he's on the same heart medicine I am. Poor man."

*Great.* Lynn thought. *TriCoast's two key guys at risk. Hope the stuff works.*

"I thought that medicine had been recalled," Sara said.

Rowan Daine started.

"Nah, just pulling your leg," Sara said.

Burl nodded at Sara and spoke to Daine. "She's like the salt you add to the water to make it boil faster."

"Being compared to salt is a new one, Burl. But I embrace it." She nodded at him and smiled cheerfully. "Just remember, you don't have the luxury of making me your enemy."

"Believe me, I wake up every morning thinking about that," he said. "Okay, look, welcome Mike to the conversation." Burl flipped on a videoconference screen. There was Mike Emerson, looking thinner and paler.

"Mike!" several in the room shouted. "How ya doing, buddy?"

"We miss you. When will you be back?" Lynn tried not to sound as anxious as she felt.

"Funny. They were all telling me how much they like *me* before you appeared," Daine said wryly.

Mike's voice was strained. "I miss being there with you."

"Lynn, let's talk while Mike's feeling up to it," Daine said.

"Mike, I was reviewing TriCoast's bid for Joost Bradshaw's company. Bradshaw's not budging, which doesn't surprise me. Based on what I'm seeing of his operations and what we know about the patented technology he's bringing to the deal, we can increase my current bid of two billion by fifteen percent."

Lynn passed out the charts she hadn't been able to before when Burl had cut her off. She held up one in front of the camera for Mike.

"This chart shows how Bradshaw Energy complements Tri-Coast's West Texas operations: adjacent acreage, high oil cut, solid production, all water slated to disposal wells or recycle, low-cost takeaway pipeline capacity and options on other pipelines, gas processing reservations, good drilling pace, good safety practices, range of customers, including one or two of the West Texas refineries. The next chart on their wells shows the geology, type curves, service costs, and several benches of reserves so their plays are three-dimensional, not two-dimensional. Their price assumptions are like ours. They don't have a lot of debt. And most importantly, the cultures of the two companies—the talent fit—is compatible."

"I like the low debt levels," Sara said. "We have to pay down debt to keep flexibility, even when paying down debt isn't cool."

"But Lynn, you're going to have to translate," Claude said. "What about this phrase 'downward trajectory on service and supply costs?'"

"Hell, I hear the same phrase all the time at my oilfield supply company," Burl said. "It means Bradshaw Energy is squeezing their suppliers dry. It could come back to bite them. It would if I were one of their suppliers."

"That's my experience, too," Rowan Daine said.

Lynn briefly gave additional details on the oil-gas mix, the number of leasehold acres Bradshaw held, how much was contiguous with their own acreage, how much was held by production, the company's very good eight-month payout on new drilling and high rates of return, and the number of rigs it was running,

"How much gas? You're not loading us up with more, are you?" Burl asked.

"You know how it is," Lynn said. "The gas is associated. It comes with the oil. We have to sell gas to produce and sell the higher-valued oil."

Claude Durand interjected—"I know they'd love more natural gas in Europe—same with anything you can do with Sara's nephew's company in Israel."

Lynn glanced at Sara.

"We're talking to him, Claude. We may be backing him up with shipments to alternate Spanish ports since the attack in Barcelona, at least until they can get permission to ship to the new ports," Sara said.

"Let me interrupt," Mike stopped and coughed. "I just want to say Lynn's done well with refining and I would expect her to make money on this acquisition also."

"You're not just buying this to destroy value, though, right?" Burl asked.

"No. Prices are decent; we've been able to export profitably despite the competition. I have an amazing team," Lynn said.

"What about their water situation? They have a bunch of disposal contracts that'll come back and bite us in the ass when the buildings in San Antonio start shaking?" Mike this time. Lynn looked at Rowan Daine. His face was a mask.

"As a private company, they've had the flexibility to incur higher costs for recycling, plus they have this new lower-cost technology. They're on track to recycle all of their water soon."

"How do you ladies pay for this?" Burl turned to Lynn and Sara.

"Cash from operations. Bradshaw Energy is capital efficient," Lynn explained.

Sara shook her head. "It could just mean their bank wouldn't loan them more money."

"I'm sure if Lynn calculates this is a good deal, it is," Daine said.

*I didn't expect support from him,* Lynn thought.

After the meeting ended, Rowan Daine asked Lynn and Burl to stay behind. When Daine was looking in another direction, Sara cocked her eyebrows questioningly at Lynn. Lynn offered a small *I-don't-know* shrug.

"Now Lynn," Daine began after the others except Burl had left and the door closed behind them. "As I said when we first met, Mike thinks highly of you. Shame what happened to your predecessor, David Jenkins. Think you can live up to his reputation?"

Lynn bristled. "His so-called girlfriend tried to kill me, too. Turns out 'his reputation' is a low bar to clear in some respects."

Instead of being angry, Daine chuckled. "You're right. But I meant how well David was operating the Permian division. Burl, you can tell Lynn what she should be doing on her new job."

*What the hell?* More leg cramps threatened Lynn's effort to stay composed.

"Since you ask, Lynn was well-suited for running the refining division, but I was surprised the board didn't ask me for people to take Jenkins' place. There are several men at TriCoast I would have recommended."

Lynn stared at Burl. *Asshole. But I should always expect knives.* "I have full faith the board knew what they were doing, appointing me—as well as appointing Rowan Daine. I'm surprised you don't, Burl." She continued, "I've met with all the field offices and have a good idea of what we need to do—"

Daine interrupted her. "But I hope you'll rely on more experienced men like Burl and others for counsel and guidance."

Even Burl looked embarrassed at Daine's remark this time.

*Daine wants me to pop off, get emotional. All his supportive comments in the meeting were for the benefit of Sara, Tyree, and Claude.* "As we discussed, over my years of experience, I've led the refining division to billions in profits. I will do the same for the drilling division."

Then Daine's tone of voice changed. "The Bradshaw Energy acquisition. I heard everything you said, but I'm still not convinced."

"Joost Bradshaw and I still have to see eye-to-eye on the price."

"My position with the board will be the acquisition is a waste of money."

Burl nodded his agreement, then pointed a finger at Daine. "Catch you later. We can both get on the company plane for some Alaska fishing soon."

Daine nodded at him and Burl left.

"I'm headed to Midland to talk to Joost further." Daine's further questions about the Bradshaw acquisition struck Lynn as slightly off. *He's just being careful about the company's money. No reason for you to get defensive.*

Then Rowan Daine produced a big smile—one that had surely won his company lots of high-dollar contracts. But his next words were chilling.

"Dayton, in my experience, the only women who work well for me are the ones underneath me in bed. I've never met a woman in the drilling business who knew her shit. I certainly never met one who could lead a roomful, or hundreds, of men."

Lynn was shocked by his frankness. She blurted, "Then it's time you get to know my superb work and leadership skills better."

She glared at him as she left. *For the sake of everyone working at TriCoast we need to understand why Daine—when he's being honest one-on-one--would try to scare me away from making a good acquisition. He's going to be horrible company on the trip to Chicago. Wish I could dump him.*

# CHAPTER 18
# DALLAS AND CHICAGO

AFTER SHE LEFT, Rowan Daine couldn't get Lynn's impertinence off his mind. Worse, she was zeroing in on his wastewater disposal business as she chased the Bradshaw acquisition.

His customers had always appreciated him keeping his costs—their costs—low, and many did not question how he had done so. When he could, he tried to palm too-curious employees off to other oilfield companies. He'd had a handful of employees who had continually raised questions, until they didn't.

At the big Park Cities mansion TriCoast was renting for him in Dallas, Daine pulled out his private cell phone, not the official TriCoast model he'd been given.

"Rowan, it's the middle of the night in London, or did you forget?" Henry Vandervoost sounded sleepy.

"I didn't forget. I'm having problems with Lynn Dayton."

"Didn't I tell you?"

"Sure. Bonus points for that. I need something to distract her. TriCoast supplies gas to Chicago?"

"Yes. So does my son. Bradshaw Energy."

"Could be a two-fer, then, a way to make his company more affordable for you. We're going to Chicago. Lynn wants me to meet TriCoast's customers there. You need to find a hacker who can get in and shut the Chicago gas down, at least part of it. A ransomware deal if it's the cover he needs."

"You overestimate me, Daine. I can't just put up a hacker job listing online."

"Henry, you can find someone. I have faith."

"Sounds like the two of them are bugging you."

"Sounds like you're in the same boat, or is Lynn your new bestie?"

"Give me a day or so."

"Has to be soon. Time it for when we're visiting Chicago, at least a test run."

❖

It became apparent to Henry that with the right credentials, a bit of time, and enough money, many of the so-called 'white hat hackers,' had never given up their black hat business and were available for special projects after verifying he was not with law enforcement. He corresponded with several to determine who could work onsite in Chicago, then hired a pair of Romanian brothers who would readily blend in with the city's Polish, Ukrainian, and Lithuanian populations. Using encrypted apps, Radu and Tihomir—at least those were the names they gave, no last name of course—agreed to insert malware into the utility's control system code. Extra because they had to go to Chicago to do so. Half up front. Nonpayment by Henry would have serious consequences.

Henry agreed.

One day and an international flight later Radu and Tihomir were "visiting relatives" in Chicago. Their destination that night was not the utility's downtown Chicago headquarters but a nondescript building housing gas distribution and pressure step-down equipment for part of the city. Cohorts they knew only by text had left them a locked car with directions to the keys in a snowy neighborhood on the north side of Chicago.

At 2 a.m. they parked near the distribution facility and donned the masks and black bloc antifa had made so useful for criminals. They climbed over the fence.

It was a cold night, so the security guard had stationed himself inside past an unlocked door.

The guard barely had time to glance up before Tihomir banged a crowbar into the back of his head, knocking him onto the floor, unconscious.

Tihomir pulled black duct tape from his pocket, first covering the lenses of several security cameras. He bound the security guard's hands behind him. Then he took over watchman duties.

Radu sat down in front of the terminals. He'd been able to breach the control system passcodes from Romania but not make any changes. He pulled the flash drive from his pocket, pre-loaded with malware, then brought up the gas distribution control program on the terminal and put it into administrative mode. Holding his breath, he inserted the flash drive into the CPU underneath the desk.

The malware Radu hadn't been able to insert from overseas loaded onto the computer as he expected.

He closed out of administrative mode on the terminal. He was satisfied that once he got the go-ahead, with just the click of a mouse back in Romania he could sabotage the gas supply of a half-dozen southside Chicago neighborhoods.

Radu signaled to his brother, and they left the gas distribution facility. The security guard was still out but could come to at any moment.

Tihomir drove the car to a pre-arranged parking lot at O'Hare where their contact would pick it up. The brothers slept in the car until daylight. They exited the car with their carry-ons, went through security at the international terminal, and boarded their return flight.

# CHAPTER 19
# CHICAGO

THE ROUTE was a fast, familiar one for Lynn—a delicious secret still known to few people—between two inner-city airports, Dallas' Love Field, and Chicago's Midway Airport. When she'd traveled so many weekends to the University of Chicago's business school program, she'd appreciated the quick, nonstop Southwest Airlines flight.

Today Lynn looked out of the window of the private TriCoast jet. Lake Michigan was green-blue but not frozen, even near the shore. Thousands of railcars, containers, and trucks were part of the study in black and white, as precise and crisp as a blueprint. After years of planning, the intermodal hub, one of the biggest in the country and where east and west met, was due to expand further in the Englewood neighborhood. Despite, or really because of, its urban location, the hub was a key to the region's annual trillions of dollars of cargo transport and delivery. Shipping and logistics—Lynn admitted to herself a passion for all the data—was important in Chicago.

Snow was on every roof but had melted or been scraped to black asphalt and black trees. Lynn felt again her love and respect for the city's brittle cold. It had never left her.

Chicago with all its lights was glamorous. Not glamorous in an imitative way or in a "lone city on the prairie way" but just as was, a mighty engine of commerce drawing to itself iron ore and corn, spitting back out steel and cereal and ideas formed during the hard ice of the bitter winters.

Buildings sprang higher and higher near the lake, but then fell away, like a parabola—a perfect distribution curve. A thin band of blue sky reminded her they'd flown east. Dusk would arrive well before 5 PM.

She needed only to look around—she didn't even look, she could hear him snoring—to realize this trip would be different, and not just because she was in a private plane. She resettled her five-foot-ten frame into a padded leather seat across the aisle from Rowan Daine, her temporary boss. She expected he would awaken a few minutes before they landed.

Sure enough, as the plane began its descent, Daine rubbed his eyes and said, "Sorry *if* I was snoring."

"C'mon Rowan. Of course you were snoring, and of course you're not sorry."

As she'd already experienced all too well, Rowan Daine wasn't one to apologize or stay on the defensive for long.

"You went to business school here?"

"Mainly the downtown campus near the river but also the main campus in Hyde Park. Chicago's beautiful. You'll see."

"Damn cold." He switched subjects. "Any more thoughts on help you might need handling your new job?"

"I could ask you that. Of course, we appreciate you stepping in for Mike." She didn't add, *but TriCoast is orders of magnitude larger and more complex than the wastewater disposal company you also head.*

*I wish Reese was here. I wish David was here to tell me what he'd been doing. He'd have insights.* Lynn felt uncertainty, and guilt. She wouldn't have this job if David hadn't died—*been murdered*—but she wouldn't say so to Daine. "David left behind a great team. As they, as all of us, get over the shock we'll continue with his momentum."

The big sweep of the city's industrial canal cut through the landscape of houses and urban forests away to the horizon. She saw Sara Paretsky's Chicago. The deceptively simple street grid hid layers of history and complexity.

They said goodbye to the pilot. A big sedan had been delivered for them at the private terminal. Lynn took the keys and checked the mirrors and lights. It was already dark.

Once in Chicago and at the I-55 north-south split near the lake, she'd gone south to UChicago's main campus in Hyde Park as often as possible, although frequently her classes had been north, at UChicago's Gleacher executive campus located right on the river.

But this time, she was not alone nor a weekend student. She was with Rowan Daine, the temporary CEO, the man who had just told her he'd never seen a woman perform well in the oil business. She was relying on *that* Rowan Daine to help her market gas to two customers.

Her assistant had arranged their stay downtown near the river in the new Jean Gang-designed Regis. More relevant, it was close to the offices of the company they'd visit in the morning. They'd stay further south, in Hyde Park, the second night. She knew the route and turned north when I-55 intersected Lake Shore Drive. Lights glittered and she felt at home.

"Tell me again why you dragged me up to Chicago in the middle of the winter? Something about a customer?"

The fresh snow was sugar-white; darker slush lined the shoulders.

"I like coming to Chicago," she explained to Daine.

"Even in winter?"

"Especially in winter."

Rowan Daine was stalling. He knew quite well why they were there. But it wouldn't hurt to walk through the schedule with him.

"This customer is one of the biggest in the country. They want to know we'll be around to sell them several billion cubic feet a year for the next twenty years. Tens of millions of dollars at least; our gas marketing manager thought your presence would help make the sale."

"Why couldn't we have this meeting in the summer?"

"It was already on David's schedule. Besides," she said slyly, "it's a test."

"Like do we want their business enough to fly up here when it's twenty below and snowing."

She nodded. TriCoast's oil wells would soon be producing not just more oil, but more gas associated with the oil–called "associated gas"—and she was anxious to find a home for it. If she didn't, it could wind up at a negative price, which meant she'd actually have to pay companies to take it. There was a worse alternative: the high-priced oil couldn't be produced at all if there was no home for the associated gas coming out of the wellbore with it.

"Then we're going to a refinery on the south side with which we do considerable business."

"The clouds are talkin' snow."

"The clouds are ALWAYS talkin' snow here," Lynn said.

In the morning, at the Regis, she awoke to a high whine. Fierce winds set off vibrations that became musical frequencies. *No time for running this morning*, she remembered. *Maybe tomorrow before we return to the airport, if it isn't too cold.*

They parked in an old, tightly spaced garage and entered a building that looked as if it had been constructed early in the last century, as indeed it had. Their first meeting at the utility company was with Denny Smith.

*Denny Smith. Why is his name familiar?* Lynn wondered.

Daine looked at the notes Lynn had given him to prepare him. "Most people in Illinois use natural gas, not propane, for heat, unless they're rural."

"And Illinois has twenty-eight underground natural gas storage fields, adding up to more than ten percent of US natural gas storage capacity. Second largest in the country. Only Michigan has more."

When the tall, lean man met them, Lynn shuddered. *Why didn't I look more closely at my notes to figure out I'd be sitting across from the boy-now-man who'd bullied me so mercilessly years ago?*

*And all I have with me is another bully. I'm sure Denny hasn't forgotten. And I'm trying to do business with him?*

Lynn Dayton rearranged her face into a smile. *Professional. Not submissive.* She opened their discussion with Smith, the head of natural gas buying for the biggest gas utility in Chicago. "Denny, so good to see you again. You've done so well since we last saw one another!"

"Lynn Dayton. Yes. I remember you from Oklahoma. Sort of. Your parents were poor and you lived in a sketchy neighborhood, right? You wound up as a scholarship student someplace?"

*Neither he nor Daine will see me grind my teeth.* "So much time since then. My folks have passed away. Yours?"

"My wife has them stashed in some assisted living place. We spring 'em once a week. So, TriCoast, hunh? What can I do for you?"

"We're here to sell natural gas, of course," Lynn said. "First, thank you for inviting us here at your busiest time. Like your other suppliers, TriCoast is pleased we can now offer you sustainably produced gas. It means none of it goes up in smoke or escapes into the air—we recover it all from the wells."

"Gonna charge me more? Other companies don't. You're saying you got green gas for me, hey? It's minus 15 degrees outside. Why do I care? All I want is for all the grandmas to stay warm. Christ, I see people like you two all the time." The utility executive leaned back in an ergonomically updated chair. "All the molecules are the same. Why should I buy from you? Didn't TriCoast just have a big scandal? A cyberattack?"

"Yes, which we overcame and resolved. All energy companies are under attack all the time. How do you protect yourselves?"

Denny shook his head. "Constant vigilance and a bunch of smart cyber nerds, thank god. So, in Texas you live in the soup of the energy biz but you're worried because you can't produce your oil if you can't sell your gas. But your methane is fighting with the methane from New Mexico, Oklahoma, Ohio, and Pennsylvania."

Lynn tried to hide her annoyance. She glanced at Daine. His face was impassive.

Denny continued. "Here in Chicago, it's extremely simple. We need heat in the winter. The less we pay, the less our customers pay."

After a few minutes and before they could talk about the terms of a deal, Denny was called out of the room.

When he rushed back in, he spoke quickly. "We've got a big leak at a distro pipe in the 'burbs so it's an all-hands situation. Near apartments. Dozens of families and young kids. Just like your kids and mine."

When she looked surprised, he said, "I did my homework too. Don't think I didn't. Look, we're always in the market for gas. Tri-Coast is a big outfit; I know you're doing all you can to cut emissions. Have your people send me a five-year proposal for a bunch of MCFs and we're good. Oh, and since you two can't take me to lunch, I'll recommend a place."

Denny remained standing.

Rowan Daine spoke up. "Thank you for your time. We'll show ourselves out so you can roll."

Lynn drove herself and Daine west and south to Pilsen. She found a parking place near 18TH Street. Smith had told them they couldn't go wrong at any of the Mexican restaurants nearby. They picked the first one they saw.

"Mexican food. This I understand," Daine murmured to her as they entered the restaurant.

After a lunch of carnitas, Lynn drove them further south and east, back across the easy, right-angle grid to I-90.

Even further south, the Calumet region of Hammond, Whiting, East Chicago, Gary, and Munster was mainly an industrial landscape of looming steel mills. At the refinery, Lynn realized how much she missed the sights, sounds, and even smells of her former position in charge of TriCoast's oil refineries.

In contrast to Smith, John Gustafson had no emergencies, so Lynn and Daine talked about TriCoast's long-term drilling plans, oil qualities, and Gustafson's sources and equipment capabilities for refining and the kinds and volumes of oil TriCoast could supply him.

*A better side of Rowan Daine*, Lynn thought. *Who was the weird ogre I saw in Dallas? Why is the Bradshaw acquisition stuck in his craw? What's he afraid of?*

## CHAPTER 20
# CHICAGO

From the air, Hannah saw the long sweep of Chicago's Industrial Canal. Houses and urban forests blanketed the landscape all the way to the horizon. A thin band of blue sky on the horizon was as precise as a line made by a ballpoint pen. The houses and trees were black against an old layer of white snow.

Chicago with vapor lights under cloud cover looked like the Northern Lights she remembered from her time in Alaska. But here, the mercury vapor lamps ran straight west toward the horizon.

She was happy to be back in her hometown, even when walking through O'Hare Airport meant dodging homeless people and cars turned on their headlights at 3:30 in the afternoon.

As she waited for her baggage, she thought about her brief research into Texas driver deaths. The answer, for such a big state, was hundreds annually. And when she focused on West Texas, despite the sparser population, the answer was still hundreds annually. She'd narrowed it further, to commercial driver deaths in the most active drilling counties in West Texas. Despite all the work of the counties, the state, and the Texas Department of Transportation to improve traffic and road safety, deaths of commercial drivers—truck drivers—still numbered in the dozens each year.

She'd heard about the burly driver from Kermit who'd picked up a load from PipePod and wondered if he was among the deaths. She'd heard about the accident—his load of pipe had shifted dangerously loose. He'd stopped and called a trucker with a forklift, but when the forklift truck arrived, the driver for the load of PipePod steel pipe was nowhere around. *What happened to him?*

Then she allowed herself to think about Joost. She increasingly dreaded this meeting in Chicago with Henry Vandervoost, Joost's father. *Despite his playboy rep, in many ways Joost is a straighter shooter than I expected. I feel like I'm ratting him out. Tattling, for God's sake.*

The north side had a few streets and highways efficiently angled off the grid, like Milwaukee and the Kennedy. The street grid's regularity felt comfortingly familiar to Hannah as both a former resident and scientist. Today she took note of the Polish Museum of History and the Lithuanian Museum. The Ukrainian Village neighborhood. Baltic LNG ports for Poland and Lithuania kept coming up in her discussions with Henry Vandervoost. *Cold here, cold there*, she thought.

Her driver left the highway and took Milwaukee, the street that cut through everything. *The answer to your traffic question is "Milwaukee,"* she thought. It was the easiest, most optimal route from industrial Goose Island to the north side, angling against the grid, but parallel to interstate I-90/I-94. However, six-spoke intersections required extra caution by the driver.

After unpacking—and dining on soup left her by her friend—Hannah settled into bed to read. High-pitched sounds whistled and howled through the apartment. Thinking it was the blinds, she raised them, leaving her friend's blackout drapes in place. She checked the steam pipes, but they weren't the source of the racket. Finally, she realized the wind was rattling the windows and sweeping around the corners of buildings in a semi-regular chorus.

She slept poorly, wishing for earplugs. Early the next morning, the sun's rays reached over the horizon and across Lake Michigan.

Not long after the sun shimmered low on the horizon, the real blizzard hit. Hannah drew on both her Chicago and Alaskan experiences. Highways and streets would be whiteout hazards.

Strong winds would pound any vehicle whose driver was foolhardy enough to be out.

She delayed her discussion with Smith for a day.

Flights were canceled. She and Henry Vandervoost had decided the safest update would be in person. Henry texted her to say he was changing his flight from London to Chicago to the following day.

She felt fortunate her friend's kitchen was stocked with cereal and protein bars as well as soup. She settled back into bed and slept for a few hours while waiting for the blizzard to pass.

When she awoke, she took turns briefly lighting the four Vicinity soy candles her friend had left out for her. Each was designed to evoke a neighborhood. The Hyde Park candle was designed to smell like a bookstore with leather, patchouli, and musk. The West Loop candle was like Blommer Chocolate: chocolate, vanilla, and walnut, while the Pilsen candle also brought chocolate to mind: Mexican hot chocolate, with smells of cinnamon, vanilla, and cream. Finally, she tried the Lincoln Park soy candle: grass, bamboo, and bergamot.

And then she was hungry.

After lunch with a glass of water so cold it felt as if it had come from the bottom of one of her favorite Alaskan glaciers, she looked outside at the weather. The cold was confining: the coming darkness of early dusk would make it feel even more so.

But the afternoon was still crystalline. Putting on every layer she owned, she left the building and walked up and down the street, and then to the empty, snowy beach. A few inches of exposed skin around her eyes felt as if they were cracking. She remembered this feeling too—brittle cold threatening to never leave. As if it would never be warm again.

She stared out at the lake for a few more minutes and began to shiver. "Cooler by the lake"—shorthand for the Lake Michigan microclimate—was no exaggeration.

Yet the lake was less hypnotic than the blue ice caves of Alaska. Those had drawn in her and her friends further and further, until someone would break the spell, point out the danger, and they would retreat. She needed no further reminder to retreat from the icy lakeshore, especially with the wind picking up again.

As she walked back from the beach to her friend's apartment building, the wind shrieked. She felt a vibration against her wrist. Her smartwatch was giving her a haptic signal. Its pulsation and accompanying text warned the decibel level of the wind was so high that more minutes immersed in it would result in her temporary deafness.

❖

The next morning was still bitterly cold, but snowplows were everywhere. Police officers issued tickets to vehicles blocking the plows.

Hannah envied no one whose car got towed. The Chicago auto pound was three dark levels underground. She'd once had to retrieve a car from the place; it looked like a circle of hell.

She hired a ride-share to take her the several miles downtown to the gas utility's headquarters. They passed a protest group of several dozen bundled-up people in front of City Hall. Temperatures dipping into the teens and a hard wind driving the wind chill below zero reinforced their signs about the poor's need for affordable heat.

Yet Chicago residents knew how to navigate the coldest weather, starting with multiple layers of clothing. They knew about heating blocks for cars. They knew the wind off the lake blew even colder and brought them even more snow. And they knew their lives depended on the natural gas that was piped in and burned into heat to keep the grand three-story buildings, and the people in them, from freezing in 30-below nights.

The protest had also already attracted television cameras. She would ask Denny what he thought. She was glad not to be part of the protest. *Occasionally, it's good to work from the inside.*

The wind sliced down the river and through the tall buildings. She hurried inside.

Denny Smith was waiting for her in the lobby. He embraced her. "Hannah! Love! It's been forever since DC! The Hawk getting you?"

"Even I don't know what you mean," she said, reluctantly freeing herself from his hug. His warmth felt good.

"The Hawk. The wind off the lake."

"Ever since I arrived. Kept me up the night before last."

"Come on, I've got coffee for you."

She took her gloves off and rubbed her hands together. In the elevator, they exchanged brief histories. Hannah left out the part about her work for Henry Vandervoost.

"Criminal forensic biologist? Cool, Hannah. We could use you here. Day before yesterday we had someone monkey with our system, took down one of our main lines. The only good thing was it was my excuse for getting a couple of Texas sales geeks out of my office."

"Who was that?" Hannah asked, suspecting she knew.

"Rowan Daine, a thick-neck way out of his lane here, and Lynn Dayton, a poor Okie-made-good I knew a long time ago. We were in high school together in Tulsa."

Hannah blinked at the coincidence but decided to keep it to herself. "C'mon Den. No need to put her on blast. Everyone matures. You're originally an Okie, too."

He smiled. "You're right. But Christ, I see their types all the time now."

"What did they want?"

"To sell me TriCoast gas, likely for a high price. Same as everyone. I'll see what they offer."

"You buy from everyone though. Even the little guys like," she hesitated as if trying to recall the name, "Bradshaw Energy."

"Yep, even them, for now." He squinted. "Their price is too high, so I'll probably have to dump them next round."

Hannah expected *that* information would be useful to Henry.

Denny had remembered her coffee preference: black with just a taste of sugar.

"So, tell me about the protests out there," she said.

"Nothing to tell. We are a hundred percent good for customer service in all weather, especially weather like this. We don't turn off the gas to customers. We can't. We won't. But lots of 'em get behind on their bills. We work with 'em. And between you and me, sometimes we just take a write-off."

"Then why are they protesting?"

"Bills are always higher in the winter. Everyone hates it. They're not out there in the summer when their bills come down."

She probed gently. "How'd you lose a distribution line a few days ago?"

"Someone reported they smelled a leak. We turned off manually but too far upstream."

"You use RB Gas Sniff? They have a machine that can detect up to thirty different gases at once. Course you're only interested in methane and the odorant, ethyl mercaptan."

"Exactly what I like about you, Hannah. Practical problem-solver. I'll tell my maintenance VP to check into RB Gas Sniff."

Hannah shifted in her chair. Henry had been pushing her to do what he called "environmental activism" to shut down city gas pipelines. She understood his objective, or the objective of whoever he was working for, had nothing to do with environmentalism.

"Too warm in here for you? Too much detail?" Denny looked at her intently.

She sputtered. "The coffee. Hot. Perfect, but hot." She sat back, then steered the conversation toward the topic of their mutual friends from Washington, D.C.

❖

*A place,* she thought, *is whatever emotions and memories we infuse it with.*

The song by Alessia drifted through the lobby of the Edgewater apartment building where she waited for Vandervoost. "Your Scars Are Beautiful."

*No, they're not.* She felt a tug of memories so strong they threatened to make her cry. *My scars are only scars. I choose not to remember. Ever.*

Henry Vandervoost got out of a taxi in the port-cochere in front of the Edgewater apartment building.

"Hold him. Have him take us to the Bloomingdale Trail, the 606. We should walk," Hannah suggested.

"Today? In this?"

"It's more private, less windy. You have gloves and a hat, yeah?" *By God, now that he's on my turf rather than vice versa, I'll use it.*

They got in the cab and Hannah gave directions to Wicker Park. The driver followed up by entering the destination in his map app, which provided the same turn-by-turn directions she'd given.

She asked where he was staying and Vandervoost said, "The Regis."

*Figures.* The Regis was the newest, grandest building in the city by star architect Jeanne Gang.

"I'm pleased you've come all the way from London for this conversation," Hannah said once they'd exited the taxi and she'd paid. She pointed toward an elevated walkway nearby.

"That looks even colder. And yes, you are worth a trip from London. Tell me how it is with my son, Joost, and his company. I believe you've met him," he said slyly.

"Aren't you going to see him?"

"It's important you get the information I requested, to prepare the trail, as it were, before I show up. He and I are not on the best terms presently."

"Uh. Yes. Joost. Impressive." They reached the Bloomingdale

Trail walking track. She strode quickly until she noticed he wasn't keeping up.

"What have you learned?"

She explained what she'd found out in Texas—"bloody well almost got myself killed in a sand dump."

He flinched. "And here in Chicago?"

"Bradshaw Energy is going to lose its biggest gas customer unless Joost drops the price way down. And if he can't sell the gas to someone else, he'll have to shut in his super-profitable oil, since they get produced together."

The winter wind sliced through every layer of -20-degree fleece Hannah was wearing. She pulled her hat down on her head more firmly.

Henry noticed. "For the record, this walk was your idea."

She could tell he wanted to say more but was fearful of putting her off. She swung her arms more vigorously to warm them.

Vandervoost wrapped the wool scarf tighter around his face. "I'll never use the phrase 'over-heated office' again."

"Say what?"

He pulled the scarf away from his face. "It's *bloody* cold up here."

"Well, tell me what else you need to tell me and can't in a text or phone call. Then we can go someplace warm for food and drinks."

"You still haven't told me what I asked you to learn. It's why I'm here." *And I don't want you to know why I need it or for whom I'm really working.*

"Which is?" Hannah prompted.

"You don't remember? The details of Joost's special water recycling process. So valuable I'm told he doesn't even want to patent it. He wants to keep the process a secret, maybe license it eventually."

"I'm on it."

"No, you're not. You don't have anything more than when you started."

"Oh, except, again for *almost getting killed in a sand avalanche* while I was accompanying Joost and Lynn while working for you, trying to find out more about the process and his company as you asked."

"I'm sorry to hear it, but for what I'm paying you, risks come with the project."

She wheeled around and stared at him. "Lynn Dayton told me about you, but she didn't tell me you were cruel, too. I should leave you to find your way across the city back to the Regis."

*Lynn Dayton. That bitch.* "Hear me out. It's business. Actually, no. It's my life. If I don't deliver, my life is over."

She shook her head. "And you're melodramatic, too. I don't believe you."

"The day I don't answer your texts, you'll believe. And Hannah, no matter what happens later, I'm telling you now I'm not suicidal." He sighed. "This job in Midland is easy. It's someplace where no one knows you. Where you"—he didn't bother to modulate his sneer—"don't have to suck up to your best friend from Washington, DC for information on Bradshaw's sale who now buys millions of dollars of gas for Chicago's major gas utility but who overlooks your environmental protests."

"Hold out your hands."

"Why?" But he did so.

She yanked the gloves off both of his hands.

"Bloody hell!"

"I know, right. Frostbite in 3-2-1. I'm not a pawn. You need to respect me, or I'm done with you. And I'll be taking your gloves."

He jammed his hands in his pockets. "Hannah. Hannah, please. Of course I respect you. I never would have talked to you in London otherwise. You're a professional. Can we please get off this damn trail and go someplace warm?"

She silently handed back his gloves and pointed toward stairs leading down from the elevated trail. Despite the cold, the stairs were clear rather than icy. *Chicago efficiency*, she thought.

"Hannah, I don't want to sound desperate, but I am. You must get the details of the water recycling process for me as soon as possible."

"But I don't mind sounding angry so I will. My nearly getting killed on your bloody project was not our arrangement."

She pointed him toward a taxi stand and walked back to the stairs up to the trail.

He shook his head in disbelief. Had he really miscalculated so badly? *Is Hannah just another barely useful idiot? Worse, will she learn I'm working for Kir Zaitsev to pay off my gambling debt? Will she betray me to my son?*

# CHAPTER 21
# HERZLIYA, ISRAEL

IN ONE CORNER of his screen, Avi caught news about loads of liquefied natural gas—*like what we were producing*, he thought sadly—arriving from Egypt into Europe, particularly Spain. "The eastern Med and North Africa could in the future be countering the energy influence of Russia's Egonov," the CNBC announcer said.

That had been before the Barcelona terminal attack, which Israel had just begun supplying. Lynn Dayton had considerately offered to make up the deliveries Israel was missing into other Spanish terminals until Avi could get permission and tankers to deliver Israeli LNG to those places—particularly Bilbao. Avi had hoped renegotiating the contract with Spanish energy minister Alejandro Garcia would be fast and easy, in recognition of the emergency. Unfortunately, Garcia was dragging his feet, *as the Americans would say*, Avi thought. Slow to respond, slow to counter.

Finally, to keep Lynn's backup offer on the table, he had lowered the LNG price, and Garcia had accepted it provisionally, for a few months. A longer contract would depend on approval from Israel's deputy energy minister. So, TriCoast had been able to load and land its LNG for Avi's Spanish contract at Bilbao, even at the lower price. Garcia had promised Avi he would soon get the new permissions for Israel to land its LNG at the new port.

But now, days later, Garcia had not delivered on his promise, despite its urgency. Avi's calls to Garcia were going unanswered.

*Is he sending a signal that since he's got TriCoast's US supplies he doesn't want to do business with us?*

And more worries. Another of Avi's screens showed Egyptian officials announcing a new, significant natural gas discovery offshore Egypt, one they expected to fast-track to production.

*That will change the Egyptians' negotiating stance,* he thought. *If they have their own offshore gas production, they'll be less interested in processing ours.*

He reviewed the next proposal. Another exploration and production company with offices in London and Tel Aviv had confirmed big new Eastern Med natural gas discoveries offshore Israel at sites named for the Greek gods of Olympus. The discoveries, big enough to be commercial with their billions of cubic meters of reserves, were northeast of Leviathan and Tamar. Mentally, he translated billions of cubic meters to the billions of cubic feet Tri-Coast used for measurement. This company wanted Avi's company's help—meaning investment—in building offshore processing units and pipelines.

*Even though it means more competition for us, the more gas, the better,* Avi thought. More gas meant more security of energy supply for Israel.

He glanced at the company's operations map. North Sea near the UK. Egypt. Offshore Israel, already with a floating production storage and offloading, or FPSO, unit was the flagship. It had already started production. Other ops in southern Europe. Italy. Greece. *Good.*

Suddenly another corner of his screen—the one showing the deck on one of the company's offshore platforms—pulsed red. An alarm blared. "Drone. Drone. Drone."

Although it could be a reconnaissance drone—and even those were illegal—he could never be sure the drone didn't have a more lethal payload.

If it got closer, the men and women operating the platform had the authorization to shoot it.

After it hovered nearby for a few minutes, they did so.

Soon, Avi heard the platform manager give the instruction to everyone to stand down.

"Where'd it originate? Who's the operator?" Avi could hear the radio traffic from the platform. He knew they were searching the horizon. A small craft was at the far edge of the frame, nearly out of camera range.

The platform manager faced the security camera to record his findings. Besides creating a video evidence trail, all with access to the security camera would get the information simultaneously, saving the manager from answering dozens of individual calls.

He sounded grim. "We recovered the drone from the water. It's Iranian-made. No ID on the craft it was launched from. But anyone watching knows Russia is a major buyer of Iranian drones."

# CHAPTER 22
# MIDLAND

LYNN WAS traveling elsewhere but Hannah decided to return to Midland. She was still bothered by the sand avalanche that could have killed her, Lynn, and Joost. If Henry asked, she would say she was doing extra due diligence on Bradshaw Energy. *Which is true. Bradshaw Energy AND Midland itself.*

She rented a car at the Midland airport, returned to her hotel on the northeast side of town several miles away, and began compiling a list of sand companies. Some of the sites also listed their full-time drivers. She didn't recognize any pictures or names.

"Joost, could I persuade you to go to lunch? I have a few more questions about your business. Of course I'm reporting everything back to Henry, but I'm still chasing what happened to us when we were almost killed by the sand avalanche."

"Yes. Let's meet at Taco di Vino on Oak at 11:30. Shall I bring Gomez? Your questions are financial?"

"Whatever you'd like, but no, I don't have financial questions. Just supplier questions."

By 11:45, they were across the table from one another at Taco di Vino. No Gomez, Hannah noted. Only Joost.

"We'll share lunches, if that's okay," Hannah said.

"Sure. But I'm notorious for eating anything that looks like a leftover. So, eat fast."

She shook her head and smiled, tucking a bra strap back into her shirt as she did so.

Joost watched her.

It was one of her signature moves, but this time she found herself blushing. *Don't be such a daft schoolgirl.* She took a bite of her coconut shrimp taco. "This is amazing. I might have to order more."

"Here, try this."

"What is it?"

"Flank steak taco."

She took a bite, smiled at him, then took another bite. "Even better."

"So, what do you want to know?"

"I have this long list of all the sand companies operating in the Permian Basin. A few of them are out of business. Are any of these suppliers to Bradshaw Energy?" She handed him a list of thirty company names.

"I've been in Midland so long I grew up with most of the guys running these companies now. The ones still here made it through the last two or three busts. Paradoxically, sand is a hard business to make money in. It's so easy to get into that everyone does, especially the real estate types. Drives the price right down. Then people like us stop drilling when the oil price drops, and it hurts the suppliers, like them."

He looked over the list. "Yeah. Gator Sand. Midland Frac Sand. Sand Dune. We use those three, or they're the ones we recommend to our drilling contractors. All solid."

She tilted her head to one side and regarded him. "But Joost—"

"Say it again. I love how you say my name..."

She laughed, despite herself. "Let's be practical. How will we ever find out who set off the sand avalanche near Monahans that was directed at us? If it had happened a few seconds sooner, you and I wouldn't be sitting here discussing your name, *Joost.*"

He nodded. "The operator said he'd momentarily lost control. Not like he slipped, but like something took over his control panel. Could have been from a remote signal, but not too remote. To be aimed at us—for whoever did it to know our precise location—it had to be set off by one of the drivers there."

"Could I get those logs, you think?"

"Just ask. For you, perhaps they would."

"Or perhaps not. Here's another question—oh no you don't." She batted his fork away. "I want the last bites of the shrimp taco. So, some of these companies list their drivers, but only their full-time drivers."

"When we were there, I didn't see any of the sand company drivers who work for us. I know them all. But these companies have a slew of part-timers. They'll pick up a few loads here, and pick up some water disposal loads for people like Rowan Daine. Depends on their schedules."

"I'll ask Daine, then. How about driver accidents? How common are they?"

He sat back and rolled his shoulders, looking at her intensely, as if he was contemplating other activities with her beyond a lunch conversation.

She smiled and rolled her eyes. Smoothed her hair. "Yeah, but seriously. Accidents your truck drivers have had? Ones you've learned about? So much traffic, so fast, and so few roads here. I thought Alaska and London were bad."

His expression turned serious. "More accidents and deaths than we realize. We both heard about the odd disappearance of the PipePod driver. He's never been found."

"Yes."

"And as I think of it," he flexed his arm and the Texas tattoo on his elbow changed shape, "we lost a driver, too. We were short on pipeline space, so we had to truck oil to a refinery near here. Terribly expensive but it's more expensive not to produce the oil at all. We'd committed to supply certain volumes to the refinery. It was late at night. Someone ran him off the road. Sounded like an accident at the time, but now I wonder."

She sat back, looked at him thoughtfully, then stood and shouldered her purse. "Thanks, Joost. You've given me new directions to pursue. If only they involved soil somehow. That's my real specialty." She gave a wry grin.

Joost got up and pushed in his chair. "Hannah. I screwed up with you at the barbecue restaurant. Will you think of giving me another chance? Go out with me again?"

She shook her head. "I'm here on business, and then I'll be leaving. It's no basis for a relationship, even if I could trust a West Texas player like you. And I don't. But thank you for the offer."

Back at the hotel that afternoon, she wondered if she should have accepted Joost's request for a simple date. *But it wouldn't be simple. On the other hand, I've had one-night stands, so it doesn't matter that I'm leaving soon. And I'm sure not ready to commit. Not after breaking up six weeks ago with a married wanker who'd promised to leave his wife. God, I was so bloody stupid.*

On her computer, she began dredging up statistics for unsolved murders, unexplained deaths, and accidental deaths in and around Midland. *I'm here. I should see what's been happening and get some context.* She looked at tables and newspaper stories online going back several years and made notes. Many deaths. Many more than she would have expected, even for a region as big as this and cities as large as Midland and Odessa.

Then she saw it. A few paragraphs from a story years ago in a newspaper that had just been digitized. Stephen Bosko, her father, found dead at a wellsite.

*Dad!*

The details were as sparse as the ones she and her mother had been provided. Words like *tragic* and *unexplained* and *accident* ricocheted around in her mind. Her eyes blurred with tears.

She stood up, went downstairs and outside. There were few places to walk—everything was a cement pad, designed for drivers—so she paced back and forth in front of the hotel.

*There must be someone who knows more.*

After a while, she returned to her room, determined to make use of the information she had gleaned from Joost. She clicked to employment websites for Permian truck drivers—jobs offered, people looking for jobs. Each had a thumbnail photo, references, and contact information, with many listing nearby man camps as their residences.

She paged through them, not expecting to see anyone she recognized.

But there he was. She'd noticed him at the sand mine, precisely because he looked like every other truck driver. His recent hauling jobs included sand, pipe for PipePod, and water, for Daine Environmental Water Services.

*Did Lynn mention him? I'll have to ask her. For now, best to go to the man he lists as a reference.*

"Rowan Daine? This is Hannah Bosko. I'm doing some due diligence in Midland for an investor, Henry Vandervoost."

"Hello, Hannah! Yes, I know Henry! And he has mentioned you. What's on your mind?"

"I have a question about someone who has listed you as a reference. What can you tell me about John Cooper?"

❖

By the time he hung up, Rowan Daine was fuming. First Lynn Dayton had asked about Cooper when she'd met him at a well site and now this uppity English bitch. *Henry really knows how to pick 'em. Hannah is way, way too nosy. Just like her old man.*

The three of them—Lynn and Hannah with their questions and attitude—and Joost with his hot-shit new water recycling process were obstacles. If they didn't go away, they were obstacles he would have to remove.

# CHAPTER 23
# LOUISIANA COAST, TRICOAST LNG TERMINAL

ZAITSEV STEEPLED HIS fingers and then quickly dropped them out of that frowned-upon western gesture. When he called Henry Vandervoost, he was dismayed the man sounded even more anxious than usual.

"No progress. I just met with my worker in Chicago. She is carrying her investigation much further than she should."

"Useful."

"She's asking me about truck driver deaths, including a bloke who just went missing, a PipePod driver."

"About which you know nothing."

"Correct. She also told me the gas utility here in Chicago is about to dump Bradshaw Energy as a supplier because they're too expensive."

"Possibly making them more desperate. Could work in our favor. But no details yet on the water recycling technology?"

"She may be hiding from me what she's learning from my son. I can't tell."

"I am sorry to hear so."

"She's met Lynn Dayton, who is telling her far too much."

"You are concerned for your reputation?"

"Of course. And what she might learn about my, and your, involvement in arranging the Barcelona attack."

"I was not there."

"No. She did say Dayton has agreed to back up Israel by supplying LNG to Spain from TriCoast's Louisiana LNG export until the Israelis can get permission to ship their LNG to other Spanish terminals."

"Important." *Very important*, Zaitsev thought.

"And Hannah is so much into her investigation, I'm concerned she will learn I'm working for you. Lynn Dayton is already asking her."

"I think you attribute far too much intelligence to this woman. You hired her for that reason, but there are many factors of which she is unaware. You will travel to Midland to meet Joost?"

"She is preparing him, so he will listen to me. I'll go soon. But not yet."

After they disconnected, Zaitsev made several more calls. Hannah's useful idiocy might still extend to her environmentalism. A hack into TriCoast's LNG terminal would serve two purposes. It could draw Hannah's attention as an environmentalist away from investigating Henry's relationship with Zaitsev. More importantly, it might discipline TriCoast against helping Israel displace Russia as the critical supplier of LNG and natural gas to Spain.

❖

A few days later, TriCoast's communications vice president, Claude Durand, voiced displeasure at the change in routine. His dismissal of Louisiana was delivered with sarcasm borne of his French background mixed with expressions reflecting his years of living in the United States. "Louisiana is French the same way Catalonia is—*un peu*, just enough to make you crazy thinking you can decipher their mixed-breed language. And every third person is named Thibodeaux or Boudreaux. Like Smith here or Li in China."

"I'll keep it in mind next time I'm in Catalonia. Which will be never. And yes, I have worked with a man named Boudreaux. Great guy," Lynn said.

She looked forward to joining several dozen day crew operators and contractors for an early holiday lunch and award ceremony at TriCoast's Louisiana liquefied natural gas terminal on the Gulf Coast. Many of the staff, expert cooks all, were due to bring their own specialties, from seafood gumbo to oyster dressing, jambalaya to turducken to bread pudding and pecan pralines.

She and Claude were on their way from Lake Charles to the terminal to give awards for two years of safe operations.

She hoped a few leftovers remained.

The plant had four enormous process "trains." It had already provided and sent hundreds of cargoes to Asia and Europe. These were in addition to the ones it was sending to Spain on behalf of Avi's company until his company could get permission to land their LNG cargoes at the Bilbao terminal instead of the now-shuttered Barcelona terminal.

The trains took billions of cubic feet each day of gaseous methane from TriCoast and other companies, removed impurities, then supercooled the gas to -260 degrees Fahrenheit. This turned it into a liquid at atmospheric pressure and reduced its volume by about six hundred times. The supercooled liquid was loaded into tankers and shipped abroad. At a foreign port such as Bilbao, the LNG was unloaded, stored, then regasified and fed into the country's natural gas grid.

Like other US energy installations, TriCoast's LNG terminal routinely fended off dozens of cyberattacks. The number and intensity of attacks, particularly from Russia, escalated when Russia was militarily active in other parts of the world. To Lynn, these were straightforward attempts by the Russians to control, infiltrate, limit, or destroy competitive non-Russian sources of natural gas and liquefied natural gas to make Russian supplies more valuable. Usually, hackers gained access through current and former employees' computers. TriCoast cybersecurity teams routinely trained the company's thousands of employees on new kinds of phishing attempts and scams.

The terminal had been operating 24/7, as had several others on the US Gulf Coast. Strong demand from countries like Finland and Estonia met limited supply after a fire had shut down one neighboring Louisiana LNG export plant. Overseas, Nigerian LNG suppliers had been unable to meet commitments due to in-country sabotage of the pipelines between the gas fields and the export terminals, driving the value of the LNG TriCoast produced even higher.

So, while Lynn's safety awards focused on the lives and health of TriCoast employees, safety was also important simply to continue operating.

Claude drove the car loaned from the Lake Charles airport FBO. In the passenger seat, Lynn reviewed her remarks for the awards.

"The agenda," Claude said, "is they eat, you talk, and then we eat."

"I'll be so hungry my stomach will do all the talking for me."

He rolled his eyes in the universal facial expression. "You will manage."

❖

Simultaneously, but several time zones away in a well-heated Moscow apartment, Zaitsev's Russian hacker finished inserting the code into TriCoast's LNG electrical system. He'd obtained the instructions from a trainee at the plant. The trainee had traded it for access back into her bank accounts after the hacker had phished them and then demanded the LNG electrical system password as ransom. The trainee had told no one, afraid of losing her new job.

With few keystrokes—electrical circuits failing open instead of closed here and there—the hacker planned to inflict the moderate damage Zaitsev had requested and for which he'd promised payment.

Within hours, as he and Zaitsev heard news of their success, hundreds of thousands of rubles landed in the hacker's accounts.

❖

After Lynn presented the safety awards, the terminal manager invited Lynn and Claude to bring their plates of food into his office.

"Very few leftovers, I'm sorry to see," Lynn said.

The terminal manager smiled.

She was taking a bite of turducken when she paused. "I smell smoke."

A half-second later, fire alarms blared.

A loud recorded voice repeated, "Evacuate the building evacuate the building."

*Moments ago, I handed out safety awards. How could the operators here have a fire?*

The manager looked at his texts. "They don't know where it is, yet. We'd better get outside though."

They walked quickly toward the exit.

Lynn was furious that her people might get injured. Amid her focused anger, she remembered an obscure study she'd read one night when she'd had trouble falling asleep. "If they can't see it, could be electrical. Put out a plantwide alert to check if any circuit relays failed, and if so, which ones and how."

The terminal manager did so.

A few moments later, his brow wrinkled. "They've found the problem and shut it down. Someone, somewhere got into the electrical system and screwed up the breaker circuits. They're supposed to fail open—that's the operating standard. Instead, someone changed the instructions, so they failed closed. We have overheating and fires in six locations. We'll shut the terminal down until we put out the fires and check everything."

The best they could do now was extinguish the dangerous fires and cool the hot spots so more wouldn't flare up.

Don Pratt, one of the onsite operators, had cross-trained for firefighting, as had most of the men and women at the terminal. He'd thrown on his gear at the sound of the alarm. A quick check showed the chillers to supercool and liquefy the gas were still working but the inlet gas field compressors had stalled and were starting to overheat, even though they were powering down.

He directed the water truck with two other men to the bank of big compressors just beyond the terminal gate. They decided to cool the compressors with lower-temperature water to bleed off the heat.

Fully geared up for a fire, Don was the nozzle firefighter, the man who opened and operated the nozzle, determined the pace of attack, and aimed the nozzle.

He got out of the truck, followed by the other two volunteer firefighters.

They checked that all connections were properly tightened, adjusting one.

They then unwound and laid out the heavy attack hose. Don crouched, pointing the nozzle so the 35-degree angle of the spray would hit the compressors directly.

A cool day, it was still Louisiana-humid. Don felt his body start to sweat. He wanted to remove his helmet to wipe his face. Instead, he blinked away at the sweat.

As the nozzle man, he was the one nearest the compressors, about fifty feet away.

Don turned his head and nodded to his backup man to start the flow of water.

As expected, high-pressure water gushed from the hose. Don adjusted the attack angle slightly.

Unfortunately, the compressors were already so hot that when gallons of firehose water hit them, the water instantly gasified into superheated steam. Like steam rising from a big field of geysers, it hit the compressors. The wind blew the superheated steam back onto the firefighters, Don first.

Don stepped back away and signaled to stop the water flow.

But it was already too late. Despite his protective gear, the hot steam found a crack in Don's face shield.

It blinded him, then burned his face and neck.

Don yelled for his backup man. He dropped back behind the truck, ripping off his helmet and cracked face shield.

When the ambulance arrived, the medic—familiar with injuries of all kinds—took a deep breath as he saw the second and third-degree burns on the young man's face.

"Can you see to get into the ambulance?"

Don shook his head.

The medic led him to a stretcher, loaded him, and rushed away, siren blaring.

# CHAPTER 24
# HERZLIYA, ISRAEL

*"Large natural gas finds in Israeli, Cypriot and Egyptian exclusive economic zones have turned the region into a global energy source."*

—*The Wall Street Journal*

AVI'S COMPANY HAD partnered with TriCoast and several other companies to develop the Tamar field, ninety kilometers west of Haifa, the first of the big offshore Med finds. Gas was produced from five wells that reached far below the seabed. The gas was brought to the surface, cleaned up (or "processed" as the engineers said) on the offshore platform, then sent via pipeline to an onshore Israeli terminal. From there it was sold in Israel, and some was exported to Jordan and Egypt. Similarly, gas from the even bigger multi-billion-dollar Leviathan field was also exported to Egypt.

It seemed sudden but wasn't. Projects and suppliers competitive to Israel's Tamar, Leviathan, and Karish fields, as well as Zohr near Egypt and Aphrodite near Cyprus, were springing up around the eastern Mediterranean. Not only were Jordan and Cyprus buying gas from Israel's fields, but Italy and Libya had signed a multi-billion-dollar deal to supply gas from offshore Tripoli to Italy and Libya.

LNG receipt storage and regas terminals were popping up everywhere, too, including one near the Port of Bilbao, one Avi had discussed with Spanish energy minister Alejandro Garcia. After the attack on Barcelona, Garcia gave Avi's company temporary approval to substitute landing its LNG in Bilbao and Cartagena, instead of Barcelona as originally contracted. But it was only temporary.

He'd just received a call from Lynn Dayton and his aunt, Sara Levin. TriCoast's Louisiana LNG terminal—which had been filling in for Avi's company in Spain—was now down for at least a few days due to electrical fires. So, he was back on his own to meet the Spanish contract.

Teos Mustafa was restive, explaining his plant would soon prioritize new Egyptian gas finds over liquefying Israel's gas. But the Israeli-Egyptian gas liquefaction agreement was still working, for now.

*Yet after all these challenges, here I am, still having to maneuver around my own country's deputy energy minister,* Avi thought.

His phone burped with the notification of an incoming text.

Señor Garcia was stalling for time, waffling, unsure his government would support the twenty-year commitment Avi and his company needed to fund an even bigger Israeli gas LNG project with Egypt. Despite Spain's clear need for natural gas, for heat, to make electricity, to back up its solar panels, and for industry, the complex politics of the Middle East, the terrible attack on the Barcelona LNG import terminal, and now the attack on TriCoast's Louisiana LNG export terminal seemed to be scaring off Garcia.

To reassure him, Avi pointed to the baseline 15-year deal that started a few years earlier between a different Israeli company with US and Egyptian partners. The deal allowed the supply of eighty-five billion cubic meters to Egypt from Israel's Tamar and Leviathan fields.

And Avi's company *had* been able to sign a trilateral deal between Israel, Egypt, and Spain. Gas from offshore Israeli fields was pipelined to Egypt where it was liquefied—since Israel didn't have its own liquefaction facilities but Egypt had spare liquefaction capacity—and then shipped by LNG carrier to Spain. The initial volume, which had gone to Barcelona, was not large, but it had been important proof of concept and a test of supply reliability.

Avi reminded Garcia that a few countries bolder than Spain, like Italy, were also becoming more serious about backing Eastern Med projects, meaning Garcia had competition for Israel's gas. He also reminded Garcia developers in Cairo, Egypt were anxious to move forward on a bigger deal to supply Cartagena and Bilbao and to become the Eastern Med's physical LNG export hub.

Avi stared at the memo. It didn't even sound like the deputy minister of energy had written it. He probably hadn't. Already, Avi had noticed various artificial intelligence tools—especially useful for writing formulaic proposals—were in heavy rotation.

Still, the meaning was clear. Avi's company was not approved to sell gas to Spain nor even to deliver it to Barcelona.

*But I see the problem.*

Avi got on his cell phone. Miraculously, he reached the man.

"I have your response to our proposal to export the natural gas we are producing to Spain, via Barcelona and now Bilbao."

"Nothing to discuss. If Señor Garcia doesn't want a twenty-year contract, we're not interested."

"Sir. You have a background as a trader. There are all kinds of spot LNG tanker capacities available. Some of Spain's utilities will sign one- or three-year deals. They're desperate. A few years ago, Europe lost over a hundred and fifty billion cubic meters a year from Russia. Israel could supply two or three billion cubic meters a year, especially in Spain, Italy, and Greece. We're already sending excess gas to Egypt to get liquefied and shipped to Asia. Even Egypt's facilities are topping out—they can only do about one LNG cargo every other day. It's good we have space there." Avi caught himself before he said *lucky*. The old man hated ascribing anything to luck.

"And waste Israel's patrimony? Better for us to keep it in the ground, under the water."

Avi took an even breath. One in. One out. "We are producing more gas now than Israel needs, than Egypt needs, than Jordan or Lebanon needs. My US friends are asking me to back *them* up, after they did the same for us. They lost an LNG plant. We need to establish credibility as a reliable supplier if we are to compete effectively with other eastern Med drillers like BP and Chevron. Chevron is racing ahead in the Leviathan field, and they've already announced they'll be selling gas to Europe. They've even got a floating liquefied natural gas plant. Since Egypt is topped out, we need something similar, or else more pipelines to Europe."

The deputy minister interrupted him. "The pipeline's already been discussed and shot down by the greens in your aunt's United States, as well as Turkey, since Turkey has a competitive pipeline to Europe. And tell me again why we Israelis should trust the Spanish."

"So, you're saying you don't want to do a deal of any length with Spain—even if we could get a twenty-year contract."

"This is our resource. This price you negotiated, which he wants to extend long-term, is too low. You just need to take the L, my friend. What's the phrase? JOMO?"

Avi bit his lip. He hated when the older man insulted him with the slang of young people. "Joy of missing out. But sir, we are already satisfying the needs of the eastern Med. It is time to fly further, establish our place in the energy trading world."

"Avi, I appreciate your enthusiasm, but no. We're done. Goodbye."

After the deputy minister clicked off, Avi glanced at the time. It was early in Dallas, but his aunt should already be at work. He called her.

His phone luck was holding. She answered. "My nephew. You must have a problem if you're calling me so early in the day."

Avi explained that the deputy minister would not approve a long-term contract for his company to sell gas to Spain.

His aunt was quiet for a moment. "No promises. I'll talk to Lynn and her group. They can usually make things happen at our end. Let me see what else I can do. You should know Don Pratt, one of the men who was burned while responding to the LNG terminal electrical fires, has died. We must resolve safety issues before we can resume shipping from our terminal. It will be down for at least a few weeks. We continue to need your backup to meet its contracts."

"You have it. And Aunt Sara, I'm sorry to hear about Don Pratt."

Towards the end of his workday a few hours later, his phone rang. The display showed only a private number.

He was shocked to hear the voice of Israel's minister of energy. Then pleased, when the man said, "Send the contract you described to Sara Levin to me. If Sara says this is something we should do, I believe her. I will approve it. Now that we are providing gas to all Israeli citizens and exporting to our neighbors in Egypt and Jordan, we should be doing business with as many other reputable companies and utilities as we can. Including Señor Garcia in Spain."

"Yes, sir."

Avi didn't stop smiling all the way home.

## CHAPTER 25
# WEST OF MIDLAND-ODESSA

Lynn met Hannah, Joost, Roy, and Beau for a promised drive to look over a few of Bradshaw Energy's well sites—sites on which she was making a bid—further west in the Permian, about a hundred and fifty miles from Midland. She was happy Beau had secured a big, reliable truck, jacked even higher off the ground with an off-road package. She'd flown over West Texas and looked at enough maps to understand there were few roads where they were headed. And none meandered: all were straight lines from one small town of a few thousand to the next: Monahans, Fort Stockton, Pecos.

They first stopped by Bradshaw Energy's office where Joost and one of his engineers showed them a wall map of Bradshaw's production.

"All those well sticks are yours?" Lynn asked.

Joost nodded.

"Look at all the green."

"Each represents a working well."

"And the red?"

"Go-stop colors of making money and losing money. Green for oil, red for gas. We don't drill gas wells, but we have oil wells that gassed out. We've already laid down gas rigs since the price keeps falling."

"Permian's huge but maturing," Lynn said. *Like the smaller basins. People want to make money fast and get out.*

"There are days when all the action is in Houston, so Midland feels like just a minor field office. But lots of other days it's good to be here and know exactly what's going on. Some stuff doesn't filter out to Houston."

They drove southwest on I-20 toward Odessa.

"You're bringing us to an H-E-B grocery store?" Hannah wondered as Joost swung the truck off I-20 on the west side of Odessa.

"Notice how big it is. They've got everything, including the best barbecue around."

Towards the front of the giant warehouse store, they placed orders at a sectioned-off counter, took seats in a red-cushioned booth, and then retrieved their orders from the counter once announced.

Their group of five, Lynn was amused to notice, ordered everything from lean and fatty brisket to burnt ends, pulled pork, and a half rack of St. Louis ribs.

Hannah made a meal of sides: coleslaw, collard greens, potato salad, and queso blanco with tortilla chips.

"The vibe out here is very male," Hannah summarized.

"What makes you say so?" Joost laughed.

Lynn looked around. "All the beards. Everyone has one except the two of us and the nice women who served us barbecue."

Joost stared across the table at Hannah and Lynn. His eyes lingered on Hannah. "You're a geologist? But you do forensics and chemistry, too?"

She nodded.

"So, what do you think of the geology around here?" he asked.

"Nothing you don't already know. It's an ancient seabed. Layer after layer. I was once called up on the case of a missing woman nearby."

"Tell us about it," Lynn said.

"I was one of many. The FBI, Texas Rangers, and county sheriff's office were all looking for a young woman."

"You help them find her?" Joost asked.

She shook her head. "I helped with soil analysis after they found her remains."

Joost and Roy winced. Lynn squinted her eyes as if she could unhear the sentence.

"So, you came out here for the investigation? You've been here before?" Beau was curious.

"The autopsy was done in Dallas County. More resources. They found sand on her body that didn't match the sand her body had been dropped in. And they had a truck they traced to a suspect, but the suspect said he knew nothing," Hannah explained.

"What was your part in the investigation?" Beau asked.

"Several. For one, there's a tool called the Munsell Soil Color Chart. It standardizes how we describe sand, dirt, and clay."

"So more than just 'brown, gray, yellow.' Seems like it would be handy out here when we talk about the prospective zones." Joost tapped his temple, miming thinking.

"Yes, and yes. Geologists use it all the time. In fact, one of the things we did was pair the Munsell chart with the geologic maps available from the USGS geologic map database all your Midland petrogeologists use.

"And there was plenty of circumstantial evidence. Turned out the sand samples in the folds of her clothes and skin had a shiny black iron-titanium oxide. This matched samples on his clothes, in his truck, on the gas pedal, and in his apartment. I won't go into all the equipment we used, but the sand linked the two of them, as did fibers that turned out to be cable frayed off a winch in the back of his truck."

"But how did you identify time of death?" Joost asked, putting down his fork and leaning toward her.

"Insects don't lie, as one biologist has told us. They smell decay. They arrive in a certain time sequence, although it depends on the temperature. If they're urban insects—and these were—but the body's out in a rural area—and it was—it suggests the body's been moved.

"Hunh. Interesting," Lynn said.

"You want me to go on?" Hannah said.

"Yes," Joost replied, leaning forward.

"Insects arrive while the person is still alive. The species come in waves. Blowflies, which are metallic-looking, are the first to arrive. Then flesh flies, which are about the size of horseflies. The house flies, coffin flies, and drain flies. Drain flies hang out in sewers, drains, and culverts. They're fuzzy, hairy, like moths."

"Okay, you got me," Lynn said. She felt her stomach twist and hoped not to have to dash for the restroom in the next few seconds. "I think I have the picture."

She noticed even Roy had started to look a bit green.

Hannah folded her hands, unperturbed.

Joost stared down at his remaining barbecue burnt ends and pushed his plate away. "Can we talk about something else? I want to be visualizing something besides flies while we're driving."

Roy said, "There are very few roads west and south. We're not going all the way to Big Bend, which is amazing, or Balmorhea. I'm hoping we see remains of wax camps or wax refineries, but we may be too far north."

"Wax refineries?" Lynn asked.

Roy smiled. "Knew *refineries* would catch your attention."

"Once a refinery engineer, always a refinery engineer," Lynn agreed.

"About a hundred years ago, people in Mexico and south Texas would harvest wax from candelilla plants. They'd bring it to locations with huge pots—nothing like a refinery today. Instead, think of an iron kettle ten feet tall and ten feet in diameter. They'd boil the wax and purify it. It still gets used today for things like chewing gum and lip balm," Roy said.

"You're right, I would like to see one of those places. We joke about small refineries being called pots and pans, but those literally were. How did the process work?" Lynn asked.

Joost turned to his phone, tapped a few buttons, and pulled up a website, showing the group the pictures. He read a few sentences. "This is how they do it. Or how they used to, anyway. The vats rest in a box made of firebricks, and butane-fired heating elements heat the bottoms to the wax melting temperature, about 160 degrees Fahrenheit."

"Not that hot. But all wax has a melting point on the low side," Lynn said, thinking of wax units she had overseen at TriCoast's oil refineries.

"Someone monitored and controlled the heat to prevent boilovers," Roy said. "Each vat held 5500 pounds of cerote, with several feet of water in the bottom. Workers would heat the vats for five to six hours to get rid of moisture. Sand settled out at the bottom. Then the wax was drained by pipes into big shallow squares in front of the vats and cooled overnight. The big wax cakes were about ten feet by sixteen feet by three inches. Workers with hammers would pull up the wax chunks and break them into smaller, fist-sized chunks, then drop about a hundred pounds worth into each burlap bag for shipping."

"Awesome!" Lynn exclaimed.

"They're mostly south of where we'll be, unfortunately," Roy said.

"Still, something to search for. Okay, break and then let's hit the road," Lynn said. She walked across the small café to a restroom at one end.

A minute or so later, Lynn overheard Hannah in the next stall, on her cell phone.

*She must know I'm right next to her! She must want me to hear her. Freudian slip?*

"Yes, Henry, I'm in Odessa with Joost and Lynn and Ray and Beau." She paused as Henry apparently voiced his reactions. "Yes, I know it's supper time there and no, Joost still has not told me much. It's a good company. You should be proud of what your ex-wife and son have put together." A longer pause. "No, nothing on the new water recycle process he wants to license. He's not very forthcoming. I should get more on it soon, though."

Lynn was torn between waiting out the conversation and exiting the bathroom before Hannah did. As Hannah kept talking, Lynn finished and left.

She returned to the booth. "I'm getting a case of bottled water and food in case we get stuck offroad somewhere. I'll meet the three of you outside at the truck."

Once outside, Joost and Beau helped Lynn lift the case of water into the truck. *How do I act with Hannah? Maybe she wanted me to hear the full update to Henry since she told me she works for him? But he wants the water recycling tech? Same thing we want but what would Henry do with it?*

"Was it you in the bathroom?" Hannah asked her.

*Christ.* "Yeah. You?" She laughed and didn't wait for Hannah to answer. Trucks roared around them. "So noisy in there I had to come out to the parking lot for the quiet."

Hannah looked at her dubiously but only said, "I see."

❖

Beau drove Joost, Hannah, Lynn, and Roy further south and west to Reeves County, where Lynn's and Joost's companies had wells on adjacent leases.

Roy ran through the checklist: "Full tank of gas? Case of water? Protein bars or jerky? Yes, to all."

Joost pointed toward Monahans Sandhills State Park. "We don't get our frac sand—our proppant to prop open the fracs—from the park, but you can see where we got the idea that out here in West Texas, we didn't need to import sand by railcar all the way from Wisconsin. These dunes are up to seventy feet tall and stretch two hundred miles into New Mexico."

Despite the cold, the wind blew a derecho of sand as the truck sped on I-20 through Monahans. Dust clouded both sides of the interstate for a few miles.

Hannah frowned, looking at the dust.

"We don't get much rain. Maybe a foot a year. Many places use tarps." Roy nodded toward one service company slide enveloped in a large cloud of sand dust. "But not all of them."

"There's so much water being put back in the ground you get earthquakes. A few 5.4 magnitude ones, I heard?" Hannah asked.

"Yes, even the uncomplaining West Texas earth bellyaches and burps sometimes," Joost said.

"—so poetic—" Hannah's eyes widened.

Joost cut his eyes to her. "Not poetry. Just too much saltwater—dirty well water—being re-injected into ultradeep wastewater wells."

"We're recycling more produced water for our fracking," Lynn said.

"Us, too," Joost responded. 'Produced water' was the water that came out with the oil and gas. It was "dirty" because it contained so much salt and so many minerals it couldn't be used for anything, even more drilling, without being cleaned up first, an expensive process.

"But let me guess," Hannah said. "It's giving you problems with your well casing."

Joost nodded, a look of astonishment and appreciation crossing his face.

"It's the contaminants in the water. You just have to experiment, maybe clean it up a bit more before you reuse it in the well," she said. "You forget—"

"You're a geochemist," Lynn and Joost chimed together.

Hannah grinned.

Lynn looked at her phone's map application. The few roads in this area *were* far apart. "Who lives here?"

"Ranching families, mainly," Roy said. "Here for generations."

Lynn decided to be blunt. "Joost, what will you do if TriCoast doesn't buy your company?"

"Someone else will. We've had other inquiries." He shrugged.

"So why are you selling?" Hannah asked.

"With the right industry partner"—he looked at Lynn—"we'd still have control, and we'd have more capital. We'd be bigger. If I'm unhappy, I'll leave and start over. There aren't many willing sellers in Midland. Private companies usually stay private. Or we'll just keep operating. Get bigger. You can't see it, but below ground there are anywhere from two to twelve benches or zones of productive shale. We have twelve years of drillable prospects. That's a long runway of inventory. Good free cash flow."

They turned off I-20 south toward Fort Stockton onto the much smaller state highway 18.

"What do you do about flaring?" Hannah asked Joost.

"Sure, we're way out here, but in Texas distances we're really operating in our own backyard. We create a problem; we suffer from it. As do all our friends and neighbors, at church, school, soccer. We don't want to put the unburned methane in the air OR flare smoke. And as we talked about earlier, we limit our use of lights so the observatory can get a clear view of the stars."

"So how do you monitor methane emissions?" Hannah insisted.

*Good woman*, Lynn thought. *I have the same questions.*

"I can't decide if you're on our side or against us," Joost said. "Bad practices will kill a well, kill a company. We don't want to lose even a single methane molecule. But here?" he waved toward the emptiness around them. "We use satellite data and drones. We catch and fix leaks and flaring within a few days."

"Impressive." Hannah nodded.

Lynn noticed Hannah warming further to Joost as he explained his careful operations.

"Fixing rogue emissions used to take months," Lynn added, "precisely because the wells are so far apart. Of course, less water here means fewer plants means better sight lines."

"We track. We use a tracking service. And we get tracked, we're sure of it. Various geolocation companies are always alert to who's building a pad and who's moving a frac crew in. Some of the services combine satellite data and cell phone tracking—for millions of cell phones—so they can see if a big crew shows up at a new lease down the road from me, or if someone is building a water line, for example. When outside contractors show up—and they do on every well—the info service lights up with the large number of mobile phones. The service can tell us about staffing changes at wells next to ours, so we know they're about to drill or frack. Other services monitor global oil inventories. Our oil's worth less if there are two tankers of it sitting offshore China. For parts of this business, that knowledge can be worth billions."

Lynn knew TriCoast also subscribed to a few such services. They'd been the first items Roy had asked her to continue when she took over for David, and she had approved them.

"What you're saying is, despite how empty it all looks, every acre has a story," Hannah suggested.

Joost and Roy nodded and grinned at one another.

"Who buys the natural gas your wells produce?" Lynn asked.

"Power companies, chemical companies, utilities like the one in Chicago, and LNG companies, like TriCoast's when it's running."

"Okay," Roy said. "Fort Stockton. We'll flip a U-turn—the rigs disappear just south of here. Plus, once we head into ranch land, the cell phone service gives out—ranchers don't pay for big cell towers on their land."

Later, as they neared the turn back onto I-20, Hannah saw a sign for the distance to Kermit.

Then Roy pointed and spoke up. "I've never seen one of the candelilla wax refineries this far north. Usually, they show up two hundred miles south of here, near Big Bend or Alpine. Looks abandoned."

*Kermit is the hometown of the missing steel pipe driver. Or was. What if he got dumped into one of those wax refinery vats?* Hannah wasn't ready to voice her suspicion but also didn't want to miss this opportunity. "Let's stop and look. I'm curious to see this place."

"I want to get back to Midland," Roy said.

"I agree with Hannah. This tiny refinery is interesting." Lynn said. "It's like the old, abandoned pots-and-pans oil refineries around Tulsa."

Beau turned the truck off the remote road and up to the side of a large, two-story adobe building.

Lynn walked around to a rusting door in the front. "I'll bet no one has been here in months."

Hannah and Lynn eased the door open. The only light came from the windows high up in the building and the door they had just opened.

To Hannah, Lynn appeared to go into engineering mode as she examined two enormous circular steel vats—like big, blackened kettles—about ten feet in diameter and ten feet tall. This was the "refinery." The adobe firebox at the bottom of the vessels still showed what Hannah presumed were the butane heating elements. In front of the pots, the cement floor was slick and shiny—this was where the cooling sections had been.

A few odd-sized chunks of refined brown wax littered the floor. Hannah picked one up. It was smaller than a brick and lighter. It appeared to have been broken off from a bigger slab.

"Originally, the pots were probably outside and then later this building was built around it," Joost said.

"There's a familiar smell," Lynn said. "Sulfuric acid."

"What I'm also noticing?" Hannah said. "A fruity smell. Still surprisingly strong. Especially around the bottom of one of these pots."

As Hannah's eyes adjusted to the gloom, she saw a barrel with a tap off to the right and remembered the description of the process: a small amount of concentrated acid had been added to the wax as it boiled.

Hannah climbed the ladder to an unsteady platform overlooking the tops of both giant vats. She screamed. With nothing to hold onto, she crouched to a squat on the open platform, putting all her energy into not vomiting.

"What is it?" Beau's voice floated up from below.

Hannah's mouth opened but she couldn't say anything.

She pointed to the vessel on the left. Finally, her words came out. "A body. A man. In this one."

Looking up at her, dead but skin preserved in the dry desert air, a man stretched his arms up against the sides of the pot he could have never scaled. Enough of his face remained that through the darkness, Hannah could see a rictus of horror and fright.

She climbed down the ladder. Beau, Joost, Roy, and Lynn took turns climbing up, seeing the same sight, and climbing down, grim expressions on their faces.

"Let's call the police," Joost said. Lynn punched in 9-1-1.

*It IS him,* Hannah thought. She recognized his face from the "missing" posters. His sprawled position suggested he had tried to climb out but failed. Yet the big, dark, faded-to-rust pooled bloodstains on his shirt told Hannah a bullet had stopped his heart.

# CHAPTER 26
# MIDLAND

Lynn, Roy, Hannah, Joost, and Beau stayed with the body at the wax refinery until they answered questions—each separated from the others—from the county sheriff and his deputies. Before the coroner arrived, the sheriff explained that although the coroner was not a medical examiner but a justice of the peace, he could pronounce death.

Roy shook his head. "As if there's a question."

After the coroner drove up, examined the scene, and officially declared the death, he said "We'll send the body to the Dallas County Medical Examiner's Office for forensics, further processing, and identification. We don't have the budget or facilities here."

After more questions from the coroner, finally he and the sheriff allowed the five of them to leave.

Lynn was relieved to get back into the truck for the return, finally, to Midland. Everyone else seemed to feel the same.

"I think they'll figure out the body is the missing driver from PipePod," Hannah said.

Lynn gasped. "Did you tell them that?"

"No, because it's just a hunch, based on where the wax refinery was, near Kermit. The driver was from Kermit, but I don't have any other evidence. If I'm right, the sheriff would wonder how I'd guessed, and I wouldn't be able to explain." Hannah looked down at her hands.

"You think someone from Kermit killed him?" Joost asked.

"So many truckers in West Texas with access to I-20, so not

necessarily someone from Kermit. And did you notice the smells?" Hannah asked.

"Just that they were terrible," Roy said.

"Musty," Lynn said. "Isn't that just the vat? Why? What do you notice?"

"Hydrocarbons, especially phenol. Some fruity smells, which was odd, as I mentioned to Lynn. Salts. Maybe metals, although they don't have an odor.

"Copper?" Roy asked.

"His blood," Hannah answered.

"What do the smells suggest to you?" Lynn said.

"Oilfield wastewater," Hannah replied.

"You mean—" Lynn started to ask.

"Yes, like something on the clothes or body of a person who hauled oilfield wastewater," Hannah said.

"John Cooper. Or Rowan Daine. Or someone who worked for Daine's company," Lynn said.

"Hannah, did you tell the sheriff or his deputies?" Joost asked.

"I did tell them that, though not that I guessed it was the Pipe-Pod driver. They can't arrest somebody based on a smell. They *bloody laughed*." Hannah looked and sounded hurt. "And yes, they already dismissed the idea of fingerprints or DNA other than the victim's."

"Did the smells seem fresh? Strong?" Lynn asked.

"Strong enough that I caught them. Weak enough the rest of you didn't," Hannah replied.

Lynn wondered if Hannah had invented the funny smell. More likely, it had been there a while and Hannah was the only one with a nose sensitive enough to catch it.

The view coming into Midland was oddly reassuring. It was flat to the horizon, but hundreds of horseheads bobbed every half-acre or so, reflecting the old days of drilling closely spaced vertical wells. They were so different from the current widely spaced horizontal wells, where an expert driller could send a toothy drill down several thousand feet and at the exact zone, turn it at a right angle to move horizontally through a formation.

Green and brown recycling and settling ponds were interspersed with a string of wind turbines, like Christmas lights. Well pads, and wells, marched out into the distance. *As if we could really look back in time to when this was all underwater and the Permian was an endless sea,* Lynn thought.

Cold clouds and narrow brown section roads gave way back to wider lanes and the standard West Texas fast, aggressive pick-up truck drivers, in a hurry to get to work or home, making sudden merges and willing to take every lane, including any not marked.

"I'm glad you're driving," Hannah said to Beau, echoing Lynn's thoughts.

After Odessa but before Midland, Beau got a call and answered it, driving one-handed. "Yes, I can be there tomorrow." When he disconnected, he said, "Let's go to the airport. Rowan Daine wants me in Dallas for a security detail tomorrow. One of you can drive on to Midland."

"Happy to," Roy said.

After they left Beau at the curb of the Midland International Air and Space Port, Roy took over the driving.

"How about The Racquet Club?" Joost said. "We could get dinner, decompress, talk about next steps. It's winter now but in the summer it's the only place in town with tall trees. Even in the winter, you get a sense of the trees."

❖

On the cold winter afternoon, the sun was speeding toward the horizon. Traffic on I-20 near Pecos was still as busy as it had been earlier in the day.

Hap Pensker was looking forward to returning home. One more wastewater delivery and then he could turn back around and drop off the tanker truck at the field office for the next shift at Daine Environmental Water Services. Then he'd climb into his own pickup truck and head home to get dinner and relieve his wife of childcare duties for a few hours. Nice work really, playing with his son and daughter. He didn't understand why she groused about being bored. *Easier than dealing with ol' Rowan Daine. Guy's not playing with a full deck. I should turn him in just for his temper. Let alone these closed wells he has us driving to. But I need the pay.*

Yet Daine had been around the office less recently. He'd taken a temporary hotshot job heading up massive TriCoast Energy. *Wonder how he landed such a sweet gig? Man gets all the luck.*

Hap pulled up to the closed gate. He had the coordinates and the unlock code. After swinging open the gate, he parked his truck near the manhole cover for the disposal well. Same code to unlock and open it.

He moved the cover aside, set his hoses and the wastewater in his truck began splashing deep into a well that seemed nowhere close to full.

Afterward, he locked up the cover and the gate.

On his way back home from the field office, he stopped at a convenience store on I-20 for a couple of Shiner Bocks. *One now, one later after the kids go to bed. Don't want to drink in front of them.*

The sounds of the highway traffic disguised the sudden silence of everything else. Even the remaining birds that hadn't yet flown south were quiet.

The floor inside the convenience store began to vibrate. Hap had felt this before and waited for it to stop. He wasn't about to run out without a protein bar and his beer. He certainly wouldn't run outside before paying. Hap liked the friendly cashier, Odini. Odini was another guy who worked late nights like Hap often did.

But the shaking didn't stop. Chip racks began to fall. Tall, heavy refrigerators pulled away from the wall, their interior lights dimming as they lost power. Overhead lights in the store darkened as the very ground kept moving.

*Earthquake. Stronger than most. I'd better get outside. Odini knows I'm good for this.*

Holding the beers and protein bar in one hand and using his other hand for balance, Hap tried to navigate around fallen racks. It was dark inside the store.

He tripped but didn't fall.

The rumbling resumed. Hap dodged around another eight-foot refrigerator that had rolled loose and tipped precariously toward him.

He scooted next to the wall in the darkness.

Yet another refrigerator blocked his exit. He set down his beers and protein bar and tried to push the steel refrigerator out of the way. He couldn't budge it over the crack opening up in the floor. He was trapped on two sides by the heavy rolling refrigerators that the earthquake had moved, but he couldn't.

He heard Odini say "Watch out, Mr. Hap!"

But it was too late. With a terrible crack, a big section of the outer wall of the convenience store shook and ripped loose, falling inward on Hap Pensker and crushing him.

The Pecos Fire Department was at the store within minutes after Odini frantically called 9-1-1.

They immediately got a forklift and a small excavator to the store and carefully removed the chunks of fallen wall. But even before they uncovered his broken body and checked his pulse, they knew from his silence that Hap Pensker was dead.

❖

Once the four of them arrived at the racquet club, they hurried out of the cold air and ordered a late dinner. Lynn and Joost sat across the table from Hannah and Roy.

Joost looked pensive. "Hannah, how is it you know so much about my business? What's your real interest?"

To Lynn, Hannah's smile looked surprisingly tentative. "There are investors—just like Lynn here for TriCoast—who've asked me to take a look. As I told you, one of them is your father."

"But who's working with him? I know him. He doesn't have enough money to buy my company."

"He hasn't mentioned that he's working for or with anyone else."

Chips and salsa arrived. Joost looked annoyed. "You don't trust us? You don't trust me? Maybe we shouldn't trust you."

Lynn decided it was time to press the point. She asked the question although she knew the answer. "Who were you talking to after our lunch at the HEB?"

Hannah rolled her eyes. "I thought you believed in the privacy of the women's restroom. And of course you know. It was evident when I joined you back at the truck, although you lied about it being too noisy."

*Yep. Nailed.*

"If you can't tell us who you and Henry are really working for, you'll need to leave Midland, no matter how I f---" Joost stopped himself, bit his lip.

"How you feel? Is that what you were going to say? You're only allowing my questions because you want to put the moves on me? Your usual approach with women? Sure seemed to be at the barbecue place. That's what your friend said." Hannah's face was red.

"Time to fish or cut bait," Roy said slowly. "What's your real deal?"

Hannah took a deep breath.

The other three waited and stared at her.

"I don't know who Henry's working for, but I know he's worried about getting information to someone else. He's worried if he doesn't, he'll get killed. I think whoever he's working for is here or has people here in the US trying to drive down the value of your company. Maybe so they can buy it. Maybe to put you out of business."

"You and my father are partners with someone hurting my people? Who tried to kill me and Lynn? Who tried to kill you?" Joost demanded.

"Henry Vandervoost recruited me in London. I swear he never told me who he's working for or why," Hannah confessed.

Simultaneously they felt, more than heard, a rumble. Lynn looked outside but didn't see lightning.

Roy shook his head and looked worried.

"My father's trying to run me out of business so he can buy it? If he was man enough to show his face here again I'd wring his fucking neck." Joost jumped up. "Get out. Get out of here now. You and my father are two snakes who deserve one another. Neither one of you deserves to do business with—"

Hannah was starting to rise as the maître d' ran over.

"I'm leaving, I'm leaving," she said.

"This isn't about you," the maître d' said. "Mr. Bradshaw, there's been an earthquake in Pecos, a bad one. One of your engineers told me to find you, to ask what they should do. He said there might be casualties."

Joost turned to leave. "I've got more important things to do now than dealing with the three of you, especially you, Hannah."

As he rushed out, punching numbers on his phone, Lynn said, "I'll get Hannah back to her hotel."

"No, don't bother," Hannah said.

Roy looked chagrined. "So dinner here's a no-go. Maybe I can scrounge leftovers at home. But before I leave, I'm checking on the earthquake news with our TriCoast guys." He stood and pulled out his phone.

Lynn pulled Hannah aside. "Let's hear what he has to say."

"I thought you didn't trust me either."

"I want you to work for us. Do a project. We need you."

"I'm sure working for Henry Vandervoost—your nemesis, you yourself said—conflicts me out. Don't see how I can."

"Let's hear what Roy tells us, first," Lynn said.

Roy rushed over and drew them in. "Five-point-four earthquake, one of the worst ever out here in West Texas. It was centered near Mentone, not too far from Pecos, not too far from where we were today."

"Aftershocks?" Hannah asked.

He nodded.

"Five miles underground. Intraplate quake. There are no tectonic fault lines around there."

"Companies must still be injecting wastewater into deep wells, even though they've been told not to exactly because of this." Lynn shook her head. "Companies like Rowan Daine's. People like John Cooper who work for him."

"This is the biggest one yet," Roy said.

"There have been many," Hannah replied. It wasn't a question.

"They slowed and stopped when people were following the water disposal rules," Lynn said.

"Our guys said blow-out preventers failed on a couple of gas wells, maybe because of the quake. Now they're on fire. One of 'em is a Bradshaw well," Roy said.

"Our people are okay?" Lynn asked. *The important question.*

"Ours, yes. But four or five were injured, maybe two killed at the well being drilled for Bradshaw Energy. Derrick's on fire. Expected to crumble any minute now."

"Roy, check in with all your field managers, make sure they and all our people are okay. Hannah and I are going back to the hotel. Call me when you've got updates."

"Yep."

Later, Hannah began thinking about what she had heard. *Is this the real story of my father's death in West Texas? Near to Kermit is what my mother and I were told. But maybe it wasn't an accidental gas pipe explosion like they told us. Wasn't he working for Daine's company at the time? My father was so honest. He would have reported illegal wastewater dumping or illegal anything. I have to find out what really happened to him!*

❖

Because of the earthquake, and the well accident, no one fully grasped the portent, the first signal of the later freeze disaster.

This wasn't woodpeckers rattling away at dead trees.

Flocks of orange-breasted robins numbering in the hundreds, thousands, were everywhere. Startling in their omnipresence, huge in size, crowding and scrabbling for seeds and berries. In Midland, they ringed the edges of fountains and when they flew, they blackened sidewalks, trucks, and mighty SUVs with droppings. They crashed into windows in pairs and wobbled off, stunned but not dead.

# CHAPTER 27
# BUDAPEST, HUNGARY

*"Since once small observation can disprove a statement, while millions can hardly confirm it, disconfirmation is more rigorous than confirmation."*

—*Nicholas Naseem Taleb*

CLANDESTINE SUPPORT TO environmental groups around the world in any country not already buying Russian oil and gas was creating dividends—to use the capitalist word—particularly once those countries outlawed hydrocarbons, particularly hydrocarbons from Russia. Kir Zaitsev played the long game and soon enough—many sooner than others—energy ministers turned back to him. They needed the oil and gas they had always needed. Others called later when their new renewables stopped producing at sundown or when the wind calmed. Fortunately for the countries desperate for hydrocarbons, Russia—Zaitsev himself—had been able to step in and again provide oil and gas.

Zaitsev also focused on making sure the newest natural gas supplier to Europe and Asia—US liquefied natural gas—was unreliable. His operative had been in the US now doing exactly that, starting with TriCoast's Louisiana terminal deliveries to Barcelona, Spain.

He hoped to meet a TriCoast executive here, in Budapest, at the second of the two important global gas conferences, to gauge the company's reaction.

The sun was bright on Zaitsev's face as he walked the streets of the city. He was glad to be away from cold, brittle Moscow.

His cell phone rang—the masked number belonged to Russian President Egonov—and Zaitsev stepped toward a building, faced outward, his back to a shop window.

"*Da, mister prezident. Da, ponyal.*" *Yes, Mr. President. Yes, understood.* Zaitsev spoke carefully in response to a torrent of invective from Egonov over why his energy minister's plans were moving so slowly. Part of the directions for his official duties were to use only Russian, no foreign words.

Egonov's loud shouting was a good sign. Cool silence could mean it was time to prepare for the sudden end of your life.

"*Da, da.*"

Egonov ended the call abruptly.

It's why Zaitsev was here at the gas conference. Evaluation, instruction, direction. He turned back to the hotel.

❖

"The weather in Budapest is cold, and so it is an optimal time to experience the baths." Avi's quick search earned only a brief, glib reply, likely composed by a tourist agency. He looked out his hotel window. The historic city on the Danube stunned him with its beauty. He was far from the only visitor. Middle Eastern, American, European, and Israeli energy executives, bankers, and fund managers—many of whom he recognized—had landed in Budapest for the second of two well-known global natural gas conferences. He'd seen some in various restaurants and at the Vasarely museum, as well as the hotel.

A frenzy of activity and deal-making was taking place under the surface, albeit all at a deliberate pace.

"Bears sound smart, bulls make money. Are you a bear or a bull?"

Avi spun around to face the speaker. Russian energy minister, Kir Zaitsev, was examining him in turn. "You again! Surely you don't expect to sell gas to others here. Your pipeline is gone," Avi said.

"Only one of our pipelines, Avi Levin. We are available, just as we have always been, to those many who need us. And even to those who have said publicly they don't. They talk to us privately. You must be unaware of our activities at Ceuta."

Avi shrugged. "Tell me."

Zaitsev looked around. "The world knows. I'm surprised you don't. I will merely say Ceuta is a helpful transshipment location for the oil we sell to China. And even though it looks like it's in Morocco and across the Strait of Gibraltar, it's as Spanish as Seville. Unfortunately, the wrong end of the Mediterranean for you."

"Are you here to compete with us or to trade with us this time?"

"I'm here to do whatever to whoever benefits my country the most." Zaitsev stood back and looked Avi up and down again. Avi tried not to flinch under the man's frank stare.

"You can't compete with us."

Zaitsev shook his head. "You and your countrymen need to look at yourself in a different mirror. One more accurate, less flattering."

"We have no business with you."

"Not true. You are already competing with me, every molecule you export. Surely you didn't expect Russia would shut in the hundreds of millions of cubic meters a day *we* are able to export. But ask your deputy energy minister. He has already approached me about buying your company. Its reserves, not its people. He wants to be out of the hydrocarbon business altogether. Net zero, you know?"

Avi's head spun at the deputy energy minister's disloyalty, but he would not voice his thoughts.

"Good day. Enjoy this weather." Zaitsev turned away from Avi and walked nonchalantly down the long, mirrored hallway.

❖

Zaitsev was impatient with Henry Vandervoost. Another European blowhard. Too sentimental about his son, Joost Bradshaw. Hell, the son had even taken his mother's last name instead of Henry's. Too emotional. Too unstable. This Hannah woman he'd told Vandervoost to recruit didn't seem up to the task either. Too intellectual to be a honey trap. In the back of Zaitsev's mine was the phenomenal success story of the water recycling process. It would be valuable for use in Russia, and for resale to China.

By the time Vandervoost arrived at Zaitsev's hotel room, Zaitsev's men had planted the bugs he would use to record the conversation and then later remove to protect his own privacy. He'd also tamped down his anger. Europeans didn't respond well to anger, not the way the Americans did. Europeans just doubled down on their innate passive-aggressiveness.

Vandervoost looked timidly around as Zaitsev welcomed him in.

"No, no security behind the door. Me alone," Zaitsev said to the man.

"In answer to your question, yes, Hannah is making progress on acquiring the water recycling process equipment plans and specs. And I am also hoping to get my son to sell his company to me."

"You mean Hannah is making progress with your son," Zaitsev said. He was momentarily distracted as he remembered the peremptory commands from President Egonov from their earlier conversation. Egonov was ready to be done with Vandervoost as the intermediary. Egonov suggested taking him out and instead dealing directly with Joost for the formula. Torture Joost if necessary. Zaitsev had patiently explained that such an approach was unlikely to succeed, but the conversation reminded him he had little time to appease Egonov.

Vandervoost blinked. "Yes. Hannah is persuasive."

"But you don't have the technology. Or an agreement to buy his company. So, she can't be as good as you say or as good as I had hoped." He debated whether to tell Vandervoost about the operative who had taken down TriCoast's LNG terminal. *Nyet*.

"TriCoast's LNG terminal?" Zaitsev asked.

"How did you know?" Vandervoost's shoe tapped an unsteady rhythm.

"Everyone does. It's public. I saw their representative, that woman, rushing around trying to explain," Zaitsev said. "The fact is her company ultimately didn't keep delivering on a short-term spot contract, so how could they be trusted to deliver on a fifteen-year contract?"

"Lynn Dayton." Vandervoost snarled. "What a witch."

"You and she have a history," Zaitsev said. It wasn't a question. It was part of the reason he'd recruited Henry Vandervoost.

"History is right. Nothing today."

"Enough of the how you call it—gossip." Zaitsev got up and walked toward the door.

Vandervoost stayed seated until Zaitsev swept a hand, motioning him to leave. "You have little time. The Russian prisons are unpleasant, but it is the Chinese to whom you owe money. I've interceded on your behalf because of your experience. Because I believe you can help us. But this is a time-limited offer. I understand the Chinese prisons are worse than ours. Their means of persuasion are at least as brutal."

# CHAPTER 28
# BUDAPEST, HUNGARY

LYNN STUMBLED OFF the airplane. No matter how much she prepared, the Dallas-to-London-to-Budapest flights could be unpredictable. She still wasn't sure how she had navigated Heathrow with so little sleep on the flight from the US.

She was glad Beau had traveled ahead. He would meet her at the hotel and provide security throughout the trip. She expected he had already checked her room for bugs.

After passport control, she waited for baggage and for the local driver Beau had arranged. This conference for LNG buyers and sellers was important for TriCoast as an LNG seller, regardless of whether she was able to buy Bradshaw Energy. She'd already missed the earlier conference that was like this one.

She glanced up at the screen by baggage claim and barely stifled a yelp.

*What's my face doing in that news report?* She looked around for a moment to see if others had matched her with the screen. Most hadn't, but a handful of people looked at her curiously. She nodded and shrugged. She quickly turned her attention back to the screen.

*My clothes are from an interview I did years ago but they're making it sound recent! I don't even own that suit anymore.*

As she focused, she noticed other oddities. *My expression isn't changing. My voice doesn't break. My hair doesn't even move!*

*But what a nightmare to have to explain when the fake video me says we're planning layoffs! I never said that! Who would go to all the trouble to do a deepfake of me, and why?*

She found her bag and saw her driver holding a sign with her name. He, too, was looking at the screen. His expression when he saw her was a question she would be answering over and over the next few days. *Best to start now. God, I'm exhausted.*

"The Gresham, please," Lynn said to the driver as he took her bag from her. "Yes, that's me. But it's not. It's a fake."

"I see." He sounded polite, but dubious.

To change the subject for the lengthy ride into the city, she said, "Please tell me about yourself, and what I should see while I'm here."

A few minutes into the drive to the hotel, she called Beau. "Could you conference in Claude and our new cyber chief?" TriCoast's new head of cybersecurity was a man she had advocated hiring only a few weeks ago. *But I didn't think I would need him for my own disaster.*

Once Beau added the other two to the call, Lynn said, "There's a fake video of me circulating. I just saw it on a news screen at the Budapest airport. Swear to God it's not me." In her exhaustion, she defaulted to mixed upstream and downstream engineering patois. "Let me swab out the situation. Give you the heart cut." Swabbing a well meant cleaning it. In refining, the heart cut was not just a middle distillation fraction, it was the essence of a thing.

"The clone, the fake, is saying TriCoast's Louisiana LNG plant will be down for months and I don't know what the problem is, but TriCoast might have to do massive layoffs. Christ, so evil. Not just for our buyers, but it could demoralize our people. Laying people off is the last thing ever." She bowed her head and rubbed her temples. "Meanwhile, I'm here to represent the company and get folks to make fifteen and twenty-year deals."

"It's easy to create a fake with the right tools and enough video and audio files of you talking," Claude explained.

The cyber chief said, "I've been expecting something like this would happen to one of you at TriCoast. Lynn, I've studied you on video and in person. Whoever it was used an early version of the software tool. They made it too long—they got greedy, if you will—the longer the fake talks the less convincing it is. It looks and sounds like you in the first few sentences, but less so after about a minute."

"That's what I noticed."

The cyber chief added, "No pauses in your speech, no hand gestures, and only two facial expressions."

Claude chimed in again. "Your real voice has more oomph, more variability."

"We've arrived at the hotel so I have to disconnect. Tell Beau what we're going to do. I'll see him in person as soon as I check in."

She thanked the driver and paid him. After getting to her suite, she tossed clothes on hangars. She texted Beau. In a few minutes, Beau had joined her at the dining table in the suite.

"We're taking the video down everywhere we can," he said. "We've split the work between me, Claude, and the new guy."

"But that still leaves me to explain it to everyone I meet here in person." She closed her eyes. *I'm so tired.*

"You'll rally. You'll be fine. Hey, I was an MP in Afghanistan and then did private security work for drilling contractors in the Middle East for a while. So much stuff was off-limits that the contractors would go crazy. Their motto was "fuck, fight, or trip pipe," which about summed up weekends. This is a video. You can totally handle this."

"I have to."

A knock sounded at the door. She looked at her phone, then at Beau, and squinted. "Damn. I forgot about the meeting with Avi Levin. I need him."

"How did he get your suite number? Surely the front desk didn't hand it out."

"I forgot I texted it to him."

"You *are* jet-lagged."

She pasted a smile on her face, opened the door, and waved Avi toward the round dining table where she and Beau were trying to undo the damage of the video clone. She introduced him to Beau.

"The video?" Avi asked.

"You've seen it?" Lynn was chagrined. *If it was on the news at the airport, it was everywhere.*

"Would have sworn it was you."

She shook her head.

"Any idea who created it?" Avi looked around suspiciously, as if the perpetrator might be in the room with them.

"Someone who wants to cause trouble for me, for TriCoast," Lynn responded.

"Maybe now isn't a good time to talk?"

Lynn shook her head. "It's a perfect time. We're almost back online. We're not firing anyone. We're locking in gas supplies from the Permian for LNG. We *are* a reliable supplier. We backed you up on the gas to Spain until you could get approval to land your LNG in Bilbao instead of Barcelona. Now we want to joint venture with your company in other long-term sales to Europe. Are you ready to go on your end?"

Beau continued tapping on his laptop, crafting appeals to take down the fake video from the many sites on which it had appeared.

Avi looked away. "Well, that's why I'm here. Zaitsev--

"—the Russian energy minister? —"

Avi nodded. "Just pointedly told me he intends to take back all his gas and oil markets, from me, from you, from everyone else."

"Have you gotten the necessary approvals to do this joint sales venture with us?"

"The ministry has been on version one-point-never of the contract."

"That bad?" She winced.

"Some people are slow-walking it. Some, I'm sorry to say, don't think Israel should be in the oil and gas business at all." Avi appeared to be making an enormous effort to stay calm. "This is our, Israel's, patrimony. Of course, we can't give it away. But we have to sell it, not keep it in the ground."

"People can't give up their fantasies, even when they're desperate. Greens in Europe are still a force, still think they're getting rid of gas and oil in the next few years, and despite everything, they still have a voice in many countries. It makes sense those countries would turn to Russia rather than make long-term gas contracts with us, no matter what they say publicly."

"I thought you were on our side." Avi stood up to leave.

"I am. I'm just the Red Team," Lynn responded, unsuccessful at stifling a yawn.

"Red Team?"

"Devil's advocate. Poking holes in your logic, in your assumptions. You've heard the term in your management or military training, right?"

"And that video of you is not real?" Avi's cheeks were red.

"The video isn't real."

"Bullshit." Avi slammed the door as he left.

"That didn't go well."

"Back to the task at hand," Beau said.

"Making deals IS the task at hand. That's what I came all this way for." Lynn put her head down for a minute.

"About the faked video. You can help by giving us names. Who do you think would have done this?"

"I don't know! Anyone. No one. A skilled outsider. People in TriCoast are loyal to one another," Lynn said. *Can I just lie down and go to sleep?*

"You may be exhausted, but you aren't naïve."

"Okay, except for Dena Tarleton." Dena was the woman who'd tried to kill Lynn and had killed David Jenkins after Dena's affair with David went sour.

"But she's dead. What about Farrell Isos?" Beau had named a former TriCoast security guard who'd been jailed for his part in a conspiracy to murder Lynn.

"Him, too. But he's still in jail."

After Beau had successfully convinced all but one site to take down the cloned video, he accompanied her to the conference's non-alcoholic mocktail party in the lounge of the hotel. Non-alcoholic in deference to the religious preferences of many of the attendees. Others had already left for the bathhouses across the Danube River.

Beau stood off to the side as Lynn circulated. She felt more curious glances. To those who asked about the video, she described the deepfake. *But many will assume that was really me,* she thought.

She found the Spanish energy minister and held out her hand for a handshake. "Señor Garcia, I'm Lynn Dayton with TriCoast. I'm pleased to meet you. I'm hoping we can further discuss supplying you with long-term LNG together with Avi Levin."

Garcia's expression did not change. He did not take her hand. "We have many suppliers who would like to do business with us. Fortunately, our arrangement with your companies is only for a brief time. Your interview did not impress me." He turned away before she could explain.

A tall, handsome man approached. Beau joined her and stiffened, examining the man for weapons.

"I am only here to shake her hand and pay my compliments to the lady. Lynn Dayton, TriCoast?" His English was lightly accented.

She looked at his nametag. "Kir Zaitsev. Good to meet you."

"But I feel as if I already know you. Your voice."

She cocked her head and raised her eyebrows. "We've never met before."

Zaitsev began moving away from her and toward their thobe-clad hosts. He turned and nodded. "Ah yes. It was the video."

*Him!* She straightened. *Is Zaitsev the video source, or is it someone nearer? Could it have been Rowan Daine?*

# CHAPTER 29
# MIDLAND, TEXAS

WHILE LYNN TRAVELED—TO an LNG conference overseas, she'd said—Hannah decided to continue her analysis of Bradshaw Energy. She was increasingly uncomfortable about Henry's motives. *But a project is a project. I need the money.*

Earlier, she'd contacted the Kermit police department, asking for a cold case file on the death of her father, Stephen Bosko. She had yet to get an answer. And now there was the death of the trucker they'd found in the wax refinery. Even if the two weren't exactly connected, Hannah realized it could be more than coincidence.

She sat in the spare office at Bradshaw Energy that had been set aside for the company's lawyers and accountants.

Joost appeared in the doorway. Hannah felt a pang of attraction, then irritation about being attracted.

"How's it going? Is Bradshaw a good investment?"

"I'm making pro—" the ring of her cell phone interrupted them. She looked at the caller ID. "Kermit PD. I need to take this."

"Mind if I wait with you?"

She did, but only shrugged as she answered her phone. "This is Hannah Bosko."

"Hannah, it's Officer Jesse Suarez with the Kermit Police Department."

"Yes, sir."

"Hannah, I was reviewing your testimony about the unique

smell you noticed at the wax refinery, the smells you connected to John Cooper."

"Yes."

"We've found and spoken with John Cooper. He has a rock-solid alibi from his boss, Rowan Daine. We cannot consider Cooper a suspect. I'm not doubting the fruit and the wastewater smells you noticed, but it could have been from any water or fruit hauler, maybe one from the Rio Grande Valley who made an unscheduled stop there."

"But Rowan Daine could be involved, too! That's why he's covering for Cooper." Hannah's voice had risen. Joost looked at her with concern.

"What evidence do you have?"

"Because Daine is alibiing Cooper!"

"Rowan Daine is a wealthy businessman who has lived and worked around here for decades. You're an outsider with a good nose who's been in West Texas a few weeks. You have no evidence, none, to justify accusing Rowan Daine of involvement in the death of the man found in the wax refinery."

"Yes, you're right, Daine's been here for decades. In fact, is it just coincidence he was here, employing my father, when my father was killed in a pipeline explosion? And have you thought more about letting me see the cold case file on his death?"

"We can't allow you to see the file."

"But Officer Suarez, now we're talking about my father!" Hannah could no longer hold back her tears. "Could you at least tell me the broad findings? What was in the file?"

Joost moved next to her and stroked her arm with his hand.

Silence. Then in a quieter voice, Suarez said, "I can tell you this. Your father did not die in a pipeline explosion, despite what you were told. That there's even still a cold case file on him reflects the fact that we considered—still consider—his death suspicious."

"Really? Oh my god! What happened? What happened to him?" Hannah tried to keep herself from screaming. It felt as if the floor had collapsed beneath her, and she was falling into a deep hole.

"I'm sorry, Hannah. That's all I can tell you." Suarez disconnected.

Hannah jumped up, grabbed Joost, and hid her face against his chest.

Joost put his arms around her and held her. Hannah clung to him and cried, heaving long sobs.

After a few minutes, Joost put one hand under her chin and lifted it. With the other hand, he wiped her face dry.

Then his lips brushed hers in a tentative kiss.

Hannah jumped back. "You are such a bloody playboy. I don't care whether this is your building or your offices. Get away from me!"

Joost slammed the door as he left.

# CHAPTER 30
# CHICAGO

ACCUSTOMED TO THE constant burden of winter, Chicagoans were surprised by the sunlight. They blinked under the respite of a cloudless sky.

But too soon the winter wind was fierce again. More snow fell. Then the city resumed its extreme tests of car functionality and parking shrewdness: cars in the most desirable street parking spots were covered in several inches of snow.

Lynn was back in Chicago to close a multi-million-dollar gas sale from TriCoast to Denny Smith's utility company for gas to keep Chicagoans warm through this and worse winters to come.

She stayed in an old, brown high-rise hotel on Ohio. It turned out to be on the direct route between I-90/I-94 and Northwestern Medical's emergency room. Ambulance sirens woke her from sleep several times.

On the positive side was in a city so vertical, her location fifty stories up coupled with her room's 180+-degree windows gave her wide, unobstructed views west past I90/I94 and east towards Lake Michigan, the Tribune Tower, NBC, and St. Regis.

❖

The embed blended in as easily here as in West Texas. John Cooper always blended in. With immigrants thronging the city, it had taken a few days to get a position on the utility repair crew, but the embed had done so with proficiency at the mechanical tests and a fake union card. He was here because while the

Romanian brothers' test run had succeeded, their promise to do more extensive damage had failed.

Within a few days he had memorized the network of the gas utility's system of distribution pipes: what large-diameter pipes went to which smaller-diameter pipes that served residential neighborhoods. Where repairs were scheduled. Which locations had security cameras. Which locations had non-working security cameras. He acquired enough control system code to pass along to his Russian programmer counterpart. *The Russians are better at this than the Romanians*, he thought.

Cooper activated new social media accounts.

Then, at an afternoon shift change, he positioned himself next to an obscure control dashboard whose security camera wasn't operating. With a silenced gun, he killed the arriving shift operator.

He signaled to his Russian programmer. The programmer used Cooper's passcode and remotely overrode a few of the utility's operating instructions.

The regulator-sensor on a main line was jammed and then fed false data, as if the line were losing pressure. Automatic systems started up, pouring high-pressure gas into distribution lines at pressures far above their maximum allowable operating pressure. The high-pressure gas would soon pour into homes in the historic south Chicago Kenwood neighborhood.

The control panel started to blare a high-pressure warning but the embed shut it off.

He laughed. He could almost hear frantic 9-1-1 calls beginning.

To further redirect attention, he painted TriCoast's name on the control dashboard and a nearby pipe, and then took pictures.

Cooper left and returned to his rented apartment. He began posting on the new social media accounts.

Rowan Daine and Kir Zaitsev would soon be smiling and paying.

❖

"No boss this time?" Denny Smith smirked at Lynn in his small, wood-paneled office at the Chicago natural gas utility.

"I'm the one who makes the contract," Lynn replied.

Denny pulled a serious face. "Basically, we're good with all of this in your contract but we have to reduce the volumes. We're replacing old cast-iron pipes in several neighborhoods, and we need flex in our take-or-pay schedule."

Lynn nodded. "Lot of utilities are. Cuts down on leaks."

A woman rushed in. Denny looked up, annoyed. "I told you not to—"

"Chicago Fire just told us they're getting dozens of 9-1-1 calls. Kenwood neighborhood. Some people don't have any gas. Their heaters are kicking off and it's twenty degrees outside. Their houses are cooling fast."

"I know the temperature."

She continued over his interruption. "Worse, some have too much gas. Way overpressured. Fires and explosions. Backflashes, especially in kitchens. Bunch of serious injuries."

"Christ. Get me maintenance. They need to turn off all the gas to the neighborhood that isn't already turned off," Denny said to the woman. To Lynn he said, "You need to leave."

Lynn drew a breath. "From what you're describing, you could have a major pipe leak—why there's no gas in many houses. Either accident or sabotage, like what happened in Aspen, Colorado."

"Tell me something I don't know."

"Overpressure? Someone either accidentally overpressured a line during a repair or again, deliberate sabotage. You're facing a bunch of fires and explosions in residences."

After a brief phone call and a few texts, Denny stared at her. His look was one of pure rage. "You were right. One of our men was shot, and killed. The report we're hearing is tampering with lines, regulators and sensors, and valves in at least two places. It was someone who knew the system. We're bringing in the FBI as well as the NTSB. And Chicago Fire and Police, although it's not as if the police don't have enough to do. We already have two hundred emergency calls."

"Have your folks found and shut off the lines and valves?" Lynn asked.

"We think so. How did you know? Is it special TriCoast green gas screwing up our lines, causing them to leak in some places, overpressure in others?" Denny's face was even redder.

"No. Our gas is on-spec—everyone's is. As for why I know, when you investigated my background, you must have noticed I'm a registered professional engineer. This is like problems I have dealt with before."

"Yet that's not what's on social media," Denny said.

"What?—" Lynn asked. Before she could ask his meaning, the utility's maintenance chief bolted in the door and stood, waiting.

"Lynn, you've done all the damage you need to. I want you to leave," Denny said.

"We use a standard recovery protocol. Want to hear it?" she asked.

"*I* do," the maintenance chief said. "Quick. We don't want people freezing to death without heat in this cold, especially with another snowstorm due tonight. We're coordinating with the Chicago Fire Department and the mayor."

"You've defined the location as limited to Kenwood and turned off the gas on the overpressured line and identified the leaking underpressured lines?" Lynn asked.

"We can't just empty out the whole neighborhood. We don't have extra housing. Plus, people don't want to risk having their houses looted," Denny said. "But we'll have thousands of people without heat or hot water, maybe for weeks. Christ Almighty. Kenwood's where the former president has a house."

"He and his family aren't in town. We checked. Only security people there," the maintenance chief said.

"How many people are affected in the neighborhood? Are

there central locations for you to distribute free electric space heaters?" Lynn asked.

"Twenty-two thousand people," the maintenance chief said. "We've requisitioned emergency space heaters and notified people to bring their gas bills to the community center or the police sub-stations to get heaters."

"Despite the risks and housing shortage, people may need to be put up in hotels or trailers," Lynn suggested.

"The cost. But yes, you are right. Depends on damage to their homes and whether it's safe for them to stay there." Denny blinked and rubbed his eyes.

"Talk to your counterparts at the electric utility, tell them about extra grid strain in Kenwood because of the space heaters," Lynn said.

Denny frowned but nodded.

"NTSB, FBI, Chicago Police, and Chicago Fire will need to look for evidence and investigate the sources," Lynn added.

"Yep."

"Without heat, water lines into houses could freeze. When they thaw, they'll crack," Lynn said.

The maintenance chief shook his head. "No. Everything is weatherproofed against the cold."

"Good. It's possible your system in Kenwood will have to be shut down at the gas meter, house by house, tested, repressurized, and rebooted the same way, house by house. And you only want your technicians doing it, not the residents."

"Yes, but we can only operate during daylight hours, also safer. It will take a while for such a big neighborhood," the maintenance chief said.

Denny stood up. "You have to stop visiting me, Lynn. Terrible things happen when you're here."

"Glad I could be of help with your recovery plan. You're welcome." Lynn ground her teeth. *The man has big problems and he's lashing out at me.* As she waited in the lobby of the building for her ride to the airport, her phone lit up. TriCoast's communications executive, Claude Durand. "Social media messaging is TriCoast's gas was the cause of the explosions and backflashes. Our name is scrawled on one of the pipelines. There's a picture of it circulating."

Lynn sighed. "Send it to me, but totally false. All gas is cleaned up to the same specs by the time it gets in the pipeline out of Texas, Oklahoma, or Pennsylvania. You can't distinguish our molecules from someone else's. Lines got overpressured and others completely lost their pressure. Appears to be deliberate. TriCoast had nothing to do with it."

Immediately after she closed the call, Joost Bradshaw's name lit up on her screen. *This can't be good either.*

"Lynn, in view of what's happening and what TriCoast is accused of—providing unsafe gas in Chicago—we are stopping negotiations between us and TriCoast. Bradshaw Energy just can't take this kind of reputational damage."

"Joost, wait. That's not what happened. The reports you're seeing are wrong."

"You. You women!"

"What do you mean?"

Silence. Joost had disconnected.

# CHAPTER 31
# LONDON, MIDLAND

In London, Henry received a text from his building's doorman about a waiting delivery.

The doorman gave him a worried look when Henry stepped out of the elevator for his package. "Don't know what you've done, mate, but take care."

The flowers—their type and number—conveyed warnings. The number—four—always avoided in China because in Mandarin it sounded like "death." There was also the Russian tradition: flowers in even numbers were used only at funerals. Two carnations and two lilies, both of which were funeral flowers in England.

When Henry's cell phone rang, he didn't have to look at the display to identify who was calling.

"Zaitsev. What is the meaning of the flowers?" Henry hoped his suspicion was wrong.

"Exactly what you interpret it to be. Early flowers for the funeral you will have if you do not follow through."

"What do you mean?"

"What has your girl in the US done? She has extracted nothing from your son except puppy love. She has not gotten him into bed. Nothing about Bradshaw Energy or its special water recycle process. *Nichego. Nichto.* Nothing."

"You should not threaten me. It is not a good look, especially for you, a modern, sophisticated Russian man."

"I am sophisticated enough to know I, too, will be dead, either from the Chinese or more likely from Egonov's guards, if you do not perform. And quickly."

"What do you want me to do that I haven't already done? Joost trusts Hannah. I'm sure she will obtain the recycling tech and everything else we want."

"It is too late, Henry. My sources say she has turned on you. If she has turned on you, she has turned on me. I thought she was your bitch. Apparently not. You need to get rid of her."

"Kill her? No. You're crazy."

"Kill her. Yes. I am crazy? Perhaps. But so what? You have three days. No, four. Four is a number that should help you remember. Kill her. If her new boyfriend or Lynn Dayton jumps in the way, kill them, too. They are no good to you or us now."

"My son?" Henry's heart contracted.

"Her boyfriend. Your son." Zaitsev ended the call.

Henry barely made it to the bathroom before throwing up in the toilet.

And then he despaired. *Goddamn. I did this to myself. I need a plan. If I don't protect Joost and Hannah from whomever Zaitsev has shadowing them, they're dead. And it will be my fault.*

❖

*This is either the smartest or the stupidest thing I've ever done.* Hannah took a deep breath and called Lynn. "We need to talk."

Lynn's voice was as chilly as the sub-zero air outside. "About what?"

"Who hired me. What I'm supposed to be doing. Joost Bradshaw. What I should do."

"I have to check on our well sites with our operators before what looks to be a big, long freeze. If half the gas goes offline, you don't have enough to make electricity and then the grid implements blackouts and people freeze to death. Happened before. It's a big deal. You can ride with me and talk, or we can talk tonight when I get back."

"I'll ride with you. Tell me where to meet you." Hannah felt relieved.

But when Hannah got into the passenger side of the pickup, Lynn was impatient. "We have so many miles to cover. You'll need to help navigate." Lynn looked at her. "We're picking up Joost at the end to see some joint sites. That okay?"

*No. How awkward.* Hannah said nothing but Lynn didn't seem to notice.

"We'll start southwest and work back so that if the wind and snow pick up, we're not trapped too far from town. So that means a lotta miles on I-20 here. Fire away. What did you want to talk about?"

Hannah took a deep breath. "You know I'm working for that guy you don't like."

"Which one?" A small smile played around Lynn's lips.

"Henry Vandervoost."

"Yes, you told me. Is it complicating things that you've fallen for his son, Joost, even though right at the moment the two of you aren't getting along?"

Hannah gulped. "So obvious?"

"I could be blind and still know, just by the tone of your voice when you talk to him and his when he talks to you."

"If I'm honest with myself, yes. I like him, even though he's just another player. I'm enough of a player, too, to recognize the moves. His father's not a bad bloke either. It's unfortunate they're estranged."

"What does the old man want you to do?"

"Well, here's the problem. I think Henry is taking orders, too. I don't think he's in charge."

"What makes you say so?"

"The way he sounds. He's in a hurry. And he's come up with at least one weird project—besides the one I'm on—that doesn't make sense."

"Start with what you're supposed to be doing," Lynn said.

*Here goes. But I can't tell her about the water recycling tech, not directly.* "Henry wants to buy Joost's company out from under him. He says he has investors. I have been honest about Henry's interest and money, but not that Henry actually wants full control of Bradshaw Energy. So, I'm supposed to find anything I can to either help Henry make the bid or reduce the value of the company, especially liabilities, like environmental liabilities. And..."

"Yes?"

*How do I say this?* "Bradshaw Energy also has a new technology that Henry's investors are especially interested in, even more than the oil and gas reserves themselves."

"Sure, everyone knows. The water recycle technology."

Lynn swerved left to avoid a big semi entering from the access road.

*Good. I didn't have to spell it out.* "Yes."

"Well, given how angry Joost seemed with you last night, you should tell Henry the project's over. You won't get anything more from Joost anytime soon because I doubt he'll talk to you right now."

"So, I'll be returning to the government grind in London, too. Henry had promised me quite a bit of money."

Lynn's answer was immediate. "We'll hire you for whatever he's paying you."

"But."

"Purely selfish. Reduces our competition to buy Joost's company. And you have geological and chemical insights we need, especially now."

"You're very generous. How do I even thank you?" Hannah relaxed.

"By doing a good job. More questions. What do you know about Henry's other investors? Can you find out who they are?"

"Yes. I mean, I'll try, the next time he calls."

"You may need to call him. And what was the weird project you alluded to?"

"Two things. I think I'm being followed by someone who works for Henry or his investors."

"The backup plan. The spy on the spy," Lynn said. "Who? What does he or she look like?"

"Like anyone and everyone who works out here."

"Not just some guy following a pretty woman?"

Hannah felt her face redden. "It's not a one-time thing. Half a dozen times."

"And the second thing?"

"Before I tell you, I want you to know I turned Henry down on this one, at least partially. Remember when you were in Chicago a day or so ago and Denny ran out of the meeting because of gas leaks and explosions?"

"You knew I was there twice?"

"I met with Denny too, but earlier. He told me you'd been there. But Henry. Henry told me he'd been asked to find a way to sabotage the entire natural gas system for the city of Chicago."

Lynn signaled right and pulled the truck off to the side of the road. Even stopped, Hannah felt the truck vibrate as other trucks rushed past on the busy interstate.

Lynn turned off the ignition and looked at Hannah. "Explain."

"I wouldn't have done it even if I could have. Depriving everyone in that big city of heat in the middle of the winter? Freeze a bunch of little kids and old people? No. But here is the issue. *Someone* asked Henry to kill people by cutting off their heat. Since Henry couldn't deliver—at least he couldn't deliver me—whoever it was found saboteurs with the capability and willingness to try to shut down heat to the whole city. At least it turned out to be only a neighborhood, not the whole city."

"Jesus! I don't like Henry, but he was never quite so evil. I agree—somebody put him up to it. And since you didn't carry it out, who did? You have to find out who's directing him. Just for my own safety knowledge, how would you have done it?"

"Couple options. Shut off the mercaptan odorant supply into the gas."

"So, no one could have smelled gas, making leaks and explosions a lot more likely. Ooof. What else?"

"Like the accident in Massachusetts. Change the settings on a few lines so high-pressure gas goes into low-pressure lines. The ones going into homes and offices."

"I think Henry got someone to use that approach. In Massachusetts, the same thing killed a person, injured others, and whole neighborhoods had fires and explosions. In Chicago, they had to cut the gas to twenty thousand people in Kenwood."

Hannah sighed, her breath starting to steam the window as the truck cooled in the frigid weather. "And there's one more problem."

"I'm turning the ignition on to warm back up." Lynn restarted the truck.

"Henry called me this morning and wants to know when my report on Bradshaw and the water tech will be finished so he can make a bid. I don't have anything finalized. Joost has told me he and his father don't get along, haven't seen one another for years, haven't talked for a month, and he doubts Henry has the private equity money he claims to have to invest in Joost's company. Yes, Bradshaw Energy used to be Henry's father-in-law's company but that was a divorce and decades ago."

Lynn flipped the turn signal. At an opening in traffic, she floored the accelerator and sped up to the standard West Texas interstate speed of eighty miles an hour.

"There he is!" Hannah was shocked. "He's the one who's been following me!"

An anonymous black truck passed on their right. It was driven by an equally non-descript man who could have been—maybe was—just another oilfield operator or driver.

Lynn took the next exit and drove to a gas station. "You fill up the truck," she told Hannah. "I'm looking for a tracker."

Lynn retrieved the flashlight from the emergency kit. First, she looked under the dash and between the seats. She looked for a box plugged into the data port. Nothing.

"Filled up. Where do you want me to look?" Hannah asked.

"The glove compartment. *Under* the seats."

Lynn lifted the hood and searched. She checked the tight spaces behind the bumpers.

"I don't see anything," Hannah reported. "If there's one underneath the truck, it will be hard to get to."

Lynn shone the flashlight into each wheel well. When she got to the third one—rear, passenger side—she saw it. The black box was a few inches wide, an inch thick, and about three inches long. The magnetized side was stuck to the wheel well. When Lynn pulled it away, its blinking green light turned red.

"You found it!" Hannah bent over to look at the tracker. "You think Daine or Cooper put it there? Should we put it back and pretend we don't see it?"

Lynn scraped grime off the tracker. Her heart fell. "No, we should leave it here at the gas station. They want us to know they're following us. It's a threat and they want us to be afraid."

"What do you mean?"

"Look here." The manufacturer's brand was visible on the tracker along with a bright green sticker printed with a logo and a name. Daine Environmental Water Services.

# CHAPTER 32
# WASHINGTON DC

LYNN ALREADY MISSED the dusty scrub and action of West Texas. But Claude Durand, TriCoast's French-born head of communications, last week had promised her a few brief appearances and an interview in Washington, D.C. could be done quickly within a day. He suggested the trip would boost her effort to acquire Joost's company. "This will give you a chance to clear the record after that AI video fake. People can see who you really are. And if Joost accepts your offer to buy Bradshaw Energy, you will be meeting with these politicians and agency heads anyway. It is better to introduce yourself now under less pressured circumstances."

At that, she relented. "But I need to keep the trip short."

To begin the day, Claude Durand told Lynn a neutral interview would help her make her case in Washington with federal regulators. *But did he say that just to get me to agree?*

Lynn had checked the interviewer's history, watched her clips, and prepared short points accordingly. "I'd still rather face an audience of hostile West Texas drillers," she told Claude.

"So, think of Missy Ferris as a roomful of drillers. But everyone you want to convince in Washington will watch your interview before they're 'in their office' to meet with you."

"Yeah, no pressure. Drillers are more straightforward than Misty." Lynn shook her head. "They just want to keep their jobs, make money, and have a good time on the weekends."

"Don't we all?"

Lynn admitted Claude was correct.

"Remember. Alert but relaxed. Engaging. Enthusiastic."

"Attentive but chill."

"*Oui.* Here we are," he said, opening the door to the Washington, D.C. studio. "I will be nearby. *Allons-y.*"

"Right. Let's go." She took a deep breath and walked into the brightly lit interview room.

"Missy Ferris, Ms. Dayton. Our make-up people will touch you up. We'll be live. We have playback options on various social media."

Lynn tried to control her expression as a man pinned back her hair and a woman added heavy foundation to her face. She bristled at having her face touched by anyone except her husband and stepchildren.

Then she thought again about her preparation. Whatever they recorded could be condensed to just a few seconds. *But I can go in whatever direction the questions go. I'm ready for any topic. I'm comfortable, just folks, smiling and having fun. Be honest: I'm nervous. It takes so much energy to relax.*

Yet Lynn found Missy's questions and manner did put her at ease as they navigated energy policy questions ranging from the end of oil—or not—to nuclear's comeback to the costs of mining for renewables. She even got time to explain that TriCoast had had no role in the Chicago gas outage, contrary to claims on social media.

All went well until the end.

"What about biomass? Isn't that the green answer we should be seeing more of?" Missy leaned forward.

"What you call biomass, most people call wood or animal dung. We've been using it for centuries and it's still the predominant fuel in poor Asian and African countries. What burns is the carbon in the wood. It's safer and healthier for women—who do most of the cooking—to use refillable LPG canisters, as they are beginning to do with TriCoast's assistance in countries like India."

"Lynn, did your therapist say it would help you, to be so confrontational?"

A hundred responses swirled through her head, all of them furious. "What? I don't...what do you mean?" Lynn said as the camera turned on her. *I will not lose control for the sake of her money shot.* "Not only do I not have a therapist, but your position that we should continue to expose women and girls to rape daily worldwide when they gather wood—biomass as you call—as happens now, is the worst kind of cruelty I can imagine. Two and a half billion people around the globe use manure for cooking inside. Many millions of them die from the diseases they get by doing so. More than from malaria and AIDs combined. Again, mostly women. That's your biomass." Lynn had not meant to sound so bitter, but Missy's disingenuousness had provoked her. As it was designed to do.

"Thank you for the lively response. All the time we have, folks."

After the cameras turned off, Lynn spun to Missy. "What were the hostile, ad hominem questions all about?"

She shrugged. "Conflict. Juices the ratings. I had to get you to react. Don't take it personally."

Lynn bit back even more angry replies, as Claude joined her from offstage.

He narrowed his eyes at Missy and said, in the native French he used rarely except when he was particularly angry. *"La trahison. La pute."*

Missy shrugged. "Whatever. You'll thank me when Lynn improves her Q score."

"The only Q score you were boosting was your own," Claude said.

❖

On the corporate plane that would return her to Midland, Lynn worried. She worried about arriving before the impending snowstorm. She worried her day in DC had accomplished nothing. *Less than nothing.*

*The interview with Missy Ferris went so poorly at the end. Even if I cleared TriCoast's name in the Chicago gas outage all anyone will remember is that Missy upset me. I didn't change a single mind at the agency meetings. Claude wasted my time.*

*And why is everything going wrong at once?* Too many other problems were piling up. She ticked them off one by one.

*I hate having Henry Vandervoost back in my orbit. He wasn't effective when he was at TriCoast. Now he's working for people we can't identify and so can't trust. And he's way too much into the Bradshaw Energy business.*

*I'm at an impasse with Joost to acquire his company. He wants to sell it, but he seems convinced it's worth far more than I think it is. I have yet to see a convincing demonstration of the water recycling technology he's so proud of.*

*Hannah's working for us now, but is she really? What's she hiding from us? She's certainly good at hiding from herself, at least when it comes to how much she likes Joost.*

*Joost and Hannah. That's a minefield of complications.*

*I don't trust Rowan Daine. It's mutual—he doesn't trust or support me. He's hurting TriCoast as the temporary CEO. He's also dragging us down by association with his wastewater company which doesn't follow the rules and may be causing earthquakes.*

*We haven't made headway on learning who set off the sand avalanche that seemed aimed to kill Hannah, Joost, and me.*

*And worst of all, I miss Cy and the kids. They need me. I need them.*

Lynn stretched and shrugged in her airplane seat, trying to squeeze tension out of her body so she could sleep.

The next she knew the pilot was waking her as the airplane spooled down at Midland's private plane FBO.

# CHAPTER 33
# ISRAEL AND SPAIN

*"Fear has big eyes but sees nothing"*

—*Russian saying*

First Avi received a text alerting him a contact would be made. All he could think was the phone call had to be one of the dozens of people he had met earlier in Budapest.

When his cell phone rang, "a friend of a friend" was how the caller identified himself. "Do not bother trying to trace me. Plans are underway to sabotage Israel's offshore platforms and pipelines. It is up to you what you do with this information. Maybe you will trade futures on it."

"When? Who are you? How do you know? Why are you telling me instead of Israeli security services or the platform and pipeline operators? I would not trade against my country!"

"Tonight. You hesitated. You thought about it." The caller hung up.

Avi first thought to tell his boss. But the man did not take him seriously.

He did have a distant relative in Shin Bet. Avi had put in his required two years of government service. Alatan, the relative, had gone on and made a career of protecting the country.

"Alatan, it's Avi Levin. We're third cousins. We started our training together, remember? I'm contacting you because I just got an alarming phone call. The caller said plans are underway to sabotage Israeli offshore platforms. Tonight."

His cousin hesitated. "Which ones? Who called you?"

"The caller didn't give me information to answer either of those questions."

"It could be a hoax. But if it isn't, Israeli lives are at risk. There are many expert saboteurs from Europe, Russia, and central Asia. I will get the word out. You may hear nothing more. If you don't, it's good news. Either there's no sabotage or we stopped it."

"Alatan, in my business we think about safety all the time. If it's a bomb, it's unlikely to be one you can see. It might be attached to one of the gas lines from the platform to the shore. Like Nordstream."

"Yes, the situation could be complicated."

Despite his cousin's warning about no news, a few hours later Avi received a three-word thank-you text from his cousin. "Malware neutralized. *Toda.*"

It wasn't until the next day he understood that the call made to him, while real, had also served as a diversion.

❖

Spain's natural gas utility was a month away from reopening the Barcelona gas import terminal, but Spanish energy minister Alejandro Garcia had certified the safety and reopening of Spain's other import terminals. More than ever, the rest of Europe now depended on the Spanish LNG regasification terminals that had once been derided as an overbuilt waste.

It was a normal morning, cooler than usual. Dozens of workers, including Diego Sanchez, just back from his honeymoon in Greece, had gathered at the gates of the Bilbao LNG import terminal for the shift change. They had been busier in the week since the reopening—more overtime than many liked—but Diego's colleagues had taken up the slack after the attack on the Barcelona terminal. The energy minister still had not announced who was responsible for the Barcelona attack, although rumors were constant.

At Bilbao's entry gate dozens of men were massed, greeting one another. His friends at the terminal greeted Diego with grins and jokes about his honeymoon. A few asked him if his wife was pregnant yet.

"Have you selected a crib?"

"Boy or girl, or one of each?"

"Many of each eventually, I hope," Diego said, smiling.

The two large shifts of dozens of men walked toward one another.

Then four men, dressed in the same uniform as the others, put on gas masks. Several of the men in the crowd turned to them in surprise.

The men in the masks began spraying liquid at Diego and the dozens of his friends and colleagues. The liquid was clear, colorless, odorless, and without taste. It quickly vaporized and spread even further in the crowd.

The vaporized liquid was a deadly nerve agent. One of its primary effects was to cause humans' muscles to contract without stopping.

Diego could feel all of his muscles twitching. There was nothing he could do for relief. Soon he was as exhausted as if he'd run a marathon, but his legs wouldn't stop moving.

He felt so tired.

"*Joder! Joder! JODER!*"

"*La hostia!*"

"*Mierda!*"

"*Hijo de puta!*"

Wide-awake men just coming on shift tried to take down the four masked men but fell before reaching them. Many were coughing and vomiting. Others clutched at their chests as their hearts stopped.

Men convulsed.

Some simply fell and died.

The masked men ran out of sight.

"Hail Mary, full of grace, the Lord is with thee; blessed are thou among women, and blessed is the fruit of thy womb, Jesus. Holy Mary, Mother of God, pray for us sinners, now and at the hour of our death." Diego Sanchez wheezed through the last words of the prayer. He tumbled to the ground, unconscious. His muscles still twitched.

The crowd of dozens of men at the Bilbao LNG terminal grew eerily quiet except for moans and curses from the injured and dying.

Ambulances arrived quickly. The medics covered themselves head to toe in hazmat suits. They sprinted in to rescue as many men as they could, men who had been felled by poisonous sarin. One ran to Diego, who was curled up in a fetal position. The medic took Diego's pulse.

Nothing.

Before running to the next downed man, the medic pinned a number and a code onto Diego's body to indicate he was now beyond rescue.

❖

Even Spain's prime minister could not restrain himself. "Alejandro, why are we so cursed? What have you done?"

"Prime Minister, the question is who? Who has done this to us? Both Barcelona and Bilbao were terminals at which we received LNG from Israel and from the USA—from TriCoast."

"You suspect them?"

"No. The planning and brutality of the attacks suggest a plan directed by a rogue country or adversary."

"No more. Alejandro. You are responsible. No more of these attacks. No more of these deaths of Spanish citizens at our LNG terminals. I don't care what gas supplies other countries in the EU need from our terminals. Our people come first. Do whatever you have to do to save them."

Alone in his office for a moment, energy minister Alejandro

Garcia fell to his knees. He prayed for the recovery of every man at the Bilbao terminal. He prayed for their families.

Then he got to his feet. He called in his press secretary.

Spanish energy minister Alejandro Garcia steeled himself to make another grim announcement to his countrymen.

## CHAPTER 34
# MIDLAND

*"Time is functionally similar to volatility: the more time, the more events, the more disorder."*

—Nassim Nicholas Taleb, *Antifragile*

So MUCH TO DO. Lynn was glad to get a call from TriCoast's cybersecurity chief. He and Beau Decatur had been working together to learn who'd sabotaged the Chicago distribution system. Accounts on social media still blamed TriCoast.

"You ever hear of a John Cooper?"

"His name is showing up in all the wrong places here," Lynn said.

"Beau and I looked at the feeds from the time of the sabotage. We think we identified this guy Cooper. He must have thought he'd blacked out or turned off all the video cameras in the control room, but he missed a few. The man who was supposed to be on shift was killed. That's not on the cameras. What investigators did find on the body of the murdered operator was enough DNA trace evidence to link to Cooper. He's no longer in Illinois, but there's a BOLO out for him. We think he's here in Texas."

"The ice storm that's coming will interrupt finding him," Lynn said. "Do you have anything that clears TriCoast?"

"Yes. We can see Cooper arriving and communicating with someone online—we haven't traced the source yet, but probably Eastern European or Russian—who was able to override the utility's operating instructions for the Kenwood service area. The regulators sensed low pressure from false data, causing high-pressure gas to be poured into the distribution system. That went right into houses and apartments, causing fires and explosions all over Kenwood.

"Then we see Cooper paint a pipeline and the control panel with the TriCoast name and logo and take pictures. The pictures showed up on new social media accounts that were active for only a few days around the time of the attack. Then they were shut down, but other accounts picked up the threat and pictures. Some real, some bots."

"What an asshole." Lynn made notes.

"Standard description of everyone in the criminal world, I'm afraid," the cyber chief responded.

After the chief disconnected, Lynn immediately called Joost Bradshaw. He did answer, but his voice sounded wary.

"Joost, we have an explanation about the Chicago pipeline sabotage. If you'll listen, then I hope you and I can restart acquisition talks."

"Okay."

Lynn took a deep breath and explained what the cyber chief had just told her: that John Cooper had been responsible for the death of the operator, for screwing up the pressure regulators leading to the Kenwood fires and explosions, and for posting pictures of TriCoast's name and logo on social media in connection with the Kenwood explosion. "Of course we were never involved, but now we know who was. There's a be-on-the-lookout out for him with law enforcement, but if he's back in Texas, the ice storm means no one will be searching for him right now."

"And the motive was to blame you?"

"We have fair competitors, and we have competitors who will stop at nothing to knock us out of the arena. The second type is who's behind this. When we've seen similar actions before, it's either domestic or a state actor from another country. Either one plays by different rules or no rules at all. Whatever it takes to win."

"That's quite an arena TriCoast is in," Joost said.

"Yes."

"I'll admit I was wrong then. We haven't talked to anyone else about the merger. Do you want to come over now and discuss it? We might end up camping out in the office for a few days, depending on the storm. Can you handle that?"

"Sure. Maybe that will help us come to an agreement faster. Hannah is with me. Shall I bring her?"

"If she wants. Yes. Bring Hannah, too. I'd like to see her."

❖

At Joost's office, everyone debated who had the thickest socks, the best gloves, the warmest long underwear, and coats. With their Chicago winter experience, Hannah and Lynn aced the warmest clothing competition.

Hannah motioned Lynn over. "Remember I told you about what Henry asked me to do in Chicago? And how I thought whoever Henry was working for got someone else to do it?" Hannah kept her voice to a whisper.

Lynn nodded.

"What are you two talking about over there?" Joost demanded.

"How cute and fit you are," Hannah replied.

Each, except Hannah, checked in with families on preparations, including propane heaters and backup generators. They discussed what to do if the electricity failed for several days and they were iced in. Though they would start off staying at Joost's Midland office, Lynn and Hannah checked on their backup hotel's preparations.

Schools were closed in anticipation of ice and snow, which started a cascade of other closures. Activities ground to a stop in a city whose impetus—whose reason for being—was transport and motion.

Lynn suggested to Roy he close the TriCoast office so people could get home easily.

"Way ahead of you. Already done so. Folks are tough but no need to take unnecessary risks."

Soon, out-of-town highway travel would cease, as everyone would be literally frozen in place. Yet again, Lynn was glad for the big trucks everyone drove Midland.

Then all made grocery store runs, dodging mad, long lines at the warehouse-sized HEB. There was a drill, a process. Everyone obeyed it after the experience a few years earlier of what jokers called The Little Texas Ice Age. No matter how accustomed Midlanders were to sustained 100-degree temperatures, sustained 0-degree temperatures required different skills. The super-cold delivered a deadly version of the locked room, from which it became impossible to escape.

At the office, each unrolled a sleeping bag and charged phones and other equipment. If the electricity quit, the cold would quickly drain batteries.

Lynn looked anxiously over her shoulders at history. The Little Texas Ice Age, or Snowpocalypse, a once-in-seventy-years prolonged, extremely cold week a few years ago meant electricity to "non-essential" gas pipes had been cut off. It turned out the gas was quite essential, first obviously for heating houses, but also for making that very electricity. Rotating equipment had frozen, thermostats had disconnected, and compressors hadn't worked, so the hard lesson had been to avoid shutting off electricity to the oil and gas fields that kept the gas flowing for heat AND to make that self-same electricity.

Nothing, not wind turbines, solar plants, gas-fired plants, or coal-fired plants had been built for days of temperatures below ten degrees in open-air Texas. About a third of generating units went offline. The whole ERCOT grid, which supplied eighty-five percent of the state, came within seconds of crashing. Had that happened, restoring the grid would have required months.

The lesson was made all the more horrible by the hundreds of people who died from the cold.

Lynn was unable to leave and go into the field. Since there were whole swaths of projects she couldn't do, being shut in by the cold made the days seem like a work retreat. She felt liberation in being away from the usual tasks and meetings.

"I have to take advantage of this situation," Hannah said.

Lynn looked at her in surprise. Joost himself allowed a smile.

"Exciting anyway for a chemistry nerd. We're here together and Joost, I want to hear about this special, secret water recycling process you have. Is it worth its weight in gold? Come on, you can tell me."

"You mean our blueprints and license potential?" Joost laughed. "Sometimes yes, sometimes no. Depends on how much oil and water people are trying to move out of the Permian basin and whether there's enough deep wastewater disposal volume. Spoiler, there isn't, No matter what Rowan Daine tells you."

"The key to the process is an inexpensive set of membranes, right?" Hannah asked. "They collect all the contaminants so you can reuse the water for fracking. With even more expensive membranes you can make the water clean enough to drink."

Joost nodded.

"It's a very different business from drilling wells. Why did you develop your own process?" Lynn asked.

"Just another line of related business. We have a staff guy and he offered to design prototypes. Our deal is he gets part of any eventual profits," Joost explained.

"And my deal is he and the process would be a part of Tri-Coast's acquisition of Bradshaw Energy," Lynn said.

"You have to convince him," Joost demurred. "He's kind of a free agent."

"So how do I know if it's worth something?" Hannah asked.

"If you're bottlenecked—not enough wastewater disposal wells in places where they won't cause earthquakes, and there are fewer and fewer of those—and you then have to shut in oil production, it can cost you millions or even billions in lost revenue. The important thing is you can use the recycle process immediately."

"The whole market for the water recycling membranes and their competitors is in the hundreds of millions of dollars. More to the point, affordable water recycling processes are a competitive advantage; companies that have them license them but don't allow them to be duplicated. In some cases, they won't discuss their process volume capabilities, the membrane chemistry, or the physics of why it works, let alone what percent of the market they have or how big the total recycle market is," Lynn said. "Although of course we can calculate it easily: at least a barrel of water for every barrel of oil, so a minimum of five million barrels of water a day have to be handled just here in the Permian basin."

"Which is how we know it's really valuable," Hannah responded, looking at Joost for confirmation.

He shrugged a non-answer.

"But it's not so valuable if you have the cheaper alternative of deep wastewater wells," Hannah said.

"Right," Joost said.

"So, your water recycle process is binary—so valuable that companies buy companies like yours just to get their hands on water recycle technology, or else worth about zero?" Hannah asked.

It was Lynn's turn to nod. She looked at Joost. "You got life insurance on your scientist?"

"Business continuation insurance for the water recycle tech. Same."

"I disagree with you. AI is one thing, but personal intellectual capital is still very valuable."

They moved on to the thermodynamics of the developing storm, specifically, how tremendously much energy was required to sublime ice—more than most people realized—to boost it from the solid stage, skip the melting stage, and go right to the gasification stage.

"More sun than we'll have for a while," Hannah said.

Still, Lynn was feeling optimistic the storm wouldn't keep them locked down for as long as she feared.

Hannah slipped away to another room for privacy. She punched a number she had memorized. She didn't expect him to answer, but he did.

"Rowan Daine here. Hannah, you're the only person who hides her telephone identification. What can I do for you? Isn't Henry keeping you busy enough?"

She tried to stay calm even though he'd immediately known that it was her. "Rowan, please tell me what you know about my father's death. He was working for your company. You told my mother it was accidental, but she never saw his body. *Was* his death an accident? Or did you kill him?"

"Ah, Hannah. The past seldom bears close inspection. Certainly true here. So long ago. So many work sites. My company has had its share of injuries and accidents, unfortunately. I wish I could remember each one, but I can't."

"I'm not finished asking questions, Rowan. I'll be back. And when I am, I'll have the police with me to arrest you for my father's murder and for all the other people you've murdered."

"But you don't have the evidence, and I'm finished giving answers. In the meantime, you'd best prepare for the snowstorm here in Midland."

When she disconnected, she was still angry, but also worried. *I never told Rowan Daine I was in Midland.*

## CHAPTER 35
# MIDLAND

AFTER THREE DAYS camped out in TriCoast's office and even though they had backup generators at the office building like those in the field, Lynn felt relieved they hadn't completely lost power. They kept connected to weather reports and grid outage maps and otherwise limited their electricity use. They monitored TriCoast and Bradshaw operations. Some workers had wound down operations and gone home as Joost, Lynn, and Roy had urged them to do. Some had insisted on staying at the job site.

Hannah and Joost seemed to be getting along. *Quite well actually,* Lynn thought. More than once late at night she'd awakened to hear them talking. She'd excused herself another time when she'd walked in on them exchanging a long kiss.

Still, the enforced togetherness was starting to tell. And as predicted, they were getting more snow.

That was yesterday. Even though the grid had lined up extra supply the last of the wind turbines froze. Solar power had been out for days. Nuclear and coal couldn't support the whole grid. And not enough gas was getting to the power plants. The local electric company announced rolling blackouts.

When the lights went out, it was the signal to move.

Battery draining after several phone calls, Lynn finally found a nearby hotel that still had both available rooms and electricity.

Hannah was even more anxious to leave. She'd been saving battery power by limiting online searches, but she felt excruciatingly close to finding the link between Rowan Daine and her father's death, despite Daine's non-answers. Warmth and steady electricity would give her the online time she needed to research what her father had been doing at Daine's company at the time of his death.

"We can take my truck. It's in the garage in the next block," Joost said. "But how do we get out? The keyless entry system fails closed."

Lynn tried not to feel panicky at the prospect of being locked in even longer, this time by mechanics instead of weather.

Hannah winced, then brightened. "You have fire doors, right?"

"That will set off the fire alarm. Those guys have enough to do without a false alarm," Joost replied.

"We'll call them and tell them," Lynn said. She realized none of them had much more than their heavy coats, gloves, hats, and phones.

They stumbled down three flights of stairs in the dark to an equally dark back hallway.

"Not chained. What a relief! Here goes." Joost pushed the door. It stuck.

"It's probably blocked by a ring of ice on the outside. Plus, it's never opened so it's sticky. Hannah, you and I need to help Joost," Lynn said.

The three of them leaned hard on the door. With a welcome crack, it swung open.

No alarm sounded.

"How far away is your truck again?" Hannah asked.

"Half a block. To the left," Joost pointed.

The sidewalk looked remarkably clear to Lynn, like it was wet. "Be careful. Black ice—"

Joost slid suddenly and fell hard, his arm only partly cushioning his fall. He gingerly pulled himself to a sitting position. "Shit. I think my arm is broken."

"We should get you to the hospital," Lynn said.

"Just a sprain. The hospital has worse cases than me. We can see how it is tomorrow."

"At least allow me to drive us in your truck to the hotel," Lynn responded.

He tossed her the keys. "Now help me up and try not to fall down yourselves."

They did.

"These next steps look super icy," Hannah said. "It won't be graceful or pretty, but we need to crab-walk through it."

"I can't," Joost said.

"Then just try to walk through without falling," Hannah said.

He slowly tested each step, while Lynn and Hannah maneuvered several yards on their hands and feet.

"We can get up, get some traction, in these clumps of grass," Hannah said.

Lynn had never been so happy to see frozen-dead landscaping plants.

They climbed a set of stairs. Joost's white truck was the only one still in the garage.

"Did anyone notice? Is the arm up or does Lynn have to bust through it?" Hannah asked.

Once they reached the exit, Lynn was happy to see this gate, at least, had failed open.

"Oh, and everyone take turns charging phones in case the drive takes a while. I have a cord right here," Joost said.

"Joost and Hannah, you navigate and watch for other trucks," Lynn said. She decided to risk the highway—it was more likely to be cleared. They could get stuck on residential side streets.

Still, she drove slowly, steering into skids and only once spinning around completely. She was glad for the heavy weight of the truck.

After an hour they'd made it to the hotel at the edge of town. Mercifully, its lights were still blazing.

They walked gingerly across the parking lot. The front desk clerk—who looked as if he'd slept at his station for the last week, as he likely had, said, "Get your showers quickly. Our pipes froze. We don't know how many or what kind of leaks we'll have once they thaw." He gave them card keys for the two rooms they had requested.

Once in the room with Lynn, Hannah turned to the sites she'd found about commercial trucking overtime violations and illegal wastewater dumping.

After an hour, Lynn asked, "Do you want me to grab something for you from the snack bar? That may be all the food they have."

"I do. Thanks."

Hannah typed furiously on her phone. *Yes!* There it was. There had been no pipeline explosions around the date of her father's death. But before that, there *had* been complaints to the state regulators about Daine's trucks running above their allowed weight and the excessive overtime required of his drivers. On the state environmental quality site were more complaints about Daine's company illegally dumping wastewater into closed wells, stock ponds, and even streams. The name at the bottom of every complaint? Stephen Bosko.

*Daine must have killed my father for reporting him. Damn that man! How do I prove it, though? Should I tell Lynn? She may not be able to do anything, but she deserves to know since Daine's also running her company now.*

When Lynn returned to their room, Hannah was surprised to see Joost accompanying her. *It was nice to hang out with Joost during the ice storm. I enjoyed being with him. But hey, I was available, so he might have been just making do. Still, I need to speak to Lynn alone.*

They talked for a while. Joost's smile was lopsided when he turned to Hannah. "I got permission from your minder to ask." He nodded at Lynn.

"Ask what?" Hannah was confused.

"Would you like to stay with me tonight? Just say yes!" Joost said.

"What? No. I mean yes. I mean, let me talk to Lynn for a few minutes first."

Joost laughed. "I told you I already have her permission. I just need yours."

Hannah was torn. She closed her eyes. "Give me half an hour. What's your room number? I'll knock."

"Good. About time you two not only figured it out but started being honest about it." Lynn laughed.

After Joost closed the door Hannah said, "Lynn, there's something you need to know."

"It will take you thirty minutes to talk about Joost?"

"No. It's about Rowan Daine. I have evidence, circumstantial anyway, a motive, that Daine killed my father, Stephen Bosko. Or had him killed."

"No! The guy leading TriCoast? He's acted suspiciously with me, but your accusation is a big leap. Are you sure?"

Hannah explained what she'd learned from her research and what the Kermit police officer had told her.

Lynn shook her head, shocked. "So much to think about. What to do."

"Yes. Sorry to dump that on you, but you need to know. So does the board."

"But as you say, the evidence is circumstantial."

"What's not circumstantial is that my father is dead." Hannah grabbed her small bag and left.

❖

By the next morning, the ice was finally melting, as was the few inches of drifting snow. Temperatures that weren't supposed to top fifteen degrees Fahrenheit reached thirty. After days of single-digit temperatures, it seemed miraculous. It was.

"I thought I'd find you here, Hannah, Lynn. My son, Joost."

Lynn was the first to recover from the shock. "Goddamn. Henry Vandervoost. What the hell are you doing here at the breakfast bar of a Midland, Texas hotel?"

Lynn smelled something she hadn't smelled for a long time: Henry's stress breath, which he had always covered by sucking on mints. His lips were stuck to his teeth as if his mouth was dry. His breath stank.

"What you"—he pointed at Hannah—"are supposed to be doing but haven't been. Getting lover-boy there—at least that's what he used to tell me when he was younger and still wanted fatherly advice occasionally—to cough up the Bradshaw water recycle process blueprints."

Joost glared at Hannah. She shrank back.

*So, Henry's telling the truth,* Lynn thought.

"You three look like shit. You sleep in those clothes?" Henry continued.

"And glad to do so," Lynn said. She pointed to other people paying attention to their raised voices. "I'd say let's take this outside, but it's still too cold."

Henry, the only one in the breakfast bar with a coat, nodded. "Perfect for me. I'm on my way out anyway. I'll keep the conversation short."

Once outside, Henry spun around and pointed again at Hannah. "You've forgotten. You work for me. You're *my* bitch."

"You asshole!" Joost launched at his father. "No wonder mom divorced you. You are such an incredible bastard. I'm not your son. Not anymore. Get your whiny Euro ass out of Texas before I call my security."

Lynn and Hannah stood and shivered, wrapping their arms around themselves.

Hannah was the first to leave. "I'm firing you as my employer, Henry. Go back to bloody England and forget we ever talked.

"You duplicitous bitch."

"Fuck you and the horse you rode in on. No, Henry, you're the one who's been keeping secrets. Secrets from your son. Go on, Joost. Ask him who he's working for. What the plan is. How he wants to take over your company. Why he hired me. Who he owes money to. Ask him who he's working for!" She ran back into the hotel's warm lobby. Lynn was so cold, but she wanted to hear Henry's answers.

Joost said, "Well? Sum it up since you brought us out here and we're freezing. Who owns you?"

Henry backed away from them. "If you say you're not my son, I don't owe you any answers except this is much bigger than me. Good luck staying alive. You'll need it."

# CHAPTER 36
# LOUISIANA

HANNAH ENDED HER contract with Henry. Her relationship with Joost had cooled again after the revelation that Henry had hired her to unearth the secrets of Joost's water recycling technology.

But Lynn kept Hannah nearby and on contract, referring frequently to the younger woman's chemistry expertise.

A few days later, Lynn received an e-mail and a phone message from Avi Levin, asking if she could meet him at TriCoast's Louisiana LNG plant so he could arrange additional backup supplies of natural gas to Israeli customers. He suggested Joost's company might also be interested, and he said the plant manager, who was copied on the message, had suggested the time and place. The plant had been on Lynn's list to visit again after it recovered from the earlier electrical fire.

She talked to Joost, and they agreed to make the trip—finding more natural gas customers was always important. She emailed the acceptance back to Avi, copying the plant manager.

Reluctantly, Hannah also agreed to go.

A sleepless night emptied into an early dawn before Lynn's flight to Lafayette, Louisiana. Her whole body hurt from lack of sleep. Every noise seemed a threat.

Joost and Hannah looked no better than she felt.

The three of them followed directions sent to them by the plant manager.

"Is Avi being extra careful? Security measure? This must be the back way," Joost said, as they threaded down a barely-two-lane asphalt road, kudzu and low trees enclosing them on both sides.

"These are the directions," Lynn said. "But last time we came through the front."

They pulled up to a guard house emblazoned with the TriCoast name, but not its logo.

A tanned, black-haired security guard approached Lynn on the driver's side of the car.

"We're here for a meeting with the plant manager and Avi Levin," Lynn said. "It's been arranged. I'm Lynn Dayton, and I have Joost Bradshaw from Bradshaw Energy and Hannah Bosko with me."

The man smiled politely. "Let me have your IDs and I will check our visitor roster."

A thought nudged the back of Lynn's mind. The man looked familiar—like someone she had seen at various job TriCoast sites—but she couldn't place him among the hundreds of employees she'd met.

Joost and Lynn handed him driver's licenses while Hannah produced her passport.

Lynn called Sara Levin. "We're in Louisiana. Looking forward to seeing your nephew."

"Lynn, no! He's not in the US. He's in Israel."

Lynn was stunned. "But I had a message and a voicemail from him to meet him at our plant. Sounds just like him. His email address."

From the back seat, Hannah whispered. "That smell. The man has the same odor as in the wax refinery where we found the dead guy. It's John Cooper. He's disguised."

In Lynn's other ear, Sara was saying, "I spoke to Avi this morning. You've been spoofed. VoCo or something like it. Whatever he told you to do, get away..." Before she could finish the call or tell the others, the guard was standing next to her open window. "We don't have a record of your meeting. I'll have to ask the three of you to step out of the car."

He pointed a Glock at them.

"Why are you pointing a gun at us?" Lynn shouted, hoping Sara could hear the conversation and wouldn't respond.

"Now, turn off your cell phones and give them to me."

Another man materialized from behind the guard shack.

"Henry Vandervoost! What are you doing here?" Lynn was stunned.

Vandervoost was also holding a gun, which he trained on Joost.

"If you'd have given me the water recycle technology instruction, I wouldn't have to do this, *son*." Vandervoost sneered the last word.

"Walk ahead of us single file. Six feet apart."

Vandervoost positioned himself to their right, John Cooper to their left. "There's a building a few hundred feet ahead, next to the pipe yard. In it we have the papers transferring your company to me, Joost. You will also either write out the details of the water recycling process, including the membrane types, or grant me written permission for it. Lynn, you're not important here, for a change. You're just collateral damage, although this makes up for you kicking me out of TriCoast. Hannah, you shouldn't have betrayed me with my son."

A cold fog rose from the ground. The huge stacks of steel pipe were a ghostly gray in the mist. *If only I could knock those over onto Vandervoost and Cooper,* Lynn thought.

Hannah looked like she had the same idea.

But each ten-foot length of pipe weighed several hundred pounds. If she had a bar, she could swat them, or distract them with the noise. *Where are tubular bells when I need them?*

"In there." Cooper directed them through a rusty door in the side of a cold warehouse. Vandervoost motioned them forward, flipped on the light, and kept his gun trained on them. He shoved them toward an interior office while Cooper stayed outside, apparently to keep watch.

Inside the office, papers were lined in neat stacks. A computer stood at the ready.

Something else, or rather someone else, was also ready. Daine.

"Rowan Daine?" Lynn was shocked. She hadn't heard him from outside. She realized the walls of the warehouse office were soundproof.

"This is more prepared than I've ever seen you, Henry," Lynn said. *Stupid but I can't help it. Some satisfaction before I die.*

"Close your mouth for once!" Vandervoost screeched.

"Who are you working for?" Lynn asked.

"Tell them, Vandervoost," Daine said.

"The Russians paid off my gambling debts to the Chinese so you could say I work for both. They didn't kill me right away because they found out I was Joost Bradshaw's father. They'll end up with the company and the recycling tech. All shell companies. Kir Zaitsev in Moscow. Of course, he doesn't get his hands dirty doing actual work. Joost, son. Sit down and start signing."

Joost shook his head and advanced on his father as Lynn calculated the odds. *Three on two. Not bad. Henry's no fighter.*

"Don't make me hurt you, Joost," Vandervoost said.

"Stop me." Joost reached for Vandervoost's gun.

"If he doesn't, I will," Daine snarled.

"Or you'll do what, you POS?" Joost said, his hands on Vandervoost's gun.

"Listen to your father, Joost." The sound of a knife whizzed. Daine slashed Joost's arm through his jacket. Joost released his hold on Vandervoost's gun.

Deep red blood began to flow. Daine had hit one of Joost's radial arteries.

A stomach-turning coppery smell hit their noses.

*Damnit. Joost could bleed out in just a few minutes!*

"Pressure! Tourniquet!" Hannah shouted.

She and Lynn pulled off Joost's jacket. His face had already turned white. They tied it as tightly as they could just below his shoulder. Hannah kept pressure on his arm.

At last, the drip of blood slowed.

Lynn stared at Vandervoost. "You'd sacrifice your son or let Rowan Daine kill him? You are a monster."

"Lynn, Lynn, Lynn. Why are you surprised? Of course, Henry would sacrifice his son. He might have a few qualms about it. I, on the other hand, don't have any hesitation about getting rid of Joost or you or Hannah," Daine said.

Vandervoost's face remained impassive except for tears leaking from his eyes.

Daine turned to Hannah. "You, for example. You're as much of a problem as your old man."

"You killed him! I have the proof!" Hannah shouted.

"So I heard. Too bad you won't have a chance to show your proof to anyone. Your father brought it on himself when he wouldn't shut up to the regulators. I only helped the process along. You called me the other day with questions."

Lynn looked with surprise at Hannah. She nodded.

"You were correct. He wasn't killed in a pipeline explosion as you were told," Daine continued. "Somehow—I wasn't there when it happened, you understand—your father became tangled in a heavy steel drill string on a well where we were removing water. I recall there wasn't enough left of his body to give to your mother to bury."

Hannah looked sick. Then furious. "You killed my mother, too."

"No. I can't take credit for that," Daine said lightly.

"You did. She was never the same after my father died."

"Keep me. Let them go." Joost's voice rasped.

The only answer from Vandervoost was a slight shake of his head as he waved the gun at them. "You're more controllable with them here."

"Okay, Vandervoost, this is where you earn what you owe Zaitsev," Daine said. He left the office, closed the door, and walked away into the dark warehouse.

"Turn around," Vandervoost said to his prisoners.

"You're going to shoot us in the back? You're a coward. Always have been. First with my mother, then with me." Joost sneered.

"Turn AROUND!" Vandervoost screamed.

Lynn heard a horrible crack of metal on bone.

Joost sank to the floor.

Hannah blinked at Lynn. Without looking, she kicked backward at Vandervoost, knocking him off-balance, but not before he'd also landed a concussive blow to her head.

As Vandervoost stumbled, Lynn whirled around and got behind him.

Hannah looked up at Lynn from the floor. "I'm going to..." She crumpled as she passed out.

Lynn slammed her right hip against Vandervoost's back and wrapped her right forearm around his neck from behind, as she remembered from her training. She put the inside of her wrist against the left side of his neck with her thumb up and other fingers curled. Before she could lock her left arm into position, he broke free.

"You bloody choking me, bitch?"

"Henry, don't sacrifice Hannah. Don't sacrifice your son," Lynn shouted at him.

"Just sacrifice you instead? Certainly," he growled in a deeper voice than she'd ever heard from him.

The last thing Lynn felt was the slamming hit to the back of her head. Then deep pain throughout her body. Her vision went black.

# CHAPTER 37
# LOUISIANA

LYNN OPENED ONE eye. She was still in the warehouse office, face-down on the floor. The light was so bright it hurt her eyes. *Concussion for sure. But I'm not dead. Yet.* She carefully opened both eyes, squinting to reduce the brightness. When she turned her head, she felt nauseous.

Her hands were bound behind her. Her fingers felt the thick rope. Joost and Hannah lay sprawled nearby. Both appeared unconscious, and both also had their hands tied loosely behind their backs.

The bulky knots gave Lynn hope. *Either Vandervoost is bad at tying knots, or he only wants to slow us down with the ropes, not keep us bound. Or both.*

Out of the corner of one eye, she saw Henry Vandervoost with his back to them. Ever the officious type, he was signing and initialing several pages of the contracts he had prepared, contracts that he had said handed control of Joost's company to him.

She looked at the knot in the rope around Joost's hands. Still lying on the floor, fingers behind her back, she began working the knot in her own rope.

After a minute, she freed her hands.

Lynn gingerly felt the back of her head. Her fingers came away sticky. Worse, she felt sick again.

Lynn risked another glance at Vandervoost. He grabbed a different pen and scribbled. It looked like he was now forging Joost's signature.

*Why hasn't he killed us yet? He must need something from one or all three of us.*

As quietly as she could, she pulled herself into a sitting position.

*He still has his gun. Can I remember my training? Can I even do anything after the knock on my head? The light seems so bright.*

Vandervoost turned in his chair. His eyes widened when he saw Lynn seated and awake. He bounced to his feet and grabbed his gun.

A Glock, Lynn confirmed. *Like Beau's, the one I practiced with a few weeks ago.*

"Do you want to die quickly or slowly? Fast, right? That's the American style." Vandervoost said.

She shook her head, and then regretted the unnecessary motion, choking down bile. "I don't want to die at all, Henry. I'm no threat to you. Look at me." She pushed against a wall to stand up. Her vision blurred.

Vandervoost was only a few feet away in the cramped office. He kept the gun pointed at her with one hand while sliding the papers into a slim leather pouch he held in his other hand.

"The boys will be wanting to know where I am. You can lead the way. Maybe I'll let them do the honor of getting rid of you." He glanced off toward his son and Hannah. He hesitated, then winced. "And them."

In that fraction of a second, Lynn summoned her energy to fight through the pain. She whacked Vandervoost's gun hand with her left arm and punched him in the nose with her right hand. His gun flew to the floor.

He stumbled and recovered, but not before Lynn had squatted and retrieved the gun.

*At least I bloodied his nose.*

She sat for a second, pointing the gun at him. But she didn't wait for the stars in her vision to clear before scrambling to her feet. *If Henry traps me on the floor I'm done.*

He shook his head at her. "There's two more out there with

guns just like mine—they gave that one to me in fact. And it looks like you might have a concussion. Sorry, not sorry."

She almost sobbed. *Hell yeah.*

"As you said, they're looking for you. Maybe worried they haven't heard shots." She shot once at his feet, and he danced backward.

Then she fired two more shots into the wall.

"You didn't kill your son. You love him. I think he still loves you, Henry. You didn't kill Hannah. You didn't kill me. You have a chance to avoid prison. Let's go."

She motioned him to walk ahead of her. "I have the gun aimed at your back. Don't give me a reason to shoot you."

She nudged him out the door of the warehouse office, turned off the light, and closed the door.

"Start walking. Call out to them." Lynn kept the gun nudged against his back. She looked around for other potential weapons and shields. Shovels? To her left was a big construction vehicle—a pipe layer. A couple of forklifts.

"Rowan. John. I'm done. Let's leave." Henry's voice quavered slightly.

Rowan Daine and John Cooper appeared out of the shadows. Daine was to Lynn's left, Cooper was to her right. Henry was still only a step in front of her.

"Bitch got you, hunh, Henry? No matter," Daine said. "You're both in time to see our finale. Take out a few terminals. Cut down the LNG exports from the US so the Russians can get a bigger lock on the market. First here, then at a few others nearby. They'll be down for months. We didn't finish the job here the first time. This time we'll get the docks, refrigerant units, and the control center. TATP is a wonder."

"You're killing people!" Lynn said.

"Collateral damage. So unfortunate. Just like your two friends in there," Daine said.

"Rowan, forget that," Vandervoost said. "We have to leave. The police could arrive any bloody moment."

"Going soft on me again, Vandervoost? You're in the way. You did this to yourself, becoming such an easy target the bitch could grab you." Daine abruptly raised his gun and fired it once at Henry's chest.

Vandervoost stumbled backward toward Lynn.

Without thinking, Lynn side-stepped several feet left into the dark, letting Vandervoost's body fall to the warehouse floor. Moving quickly hurt but she urged herself on until she could crouch behind a forklift, out of Daine's and Cooper's line of sight.

"Now it's your turn, Lynn," Daine said.

*I should try to save Henry. And Joost and Hannah. But I can't do anything if Daine or Cooper shoots me first.*

"Split up. Cooper, go left. I'll go right. We'll squeeze her." Daine's voice sounded bored.

Lynn straightened, ready to move. She heard Daine's feet shuffling as he felt his way around toward where she was hiding behind the forklift. He was approaching from her left. Cooper approached her from directly ahead, although his view of her was blocked by the forklift.

In the darkness, neither she nor Daine had an advantage.

From behind Cooper, a shaft of light lit his path.

Lynn waited until Daine was about ten feet away. Then she stood at the edge of the light band, ready to race across it.

"I've got her," Daine shouted. "Get ready. She's about to cross in front of you."

Lynn ducked down and sprinted across the shaft of light toward the shadow and the steel protection of the much larger pipe-laying construction vehicle. *If only I could get to the corner of that machine.*

A bullet whizzed just over her head. Daine was right behind her, grabbing her shirt.

There was a loud, mushy thump. Daine let go of Lynn's shirt.

Lynn didn't turn to look until she was several feet beyond, well into the shadows.

A bullet from Cooper's gun meant for her had hit Daine instead.

Daine rolled onto his side, clutching his chest. "Oh, fuck. Cooper, you fucking idiot. You fucking shot me."

She peered from behind the corner of the construction machine. Another bullet whizzed past.

"Get her." Daine started to gurgle.

She crouched down again and peeked around one huge tire. *Cooper will kill me if I don't kill him first. I have to aim for center mass. If I can even see him or shoot straight.*

Suddenly she heard choking and gasping.

"Drop the gun."

*Is that Joost's voice?*

She heard a metallic clunk.

"Hannah, get his gun. Then help me hold him down on the floor. Put your knee on his back. Lynn's probably hurt. We have to find her and help her. But we can't leave him here with just one of us."

"LYNN?" Never had Lynn heard a more welcome shout than Hannah's.

"Joost? Hannah?" Lynn peeked around the tire again. Joost and Hannah had positioned Cooper face-down on the floor, a rope around his neck—the source of the choking she'd heard. *They must have caught Cooper from behind and used one of the ropes they were tied up with.* Hannah's knee was on Cooper's back and Joost pointed Cooper's own gun at Cooper.

Hannah and Joost looked up at her. Both smiled.

"So glad to see you!" Then Lynn gasped, remembering. "Grab his phone. Call the terminal manager, then 9-1-1. Tell the terminal manager to evacuate. Tell the 9-1-1 operator to get the bomb squad out. Daine told me they were hiding bombs in the terminal. Docks, refrigerator unit, and control center. TATP."

Joost called the terminal manager, and said, "You need to evacuate now! You have bombs at the docks, refrigerator unit, and control center!"

The loud evacuation alarm immediately began honking at ear-splitting levels.

Lynn lay down on the floor, her face next to Cooper's, and shouted over the alarm. "Where else are they? What's the trigger?"

He grinned and turned his face away from her. *Killing him won't help, much as I'd like to.*

"Keep your knee on his back, Hannah," Joost said. "Lynn, get on the phone and start calling." Joost squatted, grabbed one of Cooper's wrists, and began pulling it across his back.

"The dock's the first one!" Cooper shouted. "Trigger's on my phone but I have to be ten feet or closer."

Lynn grabbed his face and turned it towards hers. "Are we within ten feet of any of the bombs you placed?"

"No."

Lynn reached the 9-1-1 operator. "I'm calling to report bombs at the TriCoast LNG terminal! We need the bomb squad. It's TATP. There's at least one each on the dock, the control center, and the refrigerant unit."

Joost kept pulling Cooper's arm into a more unnatural position. "Where else?"

They heard a sickening crack. Cooper screamed. "Stop! I'll tell you. The inlet from the main gas pipeline. That's all, I swear."

"And the inlet from the main gas pipeline," Lynn said to the operator.

"Emergency vehicles and bomb squads on the way," the operator said.

Lynn disconnected. She put her face next to Cooper's again. "What other terminals, John?"

"None. We didn't get to them."

Lynn heard sirens and ambulances.

She squinted as blindingly bright warehouse floodlights flashed around them.

# EPILOGUE
# LOUISIANA AND MOSCOW, RUSSIA

*"Time has sharp teeth that destroy everything."*

—*Simonides of Ceos, sixth century BCE*

THE REGIONAL BOMB squad found and disarmed the four TATP bombs.

Lynn and Hannah watched as John Cooper was cuffed and chained into the parish sheriff's car, a deputy guarding him. They and Joost had already given statements to the sheriff. Now he supervised the site as crime scene techs examined the warehouse, made measurements, and collected evidence.

The Calcasieu Parish Coroner's van arrived for Rowan Daine's and Henry Vandervoost's bodies. "I wish we could have saved Henry," Hannah said to Lynn as EMTs hoisted two black body bags into the van.

Since Joost's wounds were the worst, he'd been taken away in the first ambulance to Lake Charles. Another pair of ambulances arrived, one each for Lynn and Hannah.

Lying on the stretcher inside the ambulance, Lynn squinted and punched one button for the familiar number. "Cy. I'm okay but I got hit in the head. They're taking me to the hospital here in Louisiana."

He gasped. "Lynn! We'll be on the next plane."

Everyone around her was gentle and quiet, but the ride to the emergency room seemed to take forever. She felt every bump in the boxy old ambulance and tried to estimate how many miles it had on it. *Job hazard,* she thought wryly.

At the Lake Charles hospital, the ER doctor ordered a CT scan and requested Lynn be given hydrocodone and anti-nausea medicine. Then she was checked into a room as an inpatient for further evaluation. She slept.

A few hours later her eyes opened to a welcome vision of Cy, Matt, and Marika.

"Don't leave us," Marika's voice was plaintive.

"I'm right here." Guilt-filled, Lynn remembered Cy had lost his first wife, and her stepchildren their mother, to a drunk driver. Several years ago Marika had been just old enough to realize what had happened. Lynn's step-daughter's words echoed those from days earlier when Lynn had first left Dallas.

"What's worse than me getting a concussion?" Cy asked, and then answered his own question. "You or the kids getting one. I just lived through one of the most terrifying days of my life. I was afraid I'd lost you. When you called, I didn't know where you were. When I called back on your phone, they wouldn't let me talk to you. I was afraid if they hung up, you would die, and I wouldn't be there. It was the worst, longest flight we've ever been on."

"We got to the hospital. You were asleep. You slept until now." Marika began twisting restlessly, listening to "Cheeseburger in Paradise" and chiming in. "I like mine with lettuce and tomatoes! Heinz 57 and french-fried potatoes!"

"I love you all the way up to the sky," Matt whispered to Lynn.

Her heart swelled. Lynn sat up slowly, and another wave of nausea swept over her. She wrapped her arms around Matt, then Marika and Cy. The three of them enfolded her for a long, welcome few minutes.

"Any diagnosis?" Cy asked.

"The CT scans were inconclusive, which is good news. If something shows up it's bad, they told me. But the ER doctor confirmed I have a concussion."

Cy asked Matt and Marika to step outside.

He drew close to Lynn. "Matt and Marika were scared at seeing you. They lost their mother. Hell, I lost my wife. We thought they were going to lose you, too. You should think about retiring."

"Hold off on the recriminations. I'm just trying to recover."

Her husband looked abashed. "I'm sorry. The three of us were scared."

"Me, too."

❖

Since both had been diagnosed with concussions, Lynn's and Hannah's request to share a room was granted.

Any hint of sunlight was still too bright. They lay on their beds and talked across the few feet separating them in the darkness.

"I thought I knew how to avoid hitting my head," Hannah groaned.

"*You* didn't hit your head. Vandervoost did, with the butt of his gun, same as he did me," Lynn said.

"How are the concussion twins?" Joost asked, easing into the room. His head was bandaged, like theirs. So was the deep cut on his arm.

"I'm sorry about your father, Joost," Lynn said.

Joost nodded. Even in the darkness, Lynn could see tears forming in his eyes. "I wish I'd had a chance to say goodbye. He was dead by the time we came to, got out of our ropes, and got out of the office."

"It's not how we usually think about affection, but you noticed he barely tied any of us up?" Lynn asked.

"And he knocked us out instead of shooting and killing us," Hannah added.

"He wanted us to escape," Joost concluded.

Joost leaned over Hannah and gingerly pulled her into a hug. "I want more time with you."

"I'm not going anywhere at the moment," Hannah said.

"Marry me. Lynn is my witness."

"Let's talk about it after we're both released." But her wide smile gave away her answer.

Joost turned to Lynn. "And I'm sorry you had to go through so much for me to say yes, the terms your lawyers proposed are fine. I would be pleased to merge Bradshaw Energy with TriCoast at the price you have proposed. That includes the water recycle process technology."

"I think we have a deal, as long as you feel the same way when the drugs wear off and your company doesn't come with a dose of winner's curse," Lynn said. "But surely, we've exorcised the curse. Yes, if a merger works for everyone, we'd be honored to have you in charge of TriCoast's West Texas drilling operations. You wouldn't even need to leave Midland."

Relief passed over his face. "I'm sure I'll have other conditions."

After Joost left, Hannah said, "I'm accepting his proposal."

"I'm invited to your wedding?"

"Bloody yeah," Hannah said.

"You've lived in Chicago, Alaska, and London, and you want to settle down in Midland? What will you do?" Lynn asked.

"Same as in London."

Despite her aching head, Lynn laughed. "Right. Midland is exactly like London. Same size, weather, traffic, everything."

"The issues are the same. Forensics. Still too many dead bodies. Geology—Midland is about nothing but geology. And we wouldn't be too far from Big Bend."

"Not far in Texas terms. Only three hundred miles," Lynn teased.

"I've heard it's stunning. And Alpine. And Dark Skies parties at the McDonald Observatory near Fort Davis."

"And Prada Marfa," they said together, and laughed.

❖

Kir Zaitsev had returned to Moscow, even though he was concerned about his fate. He would face it. So many others had.

Egonov hated failure.

But nothing happened.

Months passed. The hard Russian winter turned to spring and summer. On the street, people bared their heads, arms, and legs.

He didn't even wonder when a few strangers—but not strangers to his friends—joined his regular Thursday night drinking group. They were introduced, they smiled, knew all the right people, jokes, references.

"*Za druzhbu,*" Zaitsev said. To friendship.

"*Za nas,*" another added. To us.

"Ah. *Za lyubov,*" countered Zaitsev. To love.

Several drinks in, he didn't think much of it when the whole party moved to a big open suite on the high floor of a hotel.

He stumbled to the suite's bathroom, pissed, and walked back out into an empty suite. Music continued to blare.

The suite wasn't empty.

Zaitsev was lifted from behind by his armpits. He kicked his legs back, trying to smash them into his attackers' kneecaps to get them to drop him.

The distance to the open window was only a few meters.

The distance to the ground was a hundred meters.

*How ordinary,* he thought. *The usual. Defenestration.*

In a last attempt at dignity, Kir Zaitsev didn't scream after he was shoved out of the open window. The only sound from Zaitsev was a loud thump when his body smashed into the pavement below.

### THE END

# NOTES

Israel Natural Gas Lines is real. The Tamar, Leviathan, and other natural gas formations in the Eastern Mediterranean are real. The Eastern Med hub is real. Avi and his company, the deputy energy minister of Israel, Teos Mustafa, and Alejandro Garcia are all fictional, as are all the characters in the book.

For US and UK readers: one billion cubic meters = 35.3 billion cubic feet or 0.83 million tons of oil equivalent (mmtoe) or 6.1 million barrels of oil equivalent

## *Levantine Basin or Eastern Mediterranean Basin (Eastern Med) per Daniel Yergin:*

a. Tamar (Israel) discovered in 2008-2009: estimated gas reserves of 300 billion cubic meters (10.6 trillion cubic feet)
b. Leviathan (Israel) discovered in 2010: estimated recoverable gas reserves of 22 trillion cubic feet (35 trillion cubic feet in place), and 40 million barrels of condensate
c. Aphrodite (Cyprus): estimated gas reserves of 4.2 trillion cubic feet
d. Zohr (Egypt): discovered in 2015, estimated gas reserves of 30 trillion cubic feet.

## ACKNOWLEDGMENTS

MANY THANKS TO editor John Paine for his patience and expertise.

Creating an interesting, reader-friendly book requires a team. I appreciate the work of New Zealand cover designer Jeroen ten Berge and pro book designer Phillip Gessert.

Marketing takes much time and energy. I was fortunate to have an expert team from Finn Partners of Kristin Clifford, Deborah Kohan, Sharon Farnell, and Nick Fontaine as well as fearless marketer Diane Feffer, who is now also Director for Theatre Owners of Mid America, Inc.

### *Forensics and research:*

Donnell Bell and Wally Lind, CrimeSceneWriter moderators

Ed Bolen, Trident Response Group

Lior Frenkel, Waterfall Security

Heather Hanna, forensic geologist

Melissa Koslin, Crimereads.co

Jeff Locklear, detective

Lee Lofland, founder, Writers Police Academy

Christian Mazur, self-defense, including Krav Maga

Phil Pierce and Judy Randall, West Texas and wax refineries

Rachael Van Horn, AKA "Wench with a Wrench" in Greasebook.com

People who wish to remain anonymous.

*Experts on energy policy and energy poverty:*

Naomi Boness

Robert Bryce

Alex Epstein

Maynard Holt

Mark Mills

Elon Musk

Irina Slav

Michael Shellenberger

Angela Stent

Scott Tinker

Daniel Yergin

Alexander Zaslavsky

*Publications:*

Capen, Edward C., Robert V. Clapp, and William M. Campbell. "Competitive Bidding in High-Risk Situations." *Journal of Petroleum Technology,* 1971. 23: 641–653.

Epstein, Alex. *The Moral Case for Fossil Fuels.* London: Portfolio, 2014.

McCloskey, Deidre. *Bourgeois Equality: How Ideas, Not Capital or Institutions, Enriched the World.* Chicago: The University of Chicago Press, 2016.

Rogan, Tom. "Did Russian hackers blow up a Texas LNG pipeline on June 8?" *Washington Examiner.* June 21, 2022.

Siegel, Laurance B. *Fewer, Richer, Greener: Prospects for Humanity in an Age of Abundance.* Hoboken, New Jersey: Wiley, 2019.

## *Organizations:*

CDC.gov

CrimeSceneWriters

All things Chicago, UChicago, and UChicago Booth School of Business

Energy Information Administration, US Dept of Energy

Hart Energy editors and authors

Mobius Risk Group

RBN Energy experts

Sibley Nature Center in Midland, TX

TPH energy analysts and bankers

Veriten energy professionals and guest experts

## *And finally:*

Thanks to Barbara Spencer, author Karen Harrington, and editor/author Barb Goffman, along with Sisters in Crime North Dallas, all of whom encouraged me past a difficult workflow point. Do read my short story, *Risk Reduction*, and all the other short stories in our group's anthology, RECKLESS IN TEXAS, Metroplex Mysteries Volume II.

I appreciate all authors everywhere. Please look over my thousand-plus Goodreads reviews for recommendations. Support from authors such as Karen Harrington and William J. Carl—check out their extraordinary writing—as well as the International Thriller Writers organization, was important. Thanks also to Jim Kipp, a family friend, finance pro, and early reader.

The former dean of the College at the University of Chicago, John Boyer, once gave the following advice: "If you ever have the idea of writing two books at once, forget it. Give it up." Yet this is what I found myself doing—this book and the annual equivalent of *not one but two more* per year (e.g. 200,000 words/year) for my non-fiction analyses of energy investments. You hold the first of these in your hands. The results of the latter can be seen on the *Seeking Alpha* website.

I am especially indebted to everyone who kept asking when I would finish writing this book and who always assumed I would.

I appreciate all the family stories. In writing one of the later chapters, I recalled the awe with which we regarded my mother's father, my grandfather. He worked full-time climbing poles as an electric lineman, with regular callouts during the fiercest Michigan winters.

I would not have completed this book without the support of my family: parents Charles and Virginia, husband Joe, daughter Kay, and son Bill. We are doubly fortunate to have added to our family son-in-law Andy, daughter-in-law Eve, and their families. And what fun it has been to join Dr. Laura Skosey as the other half of Team Laura.

# AUTHOR'S BIOGRAPHY

TEXAN L. A. Starks is the author of the award-winning Lynn Dayton thriller series. In order, they are:

1. 13 DAYS: THE PYTHAGORAS CONSPIRACY,
2. STRIKE PRICE,
3. THE SECOND LAW
4. WINNER'S CURSE.

Each book has earned five-star ratings. Starks won the Texas Association of Authors' first-place award for best mystery/thriller for **STRIKE PRICE**. She also won the Texas Association of Authors' first-place award for best international thriller for **THE SECOND LAW**.

The **SECOND LAW** was a mystery/thriller quarterfinalist in the 2019 BookLife Prize competition, an Action/Adventure finalist in the 2020 National Indie Excellence Awards, and a quarterfinalist in the 2023 ScreenCraft Cinematic Book Competition.

Amazon Shorts selected some of Starks' short stories for publication: these and others are now available as individual short stories at Amazon. Her short story, "Gumbo Filé," was published in the **DREAMSPELL NIGHTMARES** thriller anthology. "Essence of Genius, Genius of Essence" won an honorable mention in WOW!'s Spring 2021 Flash Fiction contest. Her short story, "Risk Reduction," was chosen for the second Sisters in Crime North Dallas anthology, **RECKLESS IN TEXAS,** published in March 2023.

L. A. Starks now lives in Texas. She was born in Boston, Massachusetts and grew up in northern Oklahoma—just west of Osage County as featured in the Oscar-nominated movie *Killers of the Flower Moon*. Awarded a full-tuition college scholarship, she earned a chemical engineering bachelor's degree, magna cum laude, from New Orleans' Tulane University, followed by a finance MBA at the University of Chicago Booth School of Business. While at Chicago she made time to play for a celebrated women's intramural basketball team, the Efficient Mockettes.

Working for more than a decade for well-known energy companies and consultants in engineering, marketing, and finance from refineries to corporate offices prepared Starks to write global energy thrillers.

She is multi-published on hundreds of energy investment topics, primarily at *Seeking Alpha*. Her nonfiction has appeared in *Mystery Readers Journal*, *The Dallas Morning News*, *The Houston Chronicle*, the *San Antonio Express-News*, *Sleuth Sayer* (MWA-SW newsletter), *Natural Gas*, and *Oil and Gas Journal*. She is also the co-inventor of a U.S. patent.

Starks served as development co-chair, investment oversight chair, and treasurer of the board of the Friends of the Dallas Public Library. She is a member of Sisters in Crime and an active-category member of International Thriller Writers.

Besides writing high-stakes thrillers, she is a paid contributor to *Seeking Alpha* for her energy investment articles and has run twenty-one half-marathons.

L. A. Starks is especially honored to be a 2019 inductee of the Ponca City High School Alumni Hall of Fame, among the first 25 in over 30,000 lifetime Po Hi graduates.

Visit her online at http://lastarksbooks.com, and at Goodreads, Facebook, LinkedIn, and X.

Publisher's Note: If you enjoyed WINNER'S CURSE: A Lynn Dayton Thriller, try others in the series:

- 13 DAYS: THE PYTHAGORAS CONSPIRACY: Lynn Dayton Thriller #1
- STRIKE PRICE: Lynn Dayton Thriller #2
- THE SECOND LAW: Lynn Dayton Thriller #3.